WHOSE BODY IS IT ANWAY

By

Ann Gawthorpe

*This is a work of fiction
Any resemblance to anyone,
Living or dead
Is entirely coincidental*

Copyright © 2023 Ann Gawthorpe

*In memory of
my
darling granddaughter
Jasmine Cornish
1997-2022*

PROLOGUE

The bodies lay scattered at random on the tatty Axminster Rug. Most had their arms by their sides apart from an elderly lady, more sparrow-like than human, who still clutched her handbag to her chest, and a young man who had his arms straight up in the air, looking like Dracula about to arise from his coffin. There was a huge disparity in their ages and dress, in fact the casual observer would be hard put to work out what they had in common, and why they were in number 17 Gasworks Road. And why some of them had cushions under their heads.

PART ONE – THURSDAY

CHAPTER 1

'You're going to be late again, Arnold.' He thought he could detect a slight nagging edge to Ingrid's voice, but he guessed that twenty-odd years of exchanging banalities wasn't likely to lead to sparkling conversation at breakfast time.

He lounged back with a cup of strong tea and his fourth piece of toast while he read *The Mirror's* cartoon strip, 'Andy Capp' - his role model.

'I keep telling you, I'm on flexy time. I work late in the evening to make up.'

'Does the office count time spent in the pub?'

Arnold debated whether this was worth replying to. After all, they did have this conversation on a pretty regular basis.

'Of course it does, most of my business is done in a pub.' He finished the toast, stood up, slurped the last mouthful of tea and neatly sidestepped Ingrid's attempt to give him a kiss. Using the back door as a shield he said: 'Not now, Ingrid, not on a full stomach.'

'Last night you weren't interested because you hadn't eaten enough.' There was a hint of accusation in her voice.

'Well, it's all a question of getting the right gastric balance.'

Ingrid paused for a moment. She knew the way to a man's heart was through his stomach but where did gastric balance come into it. However, there was something more important to discuss. She had waited until the last minute just in case he remembered, but it looked as if he hadn't. 'Do you know what day it is Arnold?'

Arnold paused, was this a trick question? 'Thursday…all day.'

'No, the date?'

He peered at the calendar hanging over the toaster. 'May the fourth, nineteen eighty-nine.'

But, before she could explain the significance of it, Arnold had already gone on his way to do battle with the world of insurance, blithely ignoring a barrage of horns behind him as he roared out of the garage and into the road without looking.

As he drove one-handed tapping along to Wham's 'Wake me up Before you Go, Go' on Radio One he tried to recall why May the fourth was so important to Ingrid, but decided, nope he hadn't a clue.

May the fourth might not have had any significance for Arnold Collins, but it did for David Telford. His fledgling business had landed its first big contract and he was determined to do a good job.

Full of nervous energy, he was up early, checking and re-checking his brief case and going over what had to be done. So far, he had only handled small jobs, and he was still pinching himself that he had landed such an important contract. If this was a success then who knew where it might lead.

He fervently hoped it would lead to a date being set for his wedding. He and Suzie had become engaged a year ago today and a table for dinner had been booked at the Marlborough Grange Hotel that evening to celebrate their first anniversary. So far, her parents had persuaded her that there was no rush to walk down the aisle. But surely now that he had his own business, they couldn't expect them to wait another year.

As he went to the bathroom for the fifth time in the last hour, he looked at himself in the mirror. Despite the wispy moustache he still didn't look his age, which was twenty-nine. For the umpteenth time he wondered what Suzie saw in him, but he was endlessly grateful that she found something attractive.

Fortunately, today's visit to the client was just to ensure everything was ready and that the staff understood the process. Most of the work would be done over the weekend to minimise disruption.

He checked round his flat – his bed was made and the room left tidy, his breakfast bowl, which had held muesli and fresh fruit, had been washed and left to drain, and he had put bleach down the toilet.

Taking a deep breath, he got in his car, checked his map and instructions for finding the office, and set off.

'Can I help you, sir?'

Bernard Hornby started guiltily and quickly put the brochure back on the rack. He'd hoped to sneak a selection out while the travel agent was dealing with another customer, but he'd not been quick enough. 'Ah, no, I was just browsing.'

But a seasoned travel agent never let a prospective customer off that easily. Taking his arm, she led him to a seat and quickly went round to her side of the desk. 'So, where do you want to go, sir, somewhere warm? Or did you have in mind a city break, they are very popular.'

Bernard wriggled round in his chair and looked longingly at the glossy magazines so tantalisingly out of reach. 'Could I just take a few to look at…at home.'

'Of course, you can, but perhaps we could narrow down your requirements a bit, otherwise you will be taking the whole lot with you.' She pulled a pad towards her, ready to take notes. 'I take it you want to go abroad.'

'Yes...or in this country.'

The agent frowned. 'What time of year do you have in mind?'

'Anytime, it really doesn't matter.'

The agent frowned some more. In her experience customers who were this indecisive rarely booked a holiday, they just liked the thought of them. She might have tried to pin Bernard down a bit more if two of her regulars hadn't come in at that moment. In one smooth movement she stood up, pointed Bernard towards the rack of brochures and seated the pair of cruising enthusiasts at her desk, 'So where did you two have in mind for this summer?'

Bernard grabbed as many of the magazines as he could and promptly dropped them while he struggled to open the door. The agent sighed deeply, asked to be excused and opened it for him.

But that was yesterday. Bernard was now stepping jauntily down the road carrying his brochures securely tied up with string. He stopped outside a dingy-looking building in Gasworks Road and stared proudly at the brand-new name plate on the door. ASTRAL TRAVEL.

Inside, the offices had the same run-down seediness as outside. A couple of colourful holiday posters on the walls hadn't improved the ambience one bit, but rather drew attention to the peeling paint. Bernard, however, noticed none of this.

He went into his office, carefully unknotted the string and spread the brochures across his desk. Taking one at random he flicked through it, noting the bright blue seas, happy faces and artist's impressions of hotels which hadn't yet been built.

He felt a bit guilty about taking them from another travel agency, but he certainly wasn't in the position to have his own at the moment, although he was toying with the idea of having some printed. And anyway, his clients would probably have their own ideas of where they wanted to go.

He glanced at his watch, nine-fifteen, he had forty-five minutes before his new secretary arrived. Plenty of time to get the Axminster rug he'd seen in the second-hand shop.

Ingrid and her friend and next-door neighbour Stella were seated in Stella's kitchen, drinking coffee and talking about their favourite subject – men. Or rather, one man in particular - Arnold, whose lack of husbandly virtues was an endless source conversation. Stella didn't have a husband - well she'd had one once but seemed to have lost him at some stage and she couldn't really remember how, when or why. But she made up for this by taking an inordinate amount of interest in Ingrid's marital ups and downs.

'So, he forgot your anniversary again and it's your twentieth isn't? That's china that is.' Stella had specifically looked it up. 'He doesn't deserve you, Ingrid, he really doesn't.'

Ingrid was only half listening, because she was inwardly debating whether to mention the mysteries of Arnold's gastric imbalance on their sex life. Or rather lack of sex life.

'And when was the last time he bought you flowers?'

Ingrid puzzled over that question – had Arnold ever bought her flowers? 'I can't remember, I don't think he ever has.'

Stella drew in a sharp breath, but she wasn't surprised. In her, albeit limited experience, there were men who regularly turned up with a bunch of dahlias and those who didn't. The time to worry was when those who didn't – did. In Stella's book that was a sign of a guilty conscience. 'Well, if he does come home with a bouquet from the local petrol station be suspicious, he's probably having an affair.'

'Arnold! An affair!' Ingrid roared with laughter, but inside she started worrying – was this the reason for his gastric imbalance.

Stella picked up their mugs and put them in the sink. 'Come on, we don't want to be late for our shift.'

Maurice Pargitter cradled the phone in his neck and dragged a train of paper clips round his desk with the end of a biro. 'Mmmmm, of course sweetie, where do you want to go?... Italian! But it will take ages to get through those pizzas... I know, but I have an appointment at twelve... oh, some chap who's started a travel agency... Well, if you put it like that... Yes, see you at twelve then......bye sweetie.'

Hearing footsteps, he hurriedly replaced the phone and bent industriously over some files. Out of the corner of his eye he watched Arnold enter the office, throw his briefcase on his desk and knock a pile of papers on the floor.

Trying to look as if he had been hard at work for hours, he called out, 'Morning Arnold, traffic bad again?'

Arnold glared, they, too, had the same conversation every morning so he gave his usual answer, 'I need a coffee,' and scuffled about on the floor trying to sort out claim's forms from quotes. He quickly gave up.

Lunch with the gorgeous Sandra was at stake, so for once Maurice didn't ask Arnold to make him one as well. Instead, he jumped up and offered to get them himself.

This was so out of character that Arnold was temporarily lost for words and could barely mutter, 'Okay, thanks, mate.'

Maurice was quickly back from the office restroom with two chipped mugs full of steaming grey liquid. He put one down on Arnold's desk and then half sat on the corner of it, trying to look nonchalant. 'I put some money in the tin for you,' he said, and he waved his hand to stop Arnold reimbursing him. He needn't have worried - Arnold wasn't about to. 'Actually, Arnold, old chap, I wondered if you could do this call for me?'

'So that's why you got the coffee. Well, the answer's no. What call?'

Maurice took a business card out of his pocket and passed it across. 'Some bloke starting up a travel agency, he popped in yesterday for a quote.'

Arnold glanced at the card on which was written:
**Astral Travel.
You leave everything behind
when you travel the Bernard Hornby way
17 Gasworks Road.**

'It doesn't exactly conjure up sun, sand and sex does it,' and he gave it back.

Maurice stood up and flipped it onto Arnold's teetering pile of papers from where it gently slid down between the two desks, taking the papers with it. 'Could be a free holiday in it for you and the wifey. He said his rates are very cheap and you can go anywhere in the world.'

'No, it doesn't interest me.'

'When was the last time you took her away, 1979? That was ten years ago.'

'It's not obligatory you know, and have you forgotten I took her to Bournemouth on her birthday.'

'Not this year you didn't.'

'Why the sudden interest in my holidays?' Arnold had given up on the papers, the floor was as good a place as any for them, and he started rummaging in his brief case.

Maurice watched for a while and then said casually, 'Are all your files up to date? You know some computer whizz kid is coming in today to make a start. Mr Britten was pretty insistent about it.'

'Of course, they are.' Of course, they weren't - Arnold had completely forgotten about getting ready for computerisation.

A fact Maurice well knew, and he played his trump card, 'Do the call for me and I'll help you sort out your files when you get back. In fact, I'll make a start on some of them straightaway.'

Arnold thought for a moment then scrambled under his desk. Bernard's card had cunningly concealed itself under an old tomato sandwich. 'Travel agents? Usual policy I suppose?'

'Yes, the appointment is at twelve.'

It had come as a blow to Margaret Hamilton when Goldleaf Coach Travel had finally turned up its toes and made everyone redundant. A family firm which had seen generations of the town's holiday-makers book coach trips to Brighton, Bognor and even Benidorm, it hadn't been able to compete with a new agency setting up in the same row of shops offering cheap package holidays to such far-flung places as Sri Lanka and Turkey.

She had been given a generous redundancy package, but still needed to keep working, and at her age, new jobs were not easy to come by. Which was why she had been so thrilled to see an advert in the newsagents for a secretary cum assistant for a new venture, Astral Travel.

She'd thought it was odd that her job interview had taken place in a cafe but at least Mr Hornby had bought her a cup of tea and a slice of stale madeira cake. And although he obviously knew nothing about travel agencies, he seemed pleasant enough, well harmless at any rate - and that ranked high in Margaret's estimation.

She checked her appearance in her bedroom mirror, taking in her smart suit, sensible shoes and neatly permed greying hair. Then calling goodbye to her mother she tied a scarf round her neck, squared her shoulder, and with a frisson of excitement, set off for Astral Travel.

Her enthusiasm waned somewhat on arrival at Gasworks Road - but she told herself, a job was a job and one shouldn't judge a book by its cover, or in this case the peeling paintwork of a pre-war terrace of sad-looking houses and small businesses.

The front door was ajar and her enthusiasm waned even further as she went into the narrow, dingy hallway. She called out softly for Mr Hornby, but she already knew the place was deserted, it had an air of dejected abandonment about it. But she wasn't going to let a building defeat her, after all she was an employee and had every right to be there, so she set off briskly to suss out the layout.

Of the three rooms leading off the hall one was locked, the largest one was empty apart from a couple of chairs, and one was presumably hers because it contained a desk and an ancient manual typewriter.

Margaret's heart sank even further when she saw this – at least Goldleaf Coach Travel had been able to afford an electric one.

She looked at her watch, it was well past ten-o-clock, the time Mr Hornby had said he would be there to meet her. But always one to mentally, if not physically, roll up her sleeves and get on with life, Margaret sat down at the desk to see if there was anything she could start on. In a wire basket there were a few circulars, but nothing else, not even a desk diary.

No self-respecting office could manage without a desk diary. It was an essential bulwark against the contingencies of the day. She left a note for Bernard pinned to the front door and went out in search of one - leaving one of the posters half-hanging off the wall, minus one of its drawing pins.

David was half-way to his destination when a vision flashed across his brain. A vision showing the contract, agreed but unsigned, and a list of what he had to do, lying on the worktop in his kitchen. Surely, he thought, it was safely in his brief case – wasn't it?

Then he felt sick as he remembered taking them out for another last check, before dashing off for a final visit to the bathroom and then rushing out of the flat.

He took a quick look at his watch, he just about had time to return home and get them. There was no way he could carry out all his checks without his list. David relied on lists. And lists of lists. They gave him confidence and assurance. Checking off each item soothed his soul and made everything right with the world.

He signalled left, and left again and headed back the way he'd come.

Sitting at their adjoining tills in the supermarket, Ingrid and Stella continued their conversation, or rather repeated the same conversation they'd had over coffee and during the walk to Co-op.

'Look at the way he treats you. Did he remember your birthday, no. Did he remember to collect your dry cleaning when you was laid up with that cold, no. When was the last time he wiped up?'

'I don't want him to wipe up. I'd settle for him being a bit more romantic.'

'Romantic! You don't want romantic.' Stella turned to the customer whose groceries she was scanning, 'I'm right, aren't I? She needs a bit more help around the house, some new clothes and a holiday. She doesn't need romance.'

The customer, who was more concerned that Stella was scanning the same packet of biscuits over and over, nodded quickly and snatched the bourbons from her.

'We never have a nice kiss and a cuddle these days,' Ingrid sighed and absentmindedly pushed a bag of apples through without scanning it. Her customer wasn't at all concerned by this.

'And we all know where that leads, S E X. " Stella spelt it out in case it was contagious. Then much to her customer's mortification she shouted down the shop, 'Can someone give me a price for these laxatives, the double-strength ones, the label's missing.'

But Ingrid hadn't been listening. 'He says he's gastrically unbalanced.'

'Unbalanced yes. But it's got nothing to do with his stomach,' said Stella, acidly. She picked up the laxatives and tapped in the price. 'If these don't shift it, love nothing will. Right, that will be five pounds, seventy-three pence.' Her customer had wondered whether to point out the triple-scanning of the bourbons, but decided she just wanted to get out of the shop as quickly as possible.

Ingrid's customer leaned over and patted her hand, 'Don't worry, my dear, I'm a bit psychic and I can see someone giving you some roses when you get home.'

Ingrid wasn't sure whether to be pleased or worried.

Arnold was wondering how to kill time before the noon appointment with Astral Travel, while avoiding Cyril Britten, the managing director of the Trouble-Free Insurance Agency. He settled for a coffee in the café opposite his office, after telling Maurice that he had to see another client before going to Astral Travel.

Munching his way through a large slice of lemon drizzle cake, he picked up a paper left by a previous customer. The news that Maggie Thatcher was celebrating her tenth year as Prime Minister depressed him so much that he didn't even bother to look at the page three model.

When Bernard staggered in with the ancient Axminster over his shoulder, he was relieved to see Margaret's note. He hadn't meant to spend so much time in the second-hand shop, but he'd dithered over whether to buy an electric kettle as well as the carpet, and time had slipped away from him. All the way back to Gasworks Road, he'd worried about not being there to meet her. At least it looked as if she'd only gone out for a few minutes and not for good like the first girl who'd accepted the job, but only lasted ten minutes when she found out what was involved.

He almost dropped the kettle when a voice behind him said, 'Good morning, Mr Hornby, I just popped out to get a desk diary and a few other odds and ends which we might need.'

'Ah, good morning, Miss Hamilton, sorry I wasn't here when you arrived.' He held up the kettle as a way of explanation. 'As you can see, I've been out buying as well. At least we can now have a cup of coffee.'

Margaret couldn't remember seeing any cups or jars of coffee around, but perhaps the door at the back of her office held the necessary facilities. She took the kettle from him before it slipped out of his hands and balanced it on top of the desk diary. 'I'll just pop these bits and bobs into my office.'

Bernard followed her. 'I must say, you're much more efficient than the previous girl.'

Margaret almost blushed with pleasure. 'Had she worked in a travel agency before Mr Hornby?'

'I don't think so, but she wasn't here long enough to find out.'

'There you are then. After twenty years with Goldleaf Coach Travel one does pick up a few tricks of the trade. There's not much I can't tell you about package holidays.' She then realised that Bernard was gently sagging under the weight of the carpet. 'Could I help you with that,' she said, seizing one end.

Bernard gratefully let her take it from him. 'I want to lay it down in the separating room. It's only second hand, but it will stop the splinters when the clients lay down.'

Gallantly, he opened the door into the largest room and Margaret wrestled the carpet through. They were unrolling it across the cracked and broken floor boards before it clicked with her what he'd said.

'Why do they lay down on the floor? At Goldleaf Coach Travel our clients always sat on chairs.'

Bernard, like most men, could only cope with one thing at a time, and insisted on moving the chairs out of the way before replying.

'I mean,' persisted Margaret, 'wouldn't it be more comfortable?'

'Possibly, but I'm a bit worried they'll fall off. Perhaps later on, when they're used to it.' He carried on straightening the carpet.

'Fall off! None of our clients ever fell off.' Margaret was shocked.

Bernard was surprised: 'Never?'

Margaret was adamant: 'Never.' The interchange brought back happy memories and a small tear to her eye. 'Such a pity they collapsed.'

'Woodworm I suppose,' Bernard looked at his chairs, 'I'm a bit worried these have got it too.'

'Not the chairs, the business. It was a shock to everyone when it folded. Still, I was lucky to see your advert.' Margaret usually looked on the bright side.

Bernard surveyed the room with pleasure. He had only been in business a week and things were definitely looking better. 'What sort of package deals do they...did they specialise in?'

Margaret wrenched her gaze away from the stained area in the middle of the carpet. 'Oh, five-day trips, sometimes ten-day ones, but the weekend breaks were the most popular.'

'I thought I'd concentrate on lunch breaks to start with.'

'Lunch breaks!' Margaret didn't mind admitting, she was surprised. 'Are many people interested in those?'

Bernard wandered round the room. 'Oh, yes, I have my second group of clients coming in at one-o-clock today.' He paused and stared at the floor, 'I wonder if I ought to get some cushions.'

'Good idea Mr Hornby, those seats do look a bit hard.'

'Midday is the best times to miss the crowds, especially at places like the Taj Mahal.' Bernard studied the dirty patches on the Axminster more closely. 'Yes, we could definitely do with some cushions, at least they'll cover up the stains.'

The conversation seemed to be leaping about a bit, but Margaret prided herself on her quick mind. 'How far can you go in a lunch break.'

'As far as you want.' He straightened up and rubbed his hands together. 'Right, after we've had a cup of coffee would you mind popping out again and buying some cushions, nothing too expensive.'

On firmer ground when it came to furnishings, Margaret agreed to buy half a dozen floor cushions and took the fifty pounds Bernard was holding out. After all, if he was selling holidays to hippies why should she worry. A job was a job as she kept saying to herself. 'Is there anything else we need?' she asked, wondering whether to mention the electric typewriter.

'I can't think of anything, just the insurance to sort out and I've got some chap from a local insurance broker's coming at noon. He didn't think there would be any problem about the bodies. I've got his name somewhere.' He went through his pockets. 'It must be on my desk.'

'I'll put it in the dairy, shall I?' Margaret's voice suddenly faltered, 'did you say bodies?'

CHAPTER 2

Bernard and Margaret were sitting, drinking coffee. Margaret had been correct in her supposition that the other door in her office led to a small kitchen. She had also recovered from the shock of learning there would be bodies lying around on the premises during her lunch hour. After all, she did hold a fifty-yard life-saving certificate in swimming and a Girl Guide badge for knitting so felt she could deal with anything life threw at her.

'But whatever gave you the idea of starting this business, Mr Hornby?'

Bernard passed across a book called 'Out of Body Experiences' by Zxama Zxaman. 'This! I borrowed it from the library. One of the chapters shows you how to do it, so I had a go and found I could 'come out' so-as-to speak.'

Margaret looked at the front cover which showed an amorphous human figure floating on a sea of swirling colours. She gingerly flipped it open. 'It's overdue, Mr Hornby - by several weeks.'

'Ah, yes, well, I do intend to take it back, once I've got the business off the ground.'

She turned to the back cover and read: 'Out of body experiences - true stories of people who have left their bodies.' She looked at him suspiciously, 'You mean you came out of your body and sort of floated around? That sounds terrifying.'

'It was a bit startling at first, but you soon get used to it.'

Margaret wasn't convinced. 'And that's when you got the idea for Astral Travel?'

'Yes, I quickly discovered that as soon as I was out, I could go anywhere in the world, instantaneously.'
'How?'
'Easy, you just think of where you want to go and you're there. I could show you if you like.'
But Margaret quickly decided she wanted to stay firmly in her body and take her annual two-week break in Weymouth - by train as normal. She hurriedly handed the book back to Bernard, just in case that by simply holding it she would pop out and find herself in a Moroccan bazaar or a Russian Gulag. 'No thank you Mr Hornby, I like to keep my feet firmly on the ground.'
'Well, if you're sure. Anyway, I'm teaching the technique to my clients - for a fee of course - and then they will be able to travel anywhere as well.'
Margaret wanted to get clear in her mind exactly how the business worked. 'So, all these people will be coming here in their lunch hour and, instead of eating their sandwiches or doing their shopping, they'll buzzing off to Bombay or somewhere.'
'That's the idea. Unfortunately, no one's been able to achieve separation yet, but they are very enthusiastic. I'm hoping the carpet will make them more comfortable, there were some complains about the floor boards and splinters the other day, which I think put them off.'
Margaret could instantly see a flaw in his business plan – and it wasn't anything to do with splinters. 'But, Mr Hornby, once they have learnt how to do it, they needn't come back to you again. You won't get any repeat bookings.'

Bernard hadn't thought of that - for a former bank manager he had little grasp of commerce. He frowned at the floor, but soon rallied. 'Oh well, never mind, it's more of a hobby really. I couldn't start the business while I worked for the bank of course, although I did come out of my body at the office once. But,' he quickly added, 'I'd just been told I'd been made redundant so I needed a quick break.'

Margaret started to worry - unless they could build a larger client base, she would be made redundant again, and she didn't want to lose yet another job. Once you hit the big five-O it was difficult to find employment. After all there was her mother to look after, and the car to run, not to mention the cat. She squared her shoulders. Mr Hornby might not know how to run a travel agency, but she did. 'So, how many clients do you have at the moment?'

'Only about fourteen - but anything new takes a little while to get off the ground. And I'm sure my idea for lunch breaks is going to pay off.'

'Right,' she said briskly, "I'd better go and get those cushions. And shall I pick up some travel brochures while I'm out? I could hand them out to our clients when they arrive, to try to motivate them!'

'No, that's fine, I picked up a few yesterday.'

'Right. But as soon as I get back, we need to devise a way of getting more clients.'

'Ah, no not this morning. I was planning to pop off somewhere before that insurance guy arrives. Then I can give people a first-hand description of what it's like in France at the moment, and some ideas of where to go.'

Margaret started to feel apprehensive again. 'You mean you're coming out? What, right here?'

Bernard finished his coffee. 'No, I'll be in my office.' As he headed to the door he said, 'One thing, though, it's very important my body isn't disturbed while I'm away, otherwise I may not be able to find it again.' Seeing the look on Margaret's face he hastily added he was only joking, but he didn't really know whether that was true or not. and wasn't prepared to take the risk.

Once in his office he flicked over the pages of a brochure for France and decided on Nice. He quickly pulled a pair of shorts out of his rucksack and put them on, and donned a pair of sun glasses. It wasn't strictly necessary to dress up, but it got him in the right frame of mind. Then he leaned back in his chair, came out of his body, and began a relaxing stroll along the palm-lined promenade.

David was in a panic. The journey back to his flat had taken twice as long as going. Between leaving it and returning fifteen minutes later, a set of temporary traffic lights had been set up with their guardian cones and other roadworks paraphernalia, but no workman. The lights on his side remained obstinately red, so he jumped out and waved his hand in front of the sensor. This had the desired effect – they turned green - but before he could get back in his car - they turned red again. Eventually a cyclist triggered the sensor and David whizzed through before the lights could thwart him again.

Finally, with the missing documents safely in his brief case he set off once more. If there were no more holdups he would just about arrive at the appointed time. But fate had other plans for him.

As he drove along the High Street, looking for his turning, a dog, deciding that the smells on the other side of the road were far too interesting to be ignored, shot across in front on him. David, who loved all animals, automatically swerved and missed the dog, but not the refrigerated van, coming in the opposite direction, and carrying frozen peas and other sundries to the Co-op. Despite his best attempts at braking and swerving, his Vauxhall Astra was drawn is if by a magnet into the side of the van, completely blocking the road. Traffic soon piled up in both directions and no one was going anywhere soon - including Arnold's Ford Escort.

The dog was momentarily shaken by this turn of events - but only momentarily. It was soon adding messages of its own to the tree on the opposite side, where numerous other canines had thoughtfully left theirs, and then watched with interest as the scene unfolded in front of him.

Struggling with two unwieldly bags of assorted cushions, Margaret's journey back was hindered by the crowds who had been drawn to the accident in the High Street. While they waited for the emergency services, various suggestions were made on the best way to treat the driver in the Astra. One group wanted to move him from the car in case it exploded, while the opposing faction insisted that he stay put, in case his back was broken. Margaret citing her first aid experiences in the Girl Guides, weighed in firmly on the side of those who said he should be left where he was.

The debate continued until the emergency services arrived and everyone heaved a sigh of relief and left it to the professionals. David was carefully lifted from his front seat and put on a stretcher. Once in the ambulance, he remained dead to the world. 'Poor bugger's out cold.' observed one of the paramedics. 'I'm not surprised,' observed the other, 'that's what happens when you hit a refrigerated lorry.' And they both roared with laughter.

Then they popped an oxygen mask on him and monitored his vital signs. They could see from the nasty bruise on his forehead that he had hit the windscreen with some force. But his heart rate was strong and they had every reason to believe that, not only would he survive, but would soon be sitting up in bed with nothing more than a headache, and a hefty insurance claim.

When it was clear that the car was not going to explode, much to the disappointment of three Fourth formers lounging on the corner, the firemen put away their cutting equipment, wound in their hoses, jumped on their fire truck, and went back to their station.

The police officer in charge, having found David's name and address from a Filofax in his briefcase, dispatched a young constable to inform his family and friends. Then he finished measuring skid marks, took statements from witnesses, including from two who hadn't even seen the accident, and checked the driving licence and insurance of the lorry driver. Satisfied that everything had been done to delay the traffic for as long as possible, he called for breakdown truck to take the battered Vauxhall Astra to a local garage, and opened the road.

CHAPTER 3

Back in Gasworks Road, Margaret arranged the cushions on the Axminster rug, trying to cover as many stains as possible. She could see that Mr Hornby's office door was still firmly closed so she went into her office and started knocking hell out of the typewriter. The sooner she beat the vile machine to death the sooner she might be able to have an electric one.

She was determined to set up a proper filing system where the details of each client would be filed in alphabetical order, so was typing up questionnaires for them to fill in. She was ripping a piece of paper out of the machine when she saw a man in the doorway. 'Good afternoon, can I help you?'

Arnold looked around the scruffy office in disbelief. 'I have an appointment with Mr Hornby.'

'Oh yes, Mr Pargetter.' Margaret made quite a show of checking the diary. 'You're here about the insurance. I have you diaried in for twelve noon.' She looked pointedly at her watch, 'It's now twelve minutes to one.'

'Yes, well there was an accident in the High Street, some bloke drove into a refrigerated lorry and was knocked out cold.' He waited for Margaret to fall about laughing - when she didn't, he muttered that he thought it was hilarious.

'I saw the poor driver being loaded into an ambulance so it's hardly a laughing matter, Mr Pargetter.' Margaret had once been dumped by a man who worked in insurance and this had left her with a sour impression of all who worked in that field.

Arnold wasn't particularly fussed whether the driver was okay or not he wanted to get the business over and done with so that he could have some lunch. He handed her his card. 'I'm afraid Mr P was unable to come.'

Margaret handled it as if it were something picked up out of the gutter - where in fact it had been after Arnold had accidently dropped it. 'Thank you…Mr Collins,' she stood up and headed to Bernard's office. 'I'll just see if Mr Hornby is back.' And she quietly opened the door a fraction.

Arnold followed her and was irritated to see through the gap that the boss of Astral Travel was fast asleep in his chair. He would have quite liked a snooze himself.

He was even more irritated when Margaret shut the door and informed him that Mr Hornby wasn't back yet and would he mind waiting. Yes, he would mind. It was only the thought that Maurice wouldn't sort out his files if he didn't sell the guy the holiday policy, that prevented him from turning round and walking straight out of the dump. He wondered how long it would be before his car wheels disappeared. The whole place gave him the fidgets.

For the next few minutes Margaret carried on typing and Arnold carried on fidgeting.

Bernard meanwhile was sauntering along the Promenade Anglais, admiring the deep blue sea, and oblivious of the time. That was one of the downsides of astral travel, unless there was a public clock a traveller could rely on, it was difficult to assess how long they'd been away.

'Look, I'm in a bit of a hurry, couldn't you wake him up.' By now Arnold's stomach was rumbling and he looked pointedly at his watch.

'He's not asleep, he's working.'

Arnold sighed and took two turns round the room. He then tried wheedling. 'Look, I know all about these heavy business lunches, I could often do with a bit of kip meself, but time's getting on.'

Even Margaret was now getting exasperated, the clients would be arriving any minute and she had no idea what she could say to them. She went back into Bernard's office, closing the door firmly behind her. Luckily, Bernard was just stirring. 'That insurance man is here Mr Hornby and he's getting fidgety. Here's his card. And your clients will be here any minute.'

Bernard forced himself to stop thinking about the sunny skies and the blue Mediterranean, 'Sorry, I didn't mean to be so late back. You'd better show him in.'

'But you haven't changed yet.' Margaret looked at Bernard's legs in horror. 'I'll stall him.'

Arnold, however had overheard the conversation and had no intension of being stalled. He marched into the office and looked round with a sinking heart - this office was no better than the other one. And the bloke, who was supposed to be the owner of a travel agency that could take you anywhere in the world, was wearing an old jumper, a pair of shorts and a vacant expression. Arnold didn't hold out much hope that the business would last long.

'Excuse me a moment,' said Bernard, hurriedly pulling his trousers on over his shorts. 'Sorry to have kept you waiting, I've only just got back from Nice. Won't you sit down.' He fumbled with Arnold's card while trying to tuck his shirt in, 'Mr Collins? I thought Mr Pargetter was going to handle my insurance.'

'He thought I was better equipped to deal with your requirements - I do have a lot of experience with these things.'

'And he's put you in the picture about my special needs.'

'Oh yes. So, suffering from jetlag, are you?'

'Jetlag?'

'Yes, you were spark out just now. What was the weather like in Nice?' Arnold couldn't have cared less about jetlag and the weather, but it was always good practice to take an interest in the doings of potential clients.

'Wonderful.'

'You haven't got much of a sun tan.'

'Well, I was only there an hour.'

'An hour!' Arnold thought it was a heck of a long way to go for an hour. No wonder he still had his shorts on, he must have come straight from the airport. 'Anyway, time is money Mr Hornby, so down to business. As I understand it you want our comprehensive package deal,' he spread some policies across the desk, 'covering you against unfinished hotels, airlines going bust, clients spending two weeks in the transit lounge, etc. Also, loss of luggage, loss of...'

Bernard cut him off in mid flow. 'No, no, nothing like that. I never have to worry about unfinished hotels. It's this building I want to insure.'

'Oh, I see, this is a hotel.' Arnold tried not to sound appalled. 'Right, what you need then is our hotel package.' It was no good, he had to ask. 'Do you get many people wanting to stay in Gasworks Road?'

'Oh, no, no one ever stays here, well only for an hour or so.'

Arnold raised his eyebrows, so it was that kind of hotel, but surely even the most ardent adulterer would want somewhere better than this.

He pulled another policy out of his brief case. 'Right, in that case you will need our fully comprehensive insurance, and this one covers you against fire, rising damp, falling ceilings and earth quakes, as well as any claims against your good self from guests who have been burgled, bitten by bed bugs or burnt themselves on a trouser press.' Arnold had once tangled with a hotel trouser press and it had left a mark on him – and his trousers.

Bernard pushed the policy back. 'No, let me explain. My guests, if that's what you want to call them, won't be bitten by bed bugs or suffer any other catastrophes while they are travelling freely anywhere in the world...'

'Freely! You don't charge them?' Arnold was horrified. 'You'll never make a profit that way.'

'Oh no, they are going to pay.'

'Right,' Arnold sighed and scratched his head, 'so, what are you doing, some sort of coach trip with bed, breakfast and evening meal?'

'No, they can't eat in their state.'

'Why, are they suffering from travel sickness?'

'Sometimes, but that's not the problem.'

Arnold was starting to feel depressed. 'There is a problem then.'

'Yes, it's their bodies.'

It was worse than he thought. 'Their bodies?'

'I did explain all this to Mr Pargetter and he said there wouldn't be any difficulties. You do know about insurance, don't you?'

Arnold was nettled. 'Of course, I do,' he snapped, 'just tell me what you want.'

'It's quite simple, all I want is a policy which will cover me in case of damage to my clients' bodies while they are left here empty, so as to speak. Naturally, I anticipate that when they come back to their bodies, they will be in exactly the same state as when they left them. But should a mishap occur, they may have grounds for suing me.'

Arnold made a heroic effort to comprehend. 'Let me get this straight, while they are off, gallivanting to foreign parts, struggling with airline strikes and reluctant waiters, they want to leave some bodies here.'

'Not some bodies, their bodies.'

'Do the police know about this?' The situation was getting decidedly dodgy. No wonder Maurice wanted to get shot of it.

'I don't think we have to tell the police, do we?' It was Bernard's turn to sound surprised.

'I think they might be interested.' Arnold decided to play it cool, he was obviously dealing with a potential nutter. 'But I won't tell if you don't.'

'I have got planning permission from the council.' Bernard felt this should cover all eventualities.

'The council know about this?'

'Yes, and they were perfectly happy. It's just a change of use.'

Arnold relaxed marginally. 'Well, if the council knows I suppose that's alright then.' He thought for a moment. 'We once insured a sort of left luggage office.'

'That sounds as if it may suit.'

At last thought Arnold, taking out his pen, a breakthrough, we are communicating on the same wavelength. If you can forget he's wearing shorts under his trousers he isn't a bad sort of bloke. 'Right, I shall need to know how many cases, sorry bodies, are involved, storage arrangements, security, length of stay, sizes and estimated values.'

At last thought Bernard, we're finally getting somewhere, he doesn't seem such a bad sort of bloke despite the gravy stains down his jacket. 'They come in all different sizes of course and I'm not sure how long they will stay, could be minutes, could be hours, but I shall keep them secure and the doors will be locked at night.'

'What will you do with the uncollected ones? Auction them off?'

Bernard was appalled. 'Good heavens, I hope there won't be any uncollected ones.'

Arnold carried on scribbling. 'Have you any in store at the moment?'

'No.'

'When do you intend to start?'

'Today, if possible. I tried to start earlier in the week but so far none of my clients have been able to leave them.'

'They did bring some bodies along then.'

Bernard was baffled by the line the questioning was taking. 'Yes, of course they did. Some have been more than once, but I don't know why, they just can't do it.'

Arnold felt the situation slipping away from him again. 'So, these people come along with their bodies, hang around for a while and then take them away again.'

'Yes, you could put it like that.'

'And you're charging money for this?'

'Of course, it's a holiday business.

It's a rip off thought Arnold. 'Okay, let's start again. You are running some sort of cash and carry grave yard for holiday makers with spare bodies. Is there much profit in this?'

'Actually, not at the moment,' Bernard felt a little embarrassed, 'but I didn't expect to make a killing straight away.'

Arnold's knees went funny. I knew it, he thought, he's a hit man, and he hurriedly threw his policies back into his brief case. 'Look, as I said before, I won't say anything, not a word, I'll keep shtum.' He backed towards the door, spilling the policies out on the bare boards. 'I'll forget I ever came here.'

'I can afford the premiums, if that's what you're worried about.' Bernard jumped up and held on to his arm.

Arnold held on to the door. He was in a dilemma: he wanted to get out of the place, but he also needed the business. He'd give it one more go, surely even hitmen have to cover their costs. 'If you're not making any money, how about insuring against loss of profits.' He fumbled in his case for another policy and gave it to Bernard. 'It's our special small businessman's policy. Sign on the bottom and I'll fill in the details later.' He tapped the side of his nose. 'I won't mention the bodies.'

He was about to give Bernard a pen when he heard people talking and laughing outside the door. Was this bloke running a genuine business then? After all, hit men usually make home visits, their victims didn't come to them.

Bernard let go of his arm and beamed. 'Ah, my next lot of clients have arrived. This time I am determined to get them out.'

'But they've only just got in, no wonder you're not making any money.'

'You seem to be confused, Mr Collins.'

'I'm confused!'

'Perhaps you'd like to see how it's done.' Bernard paused, 'Before I sign anything.'

Arnold could feel his knees going funny again and tried a weak joke. 'You're not going to murder anyone, are you?'

'Murder anyone!' Bernard laughed uproariously.

In Arnold's ears the laughter sounded sinister. He was never going to get out of this place alive. What would Ingrid say? What sort of funeral would she organise? He definitely didn't want the hymn 'All Things Bright and Beautiful', which was her favourite. He flinched as Bernard took his arm again and pulled him out into the hall and into a large room.

Margaret was standing talking to a small group of people. It all looked very normal and Arnold thought it was probably safe to stop choosing hymns and the order of service.

'Everyone's here, Mr Hornby.' Margaret, diary clutched to her bosom, had checked them in against the files she'd compiled from the scraps of paper she'd found in a drawer.

Bernard walked round shaking hands. 'Hello, nice to see you all again. And as you can see, we now have a carpet so no chance of getting a splinter today.'

Miss Lettice Long, a frail little soul in her seventies was positively jumping up and down with excitement. 'Today's the day, Mr Hornby, I can feel it in my bones.'

'Splendid, splendid.' Bernard patted her on the shoulder.

'I'll carry on with my typing then.' Margaret started to leave the room but was stopped by Bernard. 'Don't go,' he whispered, "I want you to keep an eye on Mr Collins, he's a bit peculiar.'

He turned to the group and briefly introduced Arnold. 'Now, for those who are here for the first time, just relax and you'll soon have the freedom to travel anywhere in the world. The most important thing is - don't forget your password.'

'Don't you mean passport.' Arnold was feeling better.

'Oh, no, we won't need those. But your password is very important because once you have mastered the technique all you have to do is say it and you will be able to pop out whenever you want. And remember once you have achieved separation just think of where you want to go and you will be there, instantaneously. So, let's all try hard, it can be done, you just have to concentrate.'

Arnold took a closer look at the group. 'Where are their bodies?' he whispered to Bernard.

Bernard looked at Margaret and whispered, 'See what I mean.' He turned back to the group. 'We are about to begin so lie down everyone.'

The aspiring travellers lay on the floor, the lucky ones grabbing the cushions. Miss Long, showing an agility which belied her years, grabbed the largest one, and then lay down clutching her handbag to her chest.

Arnold wanted to know why they were laying down and was surprised to be told by Margaret it was because they might fall off the chairs.

'Fall off the chairs, they don't look that drunk.'

'Please keep your voice down,' Margaret hissed protectively, 'Mr Hornby has to concentrate.'

Arnold snorted and started jingling the change in his pocket. How long was this farce going to go on?

'You too Mr Collins, lay down.' said Bernard.

'Oh no, I'll just watch.' Arnold crossed the room and sat on one of the chairs.

'As you please. Right, everyone, lay your arms by your sides and relax.'

'Excuse me a minute Mr Hornby, before we get started, can I ask a question?'

'Of course, Mr Evans, fire away.'

'You said we can go anywhere in the world.'

'That's right, anywhere, instantaneously.'

'But if I went to Australia, it would be the middle of the night, what good's that?'

Bernard beamed at him, 'I don't know how it works but when you get there it will be the same time as it is here.'

'What do you mean, you don't know how it works?' A middle-aged lady with a tight bun sat back up and glared him. 'I'm not paying good money if you don't know how it works.'

Some of the others then started sitting up and muttering. Bernard could see he needed to nip this in the bud. 'It's all to do with science…,' he paused and then had a brainwave, 'It's Einstein's Theory of Relativity.' He hoped they would be suitably impressed and lie back down.

And, thankfully, most of them did, apart from the woman with the bun, who was not giving up. 'And what does that mean?'

Bernard wracked his brains, he didn't know what the theory of relativity was, but had a feeling it was something to do with the speed of light and getting younger if you went faster than it. So presumably that meant the clocks went backwards. He had a vision of the hands on a clockface whirring round in reverse.

'You will be travelling at more than the speed of light and the clocks will go backwards at the same time, so that's why it will always be the same time here and where you go.' He was relieved to see her lay back down again. 'So now we've sorted that out, we'll begin.'

The room went quiet and everyone focused on what Bernard was saying. He began to intone calling on them to concentrate on letting their bodies grow heavier and their spirits to grow lighter.

One or two, including Arnold, jumped several feet in the air when the phone rang. Margaret dashed out to answer it and Bernard continued intoning. 'Focus your mind on a small pinpoint of light, feel your body getting heavier and your spirit getting lighter. Say your password and let your astral being float free.'

Arnold muttered, 'What a load of rubbish.' Threw up his arms like a drowning man, slid gracefully under the chair and came out of his body.

CHAPTER 4

Stella and Ingrid were having a quick lunch in 'The Singing Kettle' cafe before going back to finish their shift.

'Stop thinking about Arnold.'

Ingrid forced her mind back to her jacket potato topped with tuna, 'How did you know I was thinking about Arnold?'

'Because you had a daft look on your face. Don't give him another thought. He's probably hanging around somewhere up to no good.'

Stella had never shown signs of prescience before.

Arnold was, in point of fact, hanging from a light fitting. His astral body had floated up to the ceiling and was gently bouncing against the beams. His strangled cry of 'Bloody hell, what's happening.' going unheard by those below.

Bernard didn't even notice Arnold's body lying under the chair. He was staring at his clients, willing them to separate. Several were twitching and jerking and Lettice Long was shaking her head violently.

'It's not like a salt cellar, Miss Long, you can't shake your astral body out.'

Arnold made a heroic effort to look down, felt ill and closed his eyes again. He prayed the flex would hold and that no one would switch the light on. He couldn't fathom how he had got up there. What had happened to the laws of gravity, Newton's apple and all that?

A disgruntled man in a crumpled suit stood up and brushed some carpet fibres from his shoulder. He hadn't managed to get a cushion and was feeling cheated. 'This is a con,' he barked, 'I'm off.'

'You're right it is con, I've a good mind to report you to the Trading Standards.' The woman with the tight bun glared round the room, defying anyone to contradict her. She fully intended asking for her money back, quite forgetting she hadn't yet paid anything.

'Did anyone come out,' Bernard pleaded, 'just for a second.'

A younger chap in tight jeans and sweat shirt – and who had managed to get a cushion - tried to be helpful. 'I thought I was going to.'

'Good, good, next time.' Bernard's optimism inched back up again. 'Anyone else?'

The rest of the group stood up, shook their heads, brushed themselves down and collected up their bags and shopping.

'Please book your next session with Miss Hamilton,' Bernard tried to sound business-like.

Margaret met them in the doorway and rounded them up like a border collie. 'Come through to my office everyone, this way,' and like good little lambs they followed her.

All except Miss Long, who linked her arm through Bernard's and tilted her head back to talk to him. 'I shall be back this afternoon Mr Hornby,' she twittered. 'I am determined to do it - it's going to be such fun. I've always wanted to travel round the world, but on my pension, it's never been possible before.'

Bernard patted her hand. He knew he would feel guilty about taking her money - even former bank managers have hearts.

Arnold watched everyone leaving and couldn't believe they'd all ignored him. Surely a fully grown man hanging from a light fitting must have been noticed by someone. 'Oy, you lot, come back, don't leave me up here, somebody get a ladder.'

When no one returned he tried stretching his feet out to see if they could reach the floor, but the building was old and the ceiling was high. Convinced his hands were sliding down the flex, he quickly took a firmer grasp, hauled himself back up and hooked his feet round the shade.

He looked down at the floor and to his horror saw himself lying under a chair. Bloody hell? What am I doing down there when I'm up here. He quickly shut his eyes - he must be hallucinating.

Hitting the refrigerated lorry had had much the same effect on David. His corporeal body had been prevented from travelling too far by his seatbelt, although far enough to sustain the nasty knock on his forehead, while his astral body had shot out through the windscreen and landed on the pavement the other side of the lorry.

In the normal course of events, it would have rolled over, coughed, twitched and then shot back into his body again, but events today were not normal.

Passing through the lorry's freezer compartment at the speed of light, it had hit a small black hole hidden in a bag of frozen chips, which momentarily changed one of the dimensions curled up inside a 'super crunchy three-times fried oven ready', making it difficult, if not impossible, to effect a re-entry. And completely altering the taste of the chip.

David's astral body lay unmoving in a heap on the pavement, while the crowd, gawking at the accident, trod all over it oblivious to what was beneath their feet. It wasn't until the ambulance had taken his corporeal body away that he finally stood up, clutching his head, and leaned back against the tree trunk, which a little while earlier the dog had found so irresistible. He felt decidedly woozy - and couldn't remember where he was, who he was or why he was leaning against a tree.

An elderly lady dragging a shopping trolley came towards him. In his politest, how to address old ladies voice, he asked her pardon and where was he? She stared right through him - and then walked right through him.

David was indignant and glared after her, using language not suitable for addressing old ladies. It was then he discovered he didn't have a body. Well, not what you could really call a body, more an amorphous, ghostly outline. He couldn't quite put his finger on the memory, but he was fairly certain he had had a body earlier on.

The pain in his head was consistent with being struck by something hard and unyielding and wasn't getting any better. That must be it, he decided, he had been hit on the head and mugged and now he was hallucinating.

He tried to attract the attention of a postman, a woman pushing a pram and a guy coming out of a shop carrying a car battery, but they all ignored him – so much for good neighbourliness towards someone needing help. Another thought struck him - perhaps they thought he was drunk.

He staggered along the high street for a while, desperate for somewhere to sit down, but there was a distinct lack of seats so he perched on the edge of a flower tub, which had been planted up by the council in a vain attempt to win a floral award. Unsurprisingly, it wasn't that comfortable as the council didn't want people sitting on it - but he hoped someone would tell him off for flattening the geraniums and then he could ask them to direct him to the nearest hospital.

He waited for what seemed an eternity, which, in reality, was only seven and a half minutes, but although the pavement was busy everyone walked round him or through him, he might as well have been invisible.

Then it hit him – he was dead!

As a child he'd only had a hazy notion of what the celestial afterlife would be like, but he hadn't expected it to be like a normal high street, full of shops, parked cars – some half on the pavement, traffic wardens and pedestrians. Where were the pearly gates and harp-strumming angels?

Perhaps he'd gone to the other place. Hadn't he read somewhere that hell was other people, well there were certainly plenty of other people around and most of them were walking straight through him without so much as a by-your-leave. Was that supposed to happen?

He wondered what he was supposed to do next? Did he have to go on a quest to prove himself ready for...for what? Did he have to solve clues, like some kind of otherworldly treasure hunt to lead him in the right direction? Surely there would be some kind of signposting. All he could see in the immediate vicinity was a yellow sign on the pavement warning traffic that the road ahead was closed and to follow the diversion signs. Why would the afterlife need road works? And diversion signs?

The strange thing was, he didn't actually feel dead. Not having been dead before, he wasn't sure exactly what it should feel like, but surely it wouldn't be like this? Apart from his memory loss he reasoned, all that was actually missing was his body. Could he have mislaid it somewhere? Was it sitting around waiting for him? He couldn't work out how he had lost it, but it was time he started looking for it.

With shoulders braced, he set off down the road, peering under cars and wandering around shops. Then it hit him, he had no idea what he looked like so how would he recognise himself. He tried to see his reflection in puddles and shop windows but nothing showed. Had he been able to see his reflection he would have seen a shortish, slightly plump young man with curly brown hair, hazel eyes and a sweet demeanour.

He decided his only hope was to keep searching until he came across an empty body and assume it was his. But how to tell whether a body was empty or not?

He elected to go by the face. A vacant expression must mean a vacant body, and therefore his – he didn't dare contemplate the thought that there might be lots of empty bodies about.

It came as a shock to find that the first person with a vacant expression on his face was a spotty youth in trainers and a torn bomber jacket listening to a Walkman.

David wondered how to approach his body and decided to walk through it in the hope that the two parts would somehow connect.

It was with some relief that he found he couldn't get in.

The same thing happened with tramp asleep on a bench clutching a beer bottle, and a workman leaning on his shovel.

He couldn't remember ever feeling so depressed. But then, he couldn't remember very much at all.

CHAPTER 5

Arnold tried opening and closing his eyes several times – but nothing changed. He was still hanging on to the light fitting, but he was also lying under a chair. Nothing in the world of insurance had prepared him for anything like this.

He wondered if Bernard Hornby had slipped some kind of hallucinogenic drug into his coffee, but he hadn't been offered a drink. Surely the café opposite his office hadn't taken to tampering with their customers' beverages! He'd read that in Amsterdam you could buy brownies with a cannabis flavouring, but he'd had lemon drizzle cake.

His search for an explanation was cut short when Bernard and Margaret came back into the separating room. Margaret was clutching the desk diary to her bosom again and said sadly: 'Only Miss Long and one man have booked again, Mr Hornby. I really think you need to reconsider your advertising strategy.'

'Yes, you're right Miss Hamilton, but you go and have your lunch now and we'll talk about it later.'

Arnold eased his position on the flex and shouted at them, 'Blow your lunch, quick get a ladder and get me down,' and he shut his eyes and waited for help.

Margaret decided to tidy up the cushions first and noticed a leg sticking out from under one of the chairs. 'Good heavens, look at Mr Collins.' She prodded Arnold's leg with her toe, there was no reaction. 'Do you think he's drunk.'

'Well, that could explain why he didn't seem to understand what sort of policy I wanted.'

Arnold was getting more and more annoyed. Not only were these two idiots completely ignoring him, they were discussing him as if he wasn't there, and in a very derogatory manner. He wanted to be very rude - but he did need some help.

'Do you mind, I haven't touched a drop. Get something for me to stand on, this light fitting isn't going to hold much longer.'

Bernard walked across to Arnold's body and moved the chair away from it. 'Come along now Mr Collins, I'd like to get that policy sorted out.'

'I'll sort you out in a minute if you don't get me down.' Arnold's patience was wearing thin.

Margaret prodded his leg a bit harder - nothing. 'Perhaps he has, you know....' Her words petered out.

Bernard knelt down and cautiously picked up Arnold's hand, 'Mr Collins, are you there?'

'Of course, I'm here you fool, can't you see me?'

Bernard, stabbed the air with his fist and shouted, 'Yes, yes.' He'd seen people do it on television and had always wanted an excuse to try it. 'I've done it.' In the emotion of the moment, he pulled Arnold's body up and hugged him. 'Oh, thank you Mr Collins, thank you, I was beginning to lose hope.'

It was an unfortunate moment for Arnold to re-open his eyes. 'How dare you,' he screamed, 'stop hugging me at once.'

'How can you tell if he's 'come out' and not just gone to sleep. He did mention he like an after-dinner snooze.' Margaret had been suspicious of Arnold from the moment he had walked in the office and she didn't trust him not to be playing some stupid trick.

'Asleep! Of course, I'm not asleep. I'd be snoring if I was asleep, you stupid woman.'

'I'll come out of my body, and if he's still hanging around, I should be able to see his astral spirit.' Bernard was almost beside himself with excitement.

'Hanging around! Of course, I'm still bloody well hanging around and this flex isn't going to hold much longer.' Arnold groaned. Why would no one help him?

Bernard laid down on the carpet and his astral spirit shot out of his body and bobbed in front of Arnold. Arnold looked in horror at Bernard's ghostly appearance staring him in the face and then at Bernard's body lying on the carpet next to his. The world had gone insane, or perhaps it was a terrible nightmare and he'd wake up in a minute. He shut his eyes again.

'Well done, Mr Collins, you're my first success. Now, where were you thinking of going?'

'Going! I know where I'm going - I'm going out of my mind, that's where I'm going.'

'No, of course you're not,' replied Bernard, soothingly. 'Your astral spirit has come out of your corporeal body, a perfectly natural experience.' He pointed at Arnold's body, 'Look, there it is on the floor.'

'It may be natural to you, mate, but it's not natural to me.' Arnold swung a fist at Bernard in frustration, but Bernard bobbed out of the way.

'Try to relax, Mr Collins, I know how exciting it can be the first time. Now, all you have to do is think where you want to go and you will be there instantly.'

Arnold tried to reach him again, but couldn't move the flex. 'I don't want to go anywhere, instantly, I want to get back in my body.'

'Calm down, Mr Collins, there's no need to panic.'

'Panic! Who's panicking? After all, I'm only stuck on ceiling while my body's on the floor - what's there to panic about?' He tried again to move the flex but Bernard stayed tantalisingly out of reach. 'So get me back into my body - now.'

'Of course, of course. That's no problem at all,' said Bernard reassuringly. 'Let go of the light flex and float down to it.'

'I can't, I'll fall.'

'No, you won't, I promise. Look at me, I'm not falling.'

Arnold glared at him, but had to concede that the amorphous figure in front of him was floating without any visible means of support. He gingerly let go, first with one hand and then the other. Hornby was right, he didn't fall. Then half walking, half rolling he made his way to his body.

'Now lay yourself out straight,' called Bernard.

Arnold carefully laid himself in a line above his body.

'Other way round, Mr Collins – head-to-head. I want you to have the best possible experience during re-entry.' He waved his hand slowly up and down. 'Now lower yourself in gently.'

Arnold's bottom sagged downwards and disappeared.

'Left hand down a bit, and in you go.'

Margaret watched in amazement as Arnold sat up sharply, rolled over onto his knees and shook himself like a wet retriever. 'That's it, I'm getting out of here. The building I mean, not my body,' he added hastily. And picking up his brief case he dashed out of the room.

Bernard came back into his body and rushed out after him. 'But, Mr Collins, what about the insurance?'

There was a bang as the outer door slammed shut. Bernard came back into the room. 'What a strange man. Oh well, Miss Hamilton, you'd better get on to the Prudential.'

CHAPTER 6

While David's astral body was wandering up and down the High Street, his corporeal body had been found a hospital bed and it was now connected up to various high-tech machines to monitor his condition – a condition which was puzzling the medical fraternity. As far as they could see, he'd sustained a fairly nasty bump on the head, but by now should be sitting up and taking notice, albeit under observation.

Meanwhile the policeman, who had been sent round to his flat to inform his next of kin, had been told by a neighbour, that David lived there on his own and that his fiancée, Suzie worked in a nearby florist shop. In return the officer told the neighbour that David was seriously injured in hospital after a car crash.

Soon the whole block of flats knew David was on a life support system and wasn't expected to live out the day. The vicar was alerted and had provisionally pencilled in Wednesday-fortnight for the funeral.

Suzie had had a traditional childhood – ponies in the paddock, tennis parties at the local club and a private education. This was followed by a year in France to improve her languages where she stayed with her aunt in Aix-en-Provence.

Not blessed with an analytical brain, and not required to have a career or earn a living, she occupied about fifteen hours a week working in a flower shop, making wedding bouquets and flower arrangements for offices.

The owner of the boutique rarely asked her to make wreathes as Suzie spent too much time crying over them, and on one occasion actually rotted the expensive flowers specially flown in for the funeral of a much-disliked member of parliament - so no real harm done.

She was just putting the finishing touches to a spray of white lilies and baby's breath, when the uniformed officer walked up to the counter and told her that David had been involved in an accident. 'He's been taken to the Northaven Infirmary, miss.'

Suzie immediately burst into tears. 'I must go to him straight away.' The officer, who was much taken with her bouncy blonde curls and blue eyes, instantly offered to take her there.

Before long she was sitting, looking intently at her fiancé. He occasionally flinched as if he had walked into something hard and bounced off again, but otherwise he was motionless.

It didn't look as if they would be having a celebration dinner at the Marlborough Grange Hotel anytime soon.

The doctor was noncommittal. No, they didn't know why he was still unconscious as there didn't seem to be anything wrong with him. Yes, he'd had a knock on the head in the accident but it wasn't sufficient to keep him comatose. And yes, they were going to do more tests. And no, there was nothing to worry about. At which point Suzie started worrying.

She wasn't the only one who had worries. Arnold had not even stopped to get in his car. After rushing out of Astral Travel he'd legged it down the road as fast as possible and had fallen into the first pub he came across, where he ordered a double scotch, downed it in one swallow and ordered another.

'What's the matter, mate, you look as if you've seen a ghost.' The barman, who was ritually polishing a glass, couldn't have expected such a dramatic response to his customary greeting to dishevelled customers.

Arnold shot in the air, clutched his arms round his body and fell to the floor in the foetal position.

The barman peered over the counter at him. 'I'm only joking. We've only got one sort of spirit in here,' and he tapped an optic.

Having satisfied himself that he still had his body, Arnold got up, told the barman he had tripped over an empty crisp packet and took his drink to a table. He was just about to take a sip when two girls squeezing past jogged his arm.

'Sorry, didn't see you there, mister,' said the younger one

Arnold felt panic stricken. 'What, am I invisible or something?'

'Well, there's no need to be so bad tempered,' said her companion.

'You can see me, can't you?' Arnold checked his arms and legs.

'More's the pity,' one of them mumbled, as they sat down with their sandwiches and glasses of Chardonnay.

I'm not well, thought Arnold. I must go to the doctors' - or should it be a spiritualist. There must be a faulty connection somewhere. He sipped his whisky and looked round the pub.

The two girls were deep in conversation about the previous night's rave. 'So, what happened then?' The younger one was leaning forward enthralled.

'Well, he said I had the face and figure of a goddess and he wanted to take some photos, artistic ones of course.'

Arnold, who made a habit of listening to other people's conversations, muttered: 'What a load of rubbish,' came out of his body and hung above the table.

'Oh God.' He only remembered God in extreme emergencies, 'I've done it again. Help, me someone. Grab a leg, don't let me float off.' Arnold lurched and rolled just above the heads of the regulars like an unbalanced whale.

The two girls continued discussing whether or not it was a good idea to go back to a bloke's flat on the first date, and the rest of the regular clientele tucked into their pizzas and home-made lasagnas or blew the froth off their beer. No one noticed Arnold.

Once the first panic had subsided, Arnold tried to come to terms with his situation. He had got back into his body last time so, in theory, it should be possible to do it again. He lowered himself over his body, hovering like a humming bird on steroids and dropped back in. 'Bloody hell, I can't take much more of this.'

The two girls glared at his sudden outburst. 'Stop earwigging our conversation, pervert.' said the younger one.

But Arnold didn't hear her, he was far too busy trying to keep himself together - what was causing him to keep popping out? He remembered Bernard going on about passports - no, passwords, that was it, passwords. If you say the password, you came out. But what was the password?

He back-tracked over what he had been saying. The two bits of skirt had been talking about dodgy photographs and he had said what a load of rubbish. He tried it out loud, 'What a load of rubbish.'

The two girls swung round to glare at him again, but he was staring into space, while unknown to them his astral body was floating upside down over the bar.

Arnold righted himself. 'This isn't too bad once you get used to it. I'll try a bit of doggy paddle,' he muttered to himself. Then feeling more adventurous he did a forward roll, a couple of back flips and a handstand. Now he'd got over the shock and was beginning to get the hang of the phenomenon, he decided it was quite good fun. 'All I have to say is my password to come out.' He quickly swam back to his body. 'And when I'm ready I just lower myself back in.' This time he stood on his head and slid in feet first. 'Arnold my old son, I think you've hit the jackpot.'

He repeated his password several times, much to the annoyance of his neighbours, and popped in and out with ease.

'Did you hear what he keeps saying?' said the younger one.

'Ignore him,' advised her friend. 'Then what happened?'

'Let's move away, he's listening to us, the dirty old man.' Both girls turned and glared at him again. 'He's just staring into space now, creepy old git,' she added.

Arnold was incensed. 'Not so much of the old,' he hissed as he swam past on one of his lengths up and down the pub. He'd moved on from breast stroke to over arm alternating with back stroke.

In fact, Arnold had got the hang of it so quickly, he was getting bored with swimming round the bar. 'Now what shall I do?' A bloke with a bald head was too much of a temptation. But the novelty of tap dancing on the guy's pate soon wore off and Arnold decided to travel further afield. 'That Hornby bloke had said you just thought of where you want to go and you were there.' Not being of an imaginative nature, he could only think of going home and spying on Ingrid.

The transfer from pub to home was instantaneous and caught Arnold by surprise. But he soon recovered, especially when he realised how much easier it was than driving home in the rush hour. The one fly in his ointment was - no Ingrid. Then he remembered she would still be at work. He floated down the hall to the lounge and looked at the clock. Was it really only a quarter to three? He guessed time moved at a different rate in the astral mode.

He had a quick float round the rest of the house, noting the dust on top of the wardrobe and then transferred to his office where all hell had broken loose.

Cyril Britten, was incoherent with rage. He ran on a short fuse at the best of times and this was not the best of times. For the umpteenth time he looked at his watch and then shouted down the office. 'Where is he, why isn't he here.'

For a panic-stricken moment Arnold thought he was the cause of this violent outburst, but it soon became clear that it was the computer whizz kid who was causing the problem.

'If there's one thing I can't abide, it's people being late for an appointment,' shouted Mr Britten. 'Delia, ring his office and find out what the hell is going on.'

Delia, the office receptionist, and the only one who wasn't afraid of the managing director, said, 'I've already rung three times and all I get is one of those answer phones.'

'Did you leave a message?'

'Of course I did.'

'Strongly worded I hope.'

'Yes, I said you were spitting tacks.'

'And still no answer.' Britten glared round for someone to vent his spleen on. 'Pargetter, are your files up to date and ready.'

'Yes, sir, absolutely.'

'And where's Collins? Why isn't he here?'

'I really couldn't say sir.'

'I hope he's ready for computerisation.'

'I have tried to help him,' Maurice pulled open Arnold's filing cabinet drawer, 'but they are still in a bit of a mess.'

Arnold could see that Maurice had just dumped the files he'd promised to look at back into the drawer without doing anything to them. He was so enraged by this duplicity he forgot about his body.

CHAPTER 7

Arnold might have forgotten about his body, but David was thinking of his body all the time. He had lost count of the number of bodies he'd tried to get into and he was on the point of giving up.

His wanderings had brought him to a pub in the vicinity of Gasworks Road, and he peered enviously through the window at people with bodies, who were just taking them for granted and force feeding them with food and drink.

He then noticed that one, with a vacant expression on its face, wasn't joining in the general bonhomie. I'll have one more go he thought and if this isn't me, I'm giving up.

He passed through the window and stood in front of Arnold. 'Hello, is anyone in?' he said politely. He waited a few seconds, just in case, then stood on Arnold's head and slid into his body. The sense of relief was overwhelming.

He stood up and tested his arms and legs. Yes, everything seemed to be in working order although it felt tighter than he'd expected. He sat down again and looked at the half-drunk whisky. He had no recollection of ordering it. Come to that he didn't recognise the pub either.

His take-over of Arnold's body had not gone unnoticed. The two girls had watched, fascinated, as he shook his arms and legs.

'Look at him now,' said one. 'I think he's having a fit.'

Her companion was more concerned. She got up and walked across to David's table. 'Are you okay?'

'Yes, fine thanks.' David looked at her, feeling confused, 'I'm sorry, but I appear to have forgotten your name.'

The girl looked at him, equally confused, 'That's alright, don't worry about it.'

'Can I get you another drink?'

The younger one who had followed her friend was immediately suspicious. 'Who are you?'

'Why, I'm....' He realised he still had no idea. 'Excuse me a moment,' and he went through Arnold's pockets until he found a wallet containing a five-pound note, a debit card and a business card. 'Ah, yes, I'm Arnold Collins.' This took him by surprise. 'I'm not called Arnold Collins, am I?'

'It's no use asking me, I don't know,' said the younger girl.

'But we do know each other, don't we?' David couldn't imagine going drinking with young ladies he hadn't been introduced to.

'No, we bloody don't. Are you trying to pick us up or something?'

It was worse than he thought, he'd found his body but his memory was still completely missing. 'I'm dreadfully sorry, but I appear to have lost my memory.'

'How?'

'I can't even remember that. All I know is I've just found this body and I'm not sure if...'

The two girls didn't wait for him to finish his sentence and he found himself watching them scrambling through the pub door without a backward glance.

He shrugged his shoulders, he wasn't surprised by their hasty departure, it had been that sort of day. So, he carried on looking through Arnold's pockets, hoping that something would spark off a memory.

Two grubby hankies, some loose change and a key ring later he was no further forward. He went back to the business card. Apparently, he worked for the 'Trouble-Free Insurance Agency', whoever they were.

The euphoria of finding his body was rapidly wearing off. Not only had his memory not come back, but his body still didn't seem to fit properly and felt tight around the waist. He had an overwhelming urge to go home and go to bed, but he hadn't a clue where he lived.

He picked up the business card again. Of course, his office would know where he lived. He stood up to leave and knocked over Arnold's brief case. It must be mine he thought and picked it up.

He started to walk out of the pub when the landlord reminded him that he hadn't paid for his drinks. He handed over the five-pound note, hoping it would be enough - he couldn't use his debit card because he couldn't remember his PIN.

A soon as he walked out of the door his seat was taken by a large man who ordered a ploughman's.

Arnold was still wondering how to wreak revenge on Maurice when Delia, the secretary, came into the office and said that Arnold had just rung up to ask where he lived as he had forgotten his address. 'Arnold didn't sound himself at all,' she told them. 'And fancy forgetting where he lived.'

'Where is he now?' demanded Cyril Britten.

'On his way home to bed, I suppose. I don't think he's at all well.'

'I'll deal with him in the morning,' said Britten ominously.

Arnold stopped shouting ineffectively at Maurice, Cyril Britten, and the world in general. He now had a more pressing concern - his body seemed to be having a life of its own. What was it doing ringing the office? This had to be nipped in the bud, so the sooner he got back in and resumed control the better.

He checked the pub first and was horrified to find a large man sitting in his seat. He quickly checked his body wasn't squashed underneath or lying on the floor then looked round the bar. It wasn't anywhere to be seen, and neither was his brief case. He went into panic-mode until he remembered what Delia had said about him ringing the office for his address. Of course, how sensible of it.

Arriving home instantly, he found that Ingrid still wasn't there, but more worryingly, neither was his body. He immediately went into panic mode again. Supposing it couldn't find its way home. He should never have gone off and left it in that pub. Supposing he never found it again. The thought was too horrible to contemplate. He needed help and, much as he hated to admit it, Bernard Hornby seemed the best person to ask.

As soon as Miss Long had got back to her small, but comfortable flat, she'd made herself a cup of tea and a ham sandwich before opening her copy of Stephen Hawkins' 'A Brief History of Time', which had been published the year before.

She had been a physics and chemistry teacher at a small private school, where it is unlikely that any of the gels retained one scrap of what they learned once they left, primarily because she was too short to be seen over her desk. But Miss Long had retained a life-long interest in the subjects and her book shelves sagged under the weight of several incomprehensible tomes. The reason she was enjoying Stephen Hawkins' book was, it was readable if not entirely understandable.

She thought she could remember Einstein's Theory of Relativity, both the special and the general, but she wanted to check a few details, such as clocks running backwards – it might make all the difference to being able to come out of her body and start travelling. And as she had another session booked for the afternoon, she was determined to do everything possible to ensure success.

In fact, she was so certain of success she arrived early and managed to grab the biggest cushion.

Bernard's afternoon clients were a mixture of bored housewives, the unemployed and a couple of pensioners, who like Miss Long were hoping for a cheap holiday.

Having explained how it all worked, Bernard stood among the supine bodies intoning. 'Relax and let your astral body float free.' The intoning wasn't necessary, but Bernard thought it added a nice touch. 'Say your password and let your astral body come out.'

Arnold stood in front of him. 'Right, where is it? Where's my body, where would it go?'

Bernard walked right through him and lifted his arms theatrically. 'Release it from its confines.' He walked between his clients, repeating, more in hope than belief, 'Look, it's floating free.'

'Where?' Arnold looked round the room. 'No, it's not, where is it?'
'Your astral body wants to travel,' Bernard intoned. Arnold crossed the room to catch up with him 'Never mind about their astral bodies, what about my nice fleshy one?' As he stepped on one client's stomach, the man's astral body started to come out and stared at him.
'Do you mind, I've a bone to pick with Hornby,' snapped Arnold and stepped off the other side.
The man was so shocked at such rudeness he shot back in again.
'Did anyone come out?' Bernard was starting to feel desperate.
One woman said she felt a bit peculiar and an excited Lettice thought her feet had come out.
'It's got to be all or nothing Miss Long. You can't just have your feet out.'
'Are you listening to me, Hornby,' shouted Arnold, but Bernard walked straight through him again as his clients got to their feet, brushed fluff of their clothes and started for the door.
Bernard headed them off saying they still had thirty minutes of their session left and to try again.
One or two hesitated and Arnold screamed at them. 'You must be mad coming here, look what he's done to me.' But it was pointless. No one could hear him, no one could see him and he had no idea what to do next.
Meanwhile, Bernard and Margaret were trying with various degrees of success to get his clients to book another session. Lettice put her name down again for the following day, but others said they would think about it, which is the same as saying no, not on your life.

One man, however, stayed behind and followed Bernard into his office. "Eeee lad, I didn't like to say nowt in front of t'others in case I'd got it wrong. But I did start to float off and I would have gone much higher but there were this bloke standing on me stomach. Does that always happen?'

Bernard was staggered. 'Good heavens no! Are you sure you weren't imagining things?'

'No, he were definitely on me stomach, and he seemed to be shouting at you.'

CHAPTER 8

If Arnold had only waited a little longer at his house instead of rushing back to Gasworks Road, he would have met his body coming up the garden path, carrying a small bunch of flowers.

David, having got his address from Delia, had used the last of his change to buy a street map and few wilting roses - he had a vague feeling he'd planned to get some for his wife or girlfriend. But the rest of his memories were still as elusive as ever.

He could see that getting to Whitehouse Road would be a bit of a trek, but he hoped the walk would make his body feel more comfortable, like working in a new pair of shoes, but without the blisters.

He stood outside number 27, a slightly forlorn, semi-detached, pebble-dashed bungalow and shuddered – surely, he didn't live here! He eventually found the right key and opened the front door. If he thought going inside would bring back his memory he was doomed to disappointment.

Desperate to escape the flowery wall paper and geometrically-patterned carpet in the hall, he tried the door in front of him and found himself in the lounge, where the eclectic interior design was even more pronounced with the addition of Regency-striped curtains and flowery scatter cushions on a sagging sofa.

There was a mirror over the fireplace and he went and looked in it.

His reflection showed a tall, slightly pigeon-chested man in his forties with thinning brown hair, needing a haircut. He ran his fingers over his face, it felt old and wrinkly. I don't even recognise myself, he thought, surely, I'm younger than this.

In a bureau, on the other side of the room, he found some letters and started reading one. 'Dear Ingrid and Arnold, sorry it's been so long since I wrote'. Who was Ingrid? His wife? His girlfriend? His sister? He then realised he needed the bathroom and he had to find it quick. Which isn't easy when you have no idea where the bathroom is.

Suzie was still sitting in the ward, holding David's hand. He had stopped moving his legs about and now a look of utter relief had just come over his face. He was still unconscious but she thought he looked happier. Even the bump on his forehead seemed to be subsiding.

Although the consultant had said there was nothing to worry about, and that he would soon recover consciousness, Suzie wasn't convinced he was getting the best attention. She also wanted somewhere more private to sit with her fiancé.

For once she was pleased that her father had insisted on buying each of the family the latest Motorola mobile phone even though it took up most of the space in her dainty handbag. 'Daddy, would you pay for David to be moved into the private wing. I think he would be happier there.'

Her father, Cameron Baker-Brown, didn't want his future son-in-law to be happy anywhere, and the longer he stayed unconscious the better. He didn't wish him ill, but he didn't wish him to be part of the Baker-Brown family either. But if this hard-headed business man had a soft spot, it was for his only child Suzie. 'I'll see what I can do Suzie, but moving him might not be for the best.'

'But it will be so much nicer for me if I could sit with him in a private room.'

Against his better judgement Cameron capitulated.

Suzie was just saying thank you when the ward sister burst through the curtains, glaring at the mobile phone in Suzie's hand. 'You can't use that thing in here young lady, it will affect all the medical devices. Heaven knows what damage you might have done.' And she bustled over to the monitors to check on all David's vital signs.

Suzie jumped up, mortified. 'He's still alright, isn't he?'

The sister took her time checking. 'As far as I can see no harm's been done and everything is the same as before. But please do not use that phone again on hospital premises.'

Sitting back down, Suzie promised faithfully that she wouldn't, and she held on tightly to David's hand while intently watching the monitors for any signs of abnormal movement.

Once it became clear that no help was to be had at Gasworks Road, Arnold went home where to his relief, he saw his brief case in the hall. If his brief case had come home then so had his body.

He relief dissipated somewhat when he saw his body sitting in the lounge, in his dressing gown, reading letters. This independent lifestyle had to be stopped, pronto, or who knew where it could lead? He might want to go out for a quick half of best bitter in the evening and his body might have other ideas.

He hovered over it, stood on his head and prepared to lower himself in. To his amazement, he bounced straight off. He tried again with the same result. He stood in front of himself to have another go.

At that moment David looked up from the letter and saw Arnold's spectral shape hovering in front of his face. He jumped up in horror. 'What the f....' he gasped.

It was now Arnold's turn to be horrified. 'My body spoke to me. What the hell's going on?'

David rushed to the mirror. 'I'm seeing things, I must be going mad.' He turned and looked back at Arnold and then in the mirror and nearly fainted – his reflection and the spectral shape had identical facial features, although the rest of the shape was an unclothed, amorphous outline.

'Let me get back in, what the hell do you think you're playing at.' Arnold was getting annoyed.

David closed his eyes. 'Go away, go away.'

'I'm not going away, you're my body, you can't manage without me.' Arnold had another unsuccessful go at getting in.

'I'm seeing double,' mumbled David, keeping his eyes tightly closed, 'I must have had a blow on the head. I've got concussion. I need to sit down.' He sat back on the sofa and took his pulse.

Arnold floated cautiously up to David. 'Who's that talking?'

David paused with his finger pressed on his wrist. He'd never had concussion before so wasn't sure of the correct way to address a version of himself bobbing in front him. Should he answer himself or would that make matters worse? Decision made he shut his eyes and whispered 'Me, I'm talking to me.'

For a horrible moment Arnold wondered briefly if there was someone else in his body, but then dismissed the idea as fanciful. He tried cajoling, 'Look, stop messing about and let me in.'

David took a quick peep and then shut his eyes again. 'If I sit here quietly, and ignore it, it will fade away,' he muttered. 'I'm not going mad - I've just got concussion.'

'Who's got concussion?' Arnold was starting to worry. Had his body had an accident on its way home?

'I have…I think.'

'So what happened to you?'

'I can't remember.' David thought this was the oddest conversation he had ever had.

Arnold started to worry that his body had crashed the car. He looked out of the window, there was no car in the drive, had his body put it in the garage to hide the damage? 'What have you done with the car?'

'What car?'

'You know very well what car. You didn't try to drive it home without me, did you?'

'No, I walked.'

'But that's miles.' Arnold re-visited the idea of someone else being in his body – he never walked anywhere if he could help it. 'Is there someone in there?'

'Yes, me,' David whispered.

'It's no use saying, me - I want a name, come on spit it out.'

'Go away,' David whispered even more quietly.

'No, I won't go away, mate, I want to know who are you?'

David felt under the letter he'd been reading and found Arnold's business card. 'Arnold Collins.'

'Aha, gotcha, you're not Arnold Collins, I am,' He adopted a threatening stance, 'so come out with your hands up.'

It was at this point that David realised he wasn't in his own body - no wonder it didn't fit.

Arnold was still bouncing up and down, throwing air punches. 'Come on, I'm not telling you twice.'

David tried to ignore him. So, if he was in the wrong body, where was his and even more importantly, who was he.

'I don't know who you think you are taking over my body, but I'm not putting up with it,' and Arnold threw another punch.

'That's the problem,' whispered David, 'I don't know who I am, I think I've lost my memory.'

Arnold shot up to the ceiling with rage. 'You're in my body and you don't even know who you are.'

'Look could you come down off the curtain rail, I'm getting a crick in my neck.'

'My neck if you don't mind. So why did you pick on my body?'

'Because I thought it was mine,' David said, defensively, 'It was the only one I could get into. And stop bobbing up and down like that it's making me feel queasy.'

Arnold positioned himself face to face with David and glared at him. 'So, where's your body, sunshine?'

'I don't know.' David then decided attack was the best form of defence and glared right back at Arnold. 'Perhaps you shouldn't have left yours just sitting there, empty, in that pub.'

'What! You can't go around taking other people's bodies just because they look empty. You, you, body-napper, you, come out, now.'

Arnold threw more air punches, but David stood up and looked in the mirror again. Nothing had changed, but one thing he was certain about, if this wasn't his body then he wasn't giving it up until he found his. 'I need time to think.'

'Well, let's see if this helps your thought processes.' Arnold swung another punch, but his fist passed straight through David's shoulder - much to the surprise of both of them.

They looked at each other, then David sat down again and Arnold hovered in a seated position next to him. They both reflected on the situation for several minutes then Arnold said, 'Wait a minute, wait a minute, what are you doing in my pyjamas and dressing gown? It's bad enough having my body, but you've no right to wear my clothes.'

'I needed a shower and what you were wearing was pretty grubby so I couldn't put those clothes back on. I found these in the bathroom.'

Arnold couldn't fault the logic of David's argument - he'd worn the same clothes yesterday and possibly the day before.

There was another long silence while they ruminated. Then Arnold said, 'Can you see me?'

'Yes, of course I can.'

'That's funny, because no one else can. What do I look like?'

David turned and looked at him closely. 'Sort of ghostly.'

Arnold floated to the mirror, but much as he feared, there was no reflection. 'But what do I look like?'

'You look like me - or rather, you look like you. No, I look like you. Sorry, I'm a bit confused now.'

'You're a bit confused, how do you think I feel?' Arnold scratched his head, although he couldn't feel it. 'I know, there's a Polaroid camera in the sideboard, take a photo of me.'

David rummaged around and pulled out an ancient camera and a packet of films. He looked at them, but had no idea how to use the camera. 'Now what?'

Arnold sighed with exasperation and explained how to fit the packet of films in and take a photo.

David lined up the camera as best he could, pressed the button and then watched in fascination as the photo slid out of the front of the camera and an image slowly appeared. Unfortunately, not an image of Arnold.

'Take another one, you weren't pointing it at me.'

David used up all the photos in the pack and laid them out on the coffee table. They showed the wallpaper in detail, the fireplace, the curtains, the carpet and the settee, but not one of them showed Arnold. 'What shall I do with them?'

Arnold floated round the room in frustration. 'Do what you like.'

David took them into the kitchen and put them in the bin. When he returned Arnold was staring, pointlessly into the mirror. 'I wonder why you can see me when no one else can.'

David was wishing he couldn't see him either. 'I don't know.'

'Perhaps it's because you're in my body.'

'Yes, that might be it,' David said, trying to be helpful.

'Which just proves it's mine, so come out.' Arnold was starting to feel aggressive again.

'I never said it wasn't yours, but I don't want to come out until I find mine.'

They had reached an impasse, and David had the body. Arnold decided to change tack. 'So where is your body? Let's go together and look for it.'

'I told you I don't know. I've lost my memory.'

Arnold's conciliatory manner immediately vanished. 'You shouldn't go round losing your memory.'

'And perhaps you shouldn't go round losing your body.'

'I didn't lose it. I left it sitting safely in the pub. You stole it and I want it back.'

'No. I've been wandering round nearly all day. You don't know what it's like not having a body.'

'Of course, I know what it's like, what do you think I've been doing the past few hours?' Arnold's temper was rising again.

'But at least you know who you are,' reasoned David. 'Just let me stay in here until I've got my memory back.'

'And how long's that going to take?'

'I don't know.'

Arnold relapsed into spoilt-child mode. 'But that's not fair.'

'It won't be for long. As soon as I remember who I am, I'll be able to remember where my body is, and then I'll be gone. Just a few days at the most.'

'A few days! A few days!' Arnold's voice shot up two octaves. 'You're not staying in there a few days. It will be second hand when I get it back. How do I know it will still fit me. How tall are you?'

'Five foot nine.' David suddenly realised he had remembered something. 'See, it's working already, I've remembered how tall I am.'

'Five foot nine, that's terrible.'

Now David could feel the aggression rising, 'What's wrong with being five foot nine?' He did suffer slightly from shorter-man syndrome.

'Everything. I'm over six-foot, your feet will only come half way down my legs. Your toes will be sticking out just below my knee caps.'

'Rubbish.' David opened the dressing gown and rolled up Arnold's pyjama trousers. They both peered at his legs. 'See, nothing there.'

'They haven't come through yet, but they will, mate, they will. And I expect you're fatter than me, you'll stretch me. When I get it back it will be all baggy and wrinkled.'

'It feels fine to me.' Which wasn't strictly true, Arnold's body definitely pinched a bit, but David wasn't going to admit to that. 'And it will still fit you when you get it back.'

'Pop out a minute, let me just try it.'

'Oh no, you're not catching me like that.'

Again, they had reached an impasse.

Arnold floated up to the ceiling reflecting on his predicament when he had a lightbulb moment. 'I know where your body is, 17 Gasworks Road, not far from that pub.'

'Gasworks Road! What on earth would I be doing in a place called Gasworks Road? I don't even know where it is.'

'How do you know you don't, you've lost your memory – or so you say.'

David had no answer to that. 'So, what was I doing there?'

Arnold was getting excited. 'You must have gone there for a cheap holiday, don't you remember?'

'No, it doesn't ring a bell.' David couldn't say why, but he was pretty certain he'd never been to Gasworks Road for a holiday.

Arnold's excitement turned to desperation again. 'You must have been there. Astral Travel. Bernard Hornby. He shows people how to come out of their bodies.'

'He does what!' David couldn't believe anyone would want to come out of their bodies voluntarily.

'I've just told you. People pay him to get their astral bodies out.'

'What on earth for?'

'So, they can go on holiday.'

'Is that what you did, come out and go on holiday?'

'No, I went there to sell him some insurance, I came out by mistake.' Arnold hoped David hadn't heard the last bit.

But David had. 'So, if you came out by mistake in some weird travel agency, what was your body doing in that pub?'

'That's beside the point.' Arnold snapped hurriedly, and he went and peered in the mirror again. All he could see was his body sitting on the settee behind him, looking at him suspiciously. 'If you must know I popped in for a quick drink.'

'Still in your body?'

'Yes, of course I was. It would be a bit difficult to knock back a couple of whiskies if I wasn't.'

David remembered the empty glass on the table. 'I had to pay for those you know.'

Arnold glared at him, 'But with my money, sunshine.'

David conceded the point, 'But it still doesn't explain why your body was sitting there empty.'

If astral bodies can look embarrassed, then Arnold's did. 'I came out again by mistake...I didn't mean to, but it happened.'

'So, why didn't you get back in?'

Arnold could hardly admit to paying a flying visit home followed by a lengthy trip to the office. 'That's not the point.'

'I think it is. If we are being logical about the situation, this is all your fault for leaving your body empty, in that pub.' Their argument had now gone full circle and David felt he had won.

Logic had never formed part of Arnold's psyche so he resorted once again to threats of violence. And when that didn't work – to grovelling. 'Look, you can't be comfortable in there. You'll be much better off in your own. So, just come out of my body, think of Astral Travel and you'll be there in a fraction of a second. It's so easy.'

'Well,' said David, not unreasonably, 'as it's so easy, you go and see if I'm there. And if I am, come back and tell me and then I'll come out.'

'But I don't know what you look like.'

'Neither do I.'

They had reached another impasse and Arnold was livid. 'This is ridiculous, come out of my body.'

But before they could continue the argument, they were both stopped in their tracks by the sound of the front door opening.

David's heart thumped. 'Who's that?' And he jumped up and backed towards the fireplace.

'How should I know.'

'Is it your wife? Is it," he looked at the letter in his hand, 'Ingrid?'

'You want my body, mate, you work it out.' And with that triumphant parry Arnold disappeared.

Stella walked into the lounge and dropped some shopping on the settee. She had sent Ingrid into the kitchen to make a cup of tea and was about to sit down when she noticed David. Throwing her hand dramatically over her heart she said, 'Oooh, you did startle me, Arnold. What are you doing home in the middle of the afternoon - and in your dressing gown?'

David hesitated, gulped, walked across, and kissed her on the cheek. 'Hello, darling.'

'Don't you darling me Arnold Collins,' Stella hissed, and clipped him hard round the ear.

CHAPTER 9

Ingrid burst into the lounge and flung her arms round David. 'So, you didn't forget after all.'

He and Stella stared at her equally surprised. His head was still ringing from Stella's slap and he had no idea who this second woman was. He quickly decided he wasn't going to use any more terms of endearment, they led to unprovoked violence.

Stella recovered first. 'Don't tell me he remembered your wedding anniversary!'

'He did and he bought me some roses.' And Ingrid planted a large kiss on David's cheek.

Stella looked at David suspiciously. 'Did you indeed. And how many years have you been married?'

David looked from one to the other - was this woman his wife? She was older than he'd expected. 'I…can't remember,' he mumbled.

'Now why am I not surprised.' Stella turned to Ingrid, 'Don't worry about the tea, I'd rather get off home, I've had a bit of a shock.' And after a quick glare at David, she swept out of the room, calling out that she'd see Ingrid in the morning.

Ingrid, took a closer look at David, 'Are you ill Arnold, you're in your pyjamas?'

'No…umm actually I was wondering if I have any clean clothes anywhere.' David felt distinctly uncomfortable in Arnold's nightwear now that Ingrid had arrived.

Ingrid took an even closer look at David, 'Of course you have. Didn't you look in your drawers?' She patted him on the bottom, 'go on, go and get changed while I cook you something nice for tea.'

She watched him heading down the hall. 'Are you sure you're feeling okay, Arnold?'

'Yes, Ingrid, why?'

'You've just walked into the broom cupboard.'

David hurriedly extracted himself from the vacuum cleaner. 'Perhaps I'll stay in my pyjamas after all.'

Ingrid felt a wave of excitement. Then she put the roses in a vase and carried them into the lounge.

Arnold meanwhile had headed back to 17 Gasworks Road. He'd had another brilliant lightbulb moment. As soon as he found David's empty body, he would get in it and take it home, and then they could swap over. Simple.

Or it would have been if there had been any bodies lying around. Arnold couldn't believe it - the separating room was deserted. He could hear voices in Bernard's office so slid through the wall and found Bernard and Margaret looking more than a little disconsolate.

'Why are they finding it so difficult?' Bernard slouched back in his chair. 'Perhaps this was all a terrible idea.'

Margaret felt panicky, she could feel her job slipping away. 'You don't find it difficult Mr Hornby and look at that insurance guy, he popped out and he wasn't even trying.'

Bernard brightened up. 'That's true. I expect at this very moment he's enjoying a trip to some exotic clime.'

'Are you mad,' screamed Arnold, 'you should be banned.' He wasn't quite sure what Bernard should be banned from, but that didn't stop him feeling very strongly about it.

'Didn't you enjoy your tea, Arnold? I noticed you were picking at it.' Ingrid was desperately trying to correct her husband's gastric imbalance. After finding the roses in kitchen, a first as far as she could remember, she was hopeful the night would be one of wild passion or at the very least a kiss and a cuddle.

'Sorry, Ingrid, I've got a lot on my mind,' and David pushed the uneaten food to one side.

'That was my favourite meal too.' David jumped. Arnold was floating above the table glaring at him. 'Burger, chips and beans and you've hardly eaten any of it.'

Ingrid picked up the plates and headed for the kitchen, but not before she'd said, 'I thought we'd have a nice early night tonight.'

David was horrified. 'I don't think I'm tired yet.'

'Neither am I. I thought we'd, you know…' and she disappeared.

'What are you doing back here?' David hissed at Arnold. 'Why aren't you looking for my body?'

'I was but it wasn't in Gasworks Road. Now go and get that food back out of the bin. I'm starving.'

'I can't do that, that's disgusting.'

'Oh, so the thought of having an early night is disgusting is it.' Ingrid stood with two dishes of tinned rice pudding in her hands, and a look on her face which suggested that both of them could get tipped over his head, rapidly followed by the tin.

'No, of course I don't think that,' David gritted his teeth, 'there's nothing I'd like more.'
'Are you mad? I'm always telling her I can't cuddle on a full stomach. You are ruining my life.' Arnold threw a punch at David. He knew it would go straight through him, but he couldn't think of any other way of venting his anger.
'But shouldn't we eat our pudding first, Ingrid?' David was now wishing he hadn't passed on the burger, chips and beans. If he'd eaten them really slowly it would have bought him some more time. He was also wishing he hadn't bought the roses because they seemed to be the catalyst for her planned night of passion.

Margaret fanned out the holiday brochures across Bernard's desk. 'Everything new takes time to get going. Why, I remember Gold Leaf Travel struggled in the beginning.'
Bernard wasn't sure whether this was a comfort or not, after all they had gone bust in the end. 'So, what do you suggest Miss Hamilton?'
'Well, I think the first thing we should do is start calling each other by our first names, after all we are in this together... Bernard.'
Bernard, who'd never called anyone by their first names at the bank, had to mull that suggestion over for a few seconds, but Margaret saying they were in his enterprise together gave him a warm glow. 'What a good idea...Margaret.'
Margaret smiled at him, 'The next thing is our advertising campaign.'

'Do we have to do that right now?' Because of his trip to Nice, Bernard hadn't had any lunch and was starving. 'And you should get off home, it's way past six-o-clock.'

Margaret thought about her bleak little house. The cat would be out, it had a far better social life than she did, and her mother would be in her bedsit upstairs, watching telly with the sound turned up full blast and eating digestive biscuits.

Bernard thought about his empty detached Mock-Tudor four-bedroomed, two-bath-roomed house with garden room. His wife had died many years ago, and in her memory, he kept it pristine. He hardly dared use the cooker in case he made it dirty, so he existed on toast, cereal and microwave meals.

They looked at each other. 'I wonder...' Bernard said 'if we could...'

'...have a quick coffee to talk about what we do next?' Margaret said.

'Or a glass of wine...?'

'...would be lovely.'

David had made his rice pudding last longer than any other human before him, by chewing on each separate grain nineteen times. He could feel Ingrid's eyes on him, willing him to eat faster. Finally, he could drag it out no longer, his dish was cleaner than a new pin, and if he licked his spoon anymore the nickel plating would disappear. And all the while he could see Arnold's ghostly form hovering in front of him - glaring.

'I wonder if I could have a cup of coffee, Ingrid.'

Ingrid looked surprised, 'Don't you mean tea, Arnold? You always say coffee in the evening makes you want to get up in the night.' She looked at him questioningly.

David looked at Arnold questioningly. Arnold nodded so David apologised and said of course he meant tea.

While Ingrid was in the kitchen, Arnold said, 'You'd better not be thinking of going to bed with my wife.'

'That's the last thing I want to do.'

'So come out of my body and you won't have to.'

David was nearly tempted, but only nearly. The only way he was going to find his body was to use Arnold's to track it down. If necessary, he would pretend to have a heart attack to save going to bed with Ingrid - even if it meant being hauled off to hospital in an ambulance. Desperate situations called for desperate measures.

Ingrid brought in a tray of tea and put it on the low table in front of the settee. 'Why are you still sitting up at the dining table Arnold? It's much more comfortable here.' She patted the seat nearest the telly and then poured the tea.

David sat down gingerly, picked up his cup, took a mouthful and then spat it out. 'It's got sugar in it.

'You always have sugar in it, three spoon-fulls.'

'No, I don't.' David was still trying to get the taste of syrup out of his mouth. Then he realised another piece of his memory had come back. It seemed to creep up on him when he wasn't trying to remember things.

He looked up and saw Ingrid watching him suspiciously. 'Sorry I didn't realise you had already put it in…I, um thought I would try tea without it for a while.' He patted Arnold's stomach in a manner oddly familiar to him. 'I need to lose a bit of weight.' He smiled weakly and forced the rest of the tea down. 'So, no sugar from now on.'

Ingrid felt bleak inside. According to Stella, as well as buying flowers, another sign of adultery was trying to lose weight. Although why Arnold felt the need to diet was beyond her as he was as thin as a rake.

David looked up to see Arnold glaring at him again. 'How dare you change my tea-drinking habits. You might be in my body, but you have no right to make alterations without my permission.'

David acknowledged Arnold had a point so said, 'Actually, Ingrid, I've changed my mind, I won't go on a diet after all.'

Ingrid immediately brightened up and moved closer to David who was already jammed up against the arm.

Arnold, who had forced himself between them, wriggled, fidgeted and moaned. 'Oy, you're squashing me. It's only a two-seater you know.'

'Shall we have a little cuddle before going to bed?' Ingrid murmured and put her head on David's shoulder.

Arnold stared at David. 'If you want my help finding your body...'

David got the message. 'It's no good Ingrid I can't.'

Ingrid sat up and slammed the cups back onto the tray. 'Then it's obvious isn't it - someone has come between us.' And she walked out of the room.

David felt exhausted. It had been a weird sort of day. The long walk from the pub to Whitehouse Road and now avoiding Ingrid's attempts at romance were taking their toll. He looked down at Arnold's body and came to the conclusion that it was totally unfit. 'You really should take better care of yourself you know.'

Arnold glared at him. 'I know what's best for my body and it doesn't include exercise. So don't be getting any funny ideas.'

'Don't worry, I won't, all I want to do is to get to bed.'

'I've warned you sunshine, you are not sleeping with my wife.'

'I don't want to believe me.'

Arnold disappeared for a moment, but was soon back. 'She's cleaning the cooker, but that won't take long, so you'd better hurry up and work out how you are going to sleep in the spare room.'

'So just saying I would like to won't work?'

'No, believe me if it did, I'd be in there all the time.'

Another sliver of memory came back to David, and he remembered a little trick he'd perfected when he didn't want to go to school. He headed to the bathroom and ran the hot tap then held a steaming flannel on his forehead for as long as he could bear it before heading to the kitchen.

Ingrid was just rinsing the sink round. 'Yes?' she snapped.

'I don't feel well Ingrid, I think I've got flu.' He put her hand on his forehead, which was bright red, 'see how hot it is.'

'I'll get the thermometer,' Ingrid immediately turned into Florence Nightingale.

'No, that won't be necessary.' But Ingrid was already heading to the bathroom.

David quickly ran the hot tap and held the scalding liquid in his mouth as long as possible. The thermometer Ingrid held under his tongue registered hundred and three degrees. 'Arnold, you're burning up. Do you have any other symptoms?'

'Yes, I ache all over and I feel sick,' David wracked his brains, '…and I've got a headache…and toothache as well.'

'You must go straight to bed with a hot water bottle. Come along and I'll tuck you in and then make you a nice lemon drink to have with some aspirin.'

David felt bad because Ingrid was being so kind, but Arnold was glaring at him. 'That's really nice of you Ingrid...and I think I should sleep in the spare room tonight.' The atmosphere in the kitchen turned icy. 'It's just I don't want you to catch it.' The temperature plummeted even more.

'You can sort yourself out then.' And Ingrid stormed out of the kitchen, slammed into the lounge and turned on the television – full blast.

'You'd better grab some sheets out of the airing cupboard.' Arnold led the way and then showed David the guest room.

A few minutes later Ingrid snatched up the vase of roses and stormed into the kitchen. She was about to dump them in the bin when she saw the polaroid photos in there. Puzzled, she laid them out on the kitchen table. Why was Arnold taking photos of the lounge? She put them in her handbag to show Stella the following day.

PART TWO – FRIDAY

CHAPTER 10

David hadn't expected to sleep a wink. After Ingrid had gone to bed, he'd laid on the lumpy mattress, shivering as much as if he'd really did have flu because he couldn't find any blankets. Arnold refused to tell him where they were and he didn't dare ask Ingrid for any.

He finally dropped off at six-o-clock, but was woken at seven-thirty by an almighty bang, like a door slamming. He looked round the unfamiliar room and promptly put his head under the sheet hoping it was all a dream and he would wake up in his own bed.

The noise of crashing crockery forced him to have another look. The room still looked unfamiliar, and even worse he could see what appeared to be a ghost floating near the curtain rail and snoring.

Then it all came flooding back.

Arnold woke with a start, turned upside down and hung onto the curtains like a bat. He looked round, trying to get his bearings. Why was he in the spare bedroom? Why was he clinging to the curtains? And who the hell was that man in the spare bed?

When he saw it was himself, the horror of his situation all came flooding back, with a vengeance.

David sat up and glared at Arnold, who glared back and said, 'What was that loud bang?'

'I think it was your wife slamming the door.'

'Nothing new there then. Is she cooking breakfast?'

'How would I know? I've only just woken up.'

'I didn't sleep a wink you know.'

'Neither did I, it was freezing in here. Please can you tell me where can I find some blankets?'

'You won't need any blanket if you come out of my body.'

David sighed, it looked as if they were going to be having the same conversation that they'd been having for most of the night - Arnold demanding his body back and David refusing to come out until he'd found his own. 'We need an action plan.'

'Yes, well I can't do anything until I've had breakfast, I'm not going to work on an empty stomach.' It then hit Arnold that he wouldn't be going to work at all. He scowled at David, 'And you can't go to work either, you'll mess everything up. You'll have to phone in sick.'

David had no intention of going to Arnold's office. He couldn't remember what he did for a living, but he was certain he didn't work in insurance - although he had a vague feeling that there was a connection.

At that moment they heard footsteps outside the bedroom door, which was flung open revealing an angry Ingrid. 'Your breakfast is on the kitchen table Arnold. I'm going round to Stella's.'

David quickly pulled the sheet up to his chin. 'I'm really ill, 'he croaked, 'could you ring the office and say I won't be in today.' Ingrid continued to glare at him. 'Please, Ingrid.'

He certainly didn't sound himself, Ingrid thought, perhaps he really was ill. She decided to apply the acid test. 'I take it you won't want your breakfast then.' Arnold would have to be dying to turn down food.

'No, sorry Ingrid, I couldn't eat a thing.' David heard Arnold shouting at him, but ignored the invective.

'Oh my goodness, Arnold, you really are ill. Don't worry, I'll your office and then I'll ring the Co-op and say I won't be in today.' She reached over and touched David's forehead. 'You feel quite icy.'

David didn't have to pretend to shiver. 'If I could just have a blanket or two, I can't seem to get warm.'

Ingrid reverted to Florence Nightingale mode again, 'I'll get them straight away, what were you thinking of going to bed with just a sheet?'

'It was the fever, Ingrid,' David tried to make himself look as ill as possible. 'I think I was hallucinating.' Well, that part was true he thought.

'And I'll bring you a nice cup of tea and a hot water bottle as well.'

As soon as she'd gone Arnold started shouting again. 'Why did you turn down breakfast? Friday is fried egg, fried bread and bacon with black pudding.'

'I don't think I could face that. I normally have muesli and yoghurt.'

'Muesli and yoghurt!!! That won't put hairs on your chest.'

But David wasn't listening, another sliver of memory had come back, confirming that he was careful about his body, which would be in much better shape than Arnold's. He couldn't wait to get back in it.

'You do realise you can't let her stay at home to look after you, don't you?'

'I know that. And could you please stop bobbing up and down you are making me feel sea sick.' David desperately needed a cup of strong coffee.

What he got was a cup of strong tea with four spoons of sugar and a hot water bottle. Ingrid then fussed round the bed covering him in blankets and eider downs. The combination of a boiling beverage and layers of bedclothes turned him bright red.

Ingrid felt his forehead. 'Your temperature has shot up again, Arnold. Now you just lie quietly while I pop next door and tell Stella, I'm not coming into work.'

As soon as she'd gone David asked who Stella was.

Arnold pulled a face. 'The harridan from hell, she lives next door. Now get up and eat that breakfast, I'm starving and we don't have long.'

'Does she wear a bright pink shell suit with purple chevrons?'

'I don't know, but it sounds like her style. Late fifties, frizzy curls and bright blue eyeliner. Now get up.'

'It's just she slapped me round the face yesterday.' David could still feel the blow.

'What the hell did you do?'

'I gave her a kiss.'

'You did what? Are you insane?' Arnold paced up and down the bed.

'I thought she was your wife.'

'What the hell made you think that?'

'Well, she walked in as if she owned the place and asked what I was doing home from work. I don't think it was unreasonable to think she was Ingrid.'

'Reason has nothing to do with it, I'll never hear the end of this.' Arnold paced again - he'd forgotten about food. 'Perhaps Stella won't say anything,'

The bedroom door was flung open with a bang which reverberated through the house. Ingrid approached the bed, 'Arnold, Stella says you kissed her yesterday. She thinks you've turned into a sex maniac.' David and Arnold stared at her, but before either of them could speak, she added, 'I'm going to work, you can look after yourself.'

The slamming of the bedroom door was followed by the slamming of the front door. Arnold peered out of the window. 'She's gone next door again - they always walk to the Co-op together after an hour of gossip.' He rubbed his hands together. 'Well, it's an ill wind and all that...' and he headed to the kitchen where much to his disgust he found Ingrid had binned his breakfast.

He pointed out the congealed mess to David. 'This is all your fault, so you'd better start cooking sunshine because I'm starving. I'll show you where the eggs and bacon are.'

Suzie woke with a crick in her neck and looked round the unfamiliar room. David had been moved temporarily to a side ward, until a private room became available, and she'd been allowed to sleep in the chair next to him. A nurse bustled in and looked at the clipboard on the end of his bed. Then she took his temperature and blood pressure. 'All his vital signs are looking good and he's got a much better colour this morning, in fact he looks quite rosy.'

Suzie stood up and looked at him. 'He does, doesn't he. Yesterday evening he went bright red, is that a good sign?'

'You'd better ask the doctor that when he does his rounds.' The nurse snapped on a pair of rubber gloves, 'and now I have to give him a bed bath so why don't you run along and get some breakfast in the cafeteria.'

Margaret had come in early, determined to make 17 Gasworks Road, look a bit more inviting. She'd brought with her a selection of cleaning products, polishes, dusters and air fresheners as well as a carpet sweeper and a dustpan and brush, and was bent on giving the separating room a good going over.

As she worked, she thought back over the previous evening spent with Bernard. It had started with a glass of wine or two in the 'Rose and Crown' where they'd fallen into such an easy conversation that Bernard had suggested they have a Ploughman's, and they finally bonded over the spicy pickle.

She learned he was a widower with two grown-up children, one in Australia and one in Canada.

'Is that why you are so keen on astral travel?' she asked.

'It doesn't really work like that Margaret, they can't see me and I can't contact them, so I don't like to visit, it would be an invasion of their privacy.' He lowered his voice, 'but I do sometimes watch the grandchildren when they are playing in the park.'

Margaret thought that sounded very sad. 'So how often do you visit them, like, the normal way?'

'I try to see each family at least once a year, and they come here of course.'

Margaret wasn't convinced, she decided Bernard was putting a gloss on his family's visits, or rather the lack of them, but she didn't like to pursue the subject.

She pulled on her jacket and wrapped her scarf round her neck. 'I think I'd better be getting back to mother, but thank you for a lovely meal.' Then, with great daring she said, 'I insist I pay next time.'

Bernard insisted on walking her to her car, and when she was safely locked in and had driven off, he climbed into his. The day had not started too well, but it had ended much better he thought.

Arnold insisted on a full fry-up and watched eagerly while David forced it down. However, he refused the builders' tea which Arnold favoured and made himself a cup of instant coffee from a jar well past its sell-by date.

'There, doesn't that feel better.' Arnold burped and settled back, floating somewhere between the kitchen table and the back door, 'You can't tell me that yoghurt and muesli can fill you up like bacon and eggs. I have to say, you're a pretty good cook.'

David had given up trying to understand the mechanics of their situation, such as why he felt bloated, but Arnold was the one who was belching. He was glad he'd refused Arnold's request for baked beans. But now he needed to go to the bathroom and he didn't want Arnold in there with him. 'I think we need to lay down some ground rules.'

Arnold glared at him. 'The only ground rules I'm interested in is having my body back, sunshine and in good condition.'

'And that is not going to happen until I, or you, find mine.'

'Have you remembered where you left it yet?'

'No, I haven't, and neither have I remembered who I am or what my name is. But at this precise moment I would like to go to the bathroom and have a shower and put on some clean clothes. And I would appreciate it if you didn't come in to watch me doing it.'

Arnold couldn't think of any reason to argue so said, 'Okay, I'll pop back to Astral Travel and see if I can find an empty body I can borrow. You never know your luck. One of the punters has got to come out at some stage and go off for an hour or two and then I can bring it back here and you can get in it.'

David put his hands over his face. Twenty-four hours ago, that remark would have made him think he was going mad – now it seemed normal.

CHAPTER 11

Ingrid was sitting hunched over her coffee. 'I don't know what's got into Arnold he's behaving so strangely. First the flowers and then kissing you.'

Stella fanned herself, 'And he was wearing his pyjamas, I didn't know where to put my eyes. He could have flashed me at any moment.'

'And now he's refused his breakfast and yesterday he said he's going on a diet.'

'Well, it's obvious isn't it he's going through a mid-life crisis.'

'But he's only forty-seven.'

Stella nodded knowingly, 'It can happen at any age. And it's when they start thinking about other women.'

'But he's never shown any interest in you before - has he?'

'No, but I think that was a practice run.'

Ingrid was struggling to accept that Arnold had turned into a Lothario, but as Stella was not slow in pointing out – facts were facts.

'Oh yes,' continued Stella, who was now in full flow, 'I've seen it all before. They suddenly see it's all downhill from now on so they want one final fling, just to prove they've still got it.'

'I'm not sure Arnold ever had it in the first place.'

'So, he's a late starter, that's even worse, he's got a lot of catching up to do.'

Ingrid wondered if this is what had happened to Stella's husband. In all the years they'd been friends and neighbours she'd never dared ask where he was, but Stella did seem to be an authority on the subject.

Feeling a bit tearful, Ingrid reached into her bag for her hankie and found the polaroids. 'Look, I found these in the kitchen bin, Arnold has been photographing the lounge.'

Stella stared at them for a few moments 'He must have taken them to show someone what a lovely home he's got.'

'Why would he do that?'

'To attract a woman. It's like what those Birds of Paradise do, I saw it on the telly. They collect bits of stone and flowers to make their nest look attractive and if the female likes it, well you know what…'

'But Arnold's never shown any interest in collecting things.'

'He doesn't need to – you've made your home look lovely, all he has to do is show those photos to a woman to see if she likes it.'

'What am I going to do Stella?' Ingrid dabbed at her eyes, 'he must have already shown them to someone, or why throw them away?'

'Watch him like a hawk. If he starts going through the bin looking for them, you'd better let me know. And, just to be on the safe side, I won't come round to your place until he goes back to normal. I do have my virtue to think about.'

David was actually behaving quite normally - for David. He'd washed up and left the kitchen tidy, made his bed and had not left the bathroom looking as if two elephants had had a water fight in it. Now he needed to get dressed.

He hesitated outside what he assumed to be Arnold and Ingrid's bedroom. He knew he would feel extremely uncomfortable going through Arnold's clothes, and even worse, accidently coming across some of Ingrid's. The thought of it turned him hot then cold. On the other hand, he couldn't stay in Arnold's pyjamas forever and he couldn't bring himself to put back on the suit with the gravy stains down the front.

He slowly opened the door and peered in. The decoration was the same eclectic style as the rest of the bungalow - but with a lot more pink. Unmatched wardrobes stood against one wall, facing the marital bed, and an old-fashioned kidney-shaped dressing table stood in the window. David opened the first wardrobe, saw it was full of crimplene dresses and nylon trousers, and quickly shut it.

The other wardrobe was clearly Arnold's and full of baggy suits and even baggier grey flannel trousers. He couldn't remember what his fashion style was like, but he couldn't believe he'd ever worn anything like that. Eventually he found an old pair of jeans, which although they had paint stains on the knees, he felt more comfortable in.

Assuming the dressing table to be Ingrid's domain, David started rummaging through a chest of drawers which was full of brushed cotton tartan shirts and nylon jumpers.

He pulled out the least garish shirt and then found, stuffed right at the back, a lumpy sweater, which looked as if it might have been knitted by Ingrid. The stripes were a bit gaudy, but it looked warm and at least it wasn't nylon.

He quickly dressed then sat down on the bed as a wave of depression swept over him. How had this happened? How was he going to get his own body back? Even worse - would he ever get it back? The thought of being trapped in Arnold's body, wearing nylon jumpers, forever, was too horrible to contemplate.

He tried to think how and where he'd lost his body, but his memory was just a black hole. Rather like the one his astral body had passed through in the packet of frozen chips, although he had no memory of that. He sighed, no point in sitting here moping, and he certainly didn't want to be caught by Ingrid sitting on her bed, he wasn't sure he could defend his virtue. So, he stood up, smoothed down the floral eiderdown and checked to see he was leaving the room tidy before heading to the kitchen – another cup of strong coffee was needed.

He carried the mug into the lounge and started rummaging through the sideboard where he found a large glass jar of fifty-pence coins, a pen and some writing paper so sat on the settee to assess his situation.

He had hoped Arnold would have been back by now so that they could make plans together, but in his absence, he started to list what he thought needed to be done. And he guessed at the top of the list was to ring Arnold's office to say he wouldn't be in. It was only fair to do his best for his temporary body, and staying away from Arnold's place of work would be a kindness.

He fished out Arnold's calling card from between the settee cushions and rang the number. He explained to the young woman on the switchboard that he was too unwell to come into work. He itemised his symptoms and expressed his desire not to pass his illness onto his colleagues. If he expected sympathy, he was going to be disappointed.

Delia burst out laughing. 'You're not pulling that one, again, are you, Arnold?'

'No, seriously young lady, I am very ill, I'm not trying to 'pull' anything.'

'Yeah right. So, you don't want a long weekend to go to Maine Road to watch the Blues claw their way back into the first division?'

David had no idea what she was talking about. He certainly had the blues, who wouldn't in his situation, but the rest of the sentence was gibberish as far as he was concerned. 'No, I don't want to do what you're suggesting, I shall be spending the rest of the day in bed.' Then he worried they might ring Arnold to check he really was ill, while they were out looking for his body, so he added, 'Asleep. I hardly slept a wink last night so would prefer not to be disturbed.'

'I'll believe you, thousands wouldn't. I'll break the sad news to Mr Britten.'

Ingrid was finding it hard to concentrate. Was it her fault that Arnold was thinking of other women? She knew from reading women's magazines that it was important for wives 'not to let themselves go'. Perhaps she had become a bit dull and dowdy.

The queue of shoppers at her till was getting decidedly restive as she sat and stared at a packet of soap powder instead of scanning it. Had she done the right thing leaving Arnold at home alone? On the way to work Stella had said she was taking a risk, as the moment Ingrid was out the front door, he would get his 'bit of stuff' round.

Finally, the manager noticed her line of customers was snaking down one aisle and back up the next one and called another assistant down from the staff room, where she'd been enjoying a break, and was not best pleased. No sooner had she opened her till then everybody moved across, leaving Ingrid clutching the soap powder and no one to pay for it. The customer had decided they'd rather lose the detergent than another hour of their lives.

Stella continued to catalogue Arnold's crimes until her customer changed her mind about an expensive bottle of wine and demanded it be taken off her receipt.

While Stella was otherwise engaged, Ingrid came to a decision. She closed her till, walked out of the Co-op and headed for home. She knew she was risking her job, but Arnold's strange behaviour called for desperate measures.

Arnold meanwhile had forgotten all about work.

His hopes of finding an empty body to borrow were soon crushed when he saw that the only occupants in the separating room were Margaret and Bernard.

He'd watched them for a while on the off chance that Bernard would come out of his body and head for somewhere exotic, so that he could nip in and grab it, but they were just chuntering on about the Ploughman's they had the night before.

He'd then checked his car still had four wheels, which it did. Then from force of habit he'd headed to the nearest pub the 'Rose and Crown', but it was deserted apart from the cleaner washing the floors.

He didn't want to go back to his house until the usurper had come out of the bathroom so he was bored out of his mind – there didn't seem to be many opportunities for astral bodies to amuse themselves.

Then it hit him, Bernard might not want to travel, but he could. And instantaneously he was in Benidorm - completely forgetting that the one and only time he and Ingrid had visited the place he'd got sunburn, sunstroke and food poisoning.

Meanwhile, Margaret and Bernard had moved on from discussing the ploughman's and Margaret was now trying to persuade him to give his clients a more fulfilling experience. Last night, tucked up in her virginal bed, she had started making a list, which she now produced. 'I think we should offer them a cup of coffee when they arrive, and possibly even a biscuit.'

'I don't want to eat into their travel time, they only have an hour at the most.' Bernard had yet to be convinced.

'On their first occasion, yes, but after that they will have all the time in the world. And I think it would help to relax them.'

'You could be right Margaret.' Bernard was starting to get into the swing of it. 'What sort of biscuits would you suggest?'

'Nothing coated in chocolate, it could get all over the cushions.' She went through all her favourites and finally settled on jammy dodgers.

'And I was also wondering about some background music, something oriental perhaps, but soothing.'

Bernard was impressed. Not only had Margaret cleaned the Axminster rug until it looked, well not like new, but at least a little less disgusting, but she had all these wonderful ideas.

But Margaret wasn't finished. 'And if a client brings along a friend, they can have a free session as a reward.'

'And loyalty cards, we could also have loyalty cards.' Bernard had one for his local village coffee shop which entitled him a free cappuccino once all the little squares had been stamped.

Margaret wasn't sure that clients would be prepared to attend twelve sessions without achieving separation, just to get a freebee, but she didn't want to rain on his parade so as to speak. 'Yes, that's something we could consider as well.'

The second item on David's list was where to start looking for his body. Under this he added subheadings of what he could remember about himself, which so far was his height, what he liked for breakfast, how to fake a temperature and a conviction he used to be well-dressed and health conscious. None of which helped him to pinpoint where he'd left his body - or why.

The third item was what to do about Ingrid, and possibly Stella, in the event that his body wasn't found before Ingrid came home from work. Now that was a tricky one. He wondered whether to tell her what had happened and that he wasn't really Arnold, but was just borrowing his body.

Used to assessing the pros and cons before making a decision, he wrote down the two possible outcomes. One: she would be surprised, but once over the shock she would help him. Or two: she would throw a fit and have him taken away in a straightjacket.
Writing lists and subheadings had a calming effect on him. He returned to item two. He could add another subheading - possible scenarios which would cause him to exit his body. He wrote down being mugged, but couldn't think of anything else.
To make more progress he needed another cup of coffee, but not the ghastly stuff he'd found at the back of the cupboard. So, he added another heading to his list, essential food items, and under it wrote down muesli, yoghurt, wholemeal bread, avocados and Brazilian-blend ground coffee. It never occurred to him that Arnold wouldn't have a cafetiere in which to make it.

Margaret now moved on to the next item on her list – advertising. 'We could put an advert in the local paper.'
'Wouldn't that be expensive?' So far, his venture had been all out goings and no incomings as Bernard felt it wasn't fair to charge until the clients managed to achieve separation.
Margaret chewed on her pen for inspiration and it worked. 'I know, we could invite one of the local reporters along to have a free go and they could write about in the weekly paper and that wouldn't cost anything.'
Bernard was very impressed, and not to be outdone he suggested having T-shirts printed with a slogan he'd devised.

Margaret sighed quietly and the pointed out that T-shirts would probably cost far more than an advert and she wasn't sure many people would be prepared to walk about with 'Come Out Today, You Know You want To', printed across their chest.

'Where the hell have you been? I need you to…'

But Arnold was over excited and couldn't wait to share what he'd been doing. 'Guess, come on guess where I was,' and he started paddling an imaginary canoe and humming the 'Hawaii Five-O' theme tune. When he saw he didn't have David's full attention, he started singing in a broken baritone, 'Hula, hula, hula, hula, hula ha,' while swaying his hips, 'Have you guessed yet?

David put his hands over his eyes to shut out the sight. 'Will you stop that you look like a palm tree on Prozac, you're making me feel queasy again.'

'You're getting closer with palm trees,' Arnold added in some arm movements. 'So, what am I doing now?'

'Well, it's obviously something obscene, but apart from that I have no idea.'

'Hawaiian dancing. I've been to Hawaii, mate. You know grass skirts and all that.'

'Well lucky you.' David consulted his list. 'Now, if you could just stop swinging your hips, we have an agenda to work through.' He glared at Arnold, 'are you listening to me?'

But Arnold was on a roll. 'I went to Benidorm first, full of tourists, all walking straight through me. So, I says to meself, I don't have to stay here with all these package holiday plonkers, I'm going somewhere up market.' He carried on gyrating. 'Flipping marvellous. You should go there sometime, take the missus, if you've got one.'

David waved his list at him. 'I've already phoned your office to say you wouldn't be in.'

'I didn't really want to come back, mate, but I thought I'd better see how you're doing.'

'Your young receptionist didn't believe you were ill, she reckoned you were going to a main road in blue.'

Arnold stopped wiggling. 'I don't know what she's talking about, what main road? Oh, Maine Road the football match of the season. No, I haven't got a ticket, they're like gold dust.'

David continued to wave his list. 'The next item is finding my body. I've noted down a few ideas, but we need to think outside the box on this. Clearly, I didn't take part in some dubious astral travel holiday scheme. I really can't see me doing that.' He glared at Arnold. 'Feel free to add your thoughts to the discussion.'

But once again, Arnold was on a roll. Of course, he didn't need a ticket to go to the football match. He could have the best seat in the house. He could sit in the director's box. He could stalk the manager. He could stand on the touch line. All he had to do was keep David in his body until the game was over Saturday evening. He had completely forgotten how desperate he'd been to get it back. If the usurper was a fan of the beautiful game he'd understand, surely. 'Do you like football?'

'No,'

'How do you know you don't?'

'I can't imagine me standing in the freezing rain cheering on a squad of muddy blokes kicking a ball about. Anyway, why do you ask? Do you think I came out at a football match?'

'No, it doesn't sound as if you did.'

'So, let's just concentrate on the matter in hand. Do you have any other ideas?'

'What? Oh right, ideas.' Arnold held his fist to his head as if in deep concentration. 'No, sorry, sunshine, I can't think where your body could be...but there's no rush is there?'

David looked at him incredulously, 'You've changed your tune.'

'No, you're right we need to find it.' Arnold thought it wise to pretend he was still keen even though he wasn't.

'I have made a list of scenarios in order of possibility.' David peered at the paper. 'Your handwriting is appalling, but I think the first one says mugged and the second one says some kind of accident.'

'Accident! You think you may have been in an accident? What sort of accident?'

'How do I know?' David peered at the list again, 'Or I have a serious illness - you know, unconscious, high temperature, hallucinations.'

Arnold shrugged, 'Yeah I suppose that's a possibility.'

'And if we follow this line of reasoning, all of those could mean I'm in a hospital somewhere.'

The only line of reasoning Arnold wanted to follow was how to pass the time until Manchester City played Bournemouth in the final home game of the season. If City won and Crystal Palace lost their match, or had a draw, then City would be promoted to the first division. It was all City fans could talk about, dream about. It was all Arnold had been thinking about for weeks.

'So, we need to start calling all the hospitals to check out my hypothesis.'

'There's just one flaw in your *hypothesis* sunshine, you don't know what your name is.'

David paused and then snapped his fingers. 'Ah, but you could go round all the hospitals to see where I am.'

'No, I couldn't.'

'Why not, you have a vested interest in this too. As soon as you find me, come back here and let me know and I will visit myself and we can do the swap over.'

'Because I have no idea what you look like - and neither do you.' Arnold smirked to himself, Maine Road here I come.

David paced the room in frustration. 'Okay, *sunshine*, let's have your input.'

But Arnold had gone. He needed to pass the time until tomorrow afternoon well away from the usurper and his ideas, and those grass skirts and swaying palm trees were just too irresistible.

Left with his list and no help from Arnold, David carried on pacing. Then it struck him, he didn't need to know his name, he could just ring the hospitals and ask if a man had been brought in yesterday, following an accident or an illness.

He found the telephone directory on a shelf under the hall table, but before he could look for the numbers, the phone rang. He ignored it for a while, but whoever was calling wasn't giving up. 'Hello.'

'Arnold? it's Delia, Mr Britten says if you don't come in straight away, you'll get the sack.'

CHAPTER 12

Ingrid came in the front door just as David put the phone down - both were equally surprised to see each other. Ingrid recovered first. 'What are you doing out of bed Arnold, I thought you were supposed to be ill.' She glared at the telephone directory he was holding. 'And who were you ringing?'

David quickly put the directory back on the shelf. 'No one, Ingrid.' He decided it would be too complicated to explain about hospitals and missing bodies.

'And why are you wearing those filthy jeans?'

David glanced down at his legs, 'They were all I could find that fitted.'

Ingrid gave him a suspicious look - all Arnold's clothes fitted him. 'Well, I suppose if you're not going into work, they'll do.'

'Ah, about going into work. A woman rang and said a Mr Britten, I think that's his name, said I'd get the sack if I didn't go in.'

Ingrid was now convinced Arnold was seriously ill - and also hallucinating, fancy not being sure of his boss's name, Arnold moaned about him most days. 'Why don't you go and sit down, Arnold, and I'll bring you a nice cup of tea.'

'But what about Mr Britten?' David felt he owed it to Arnold not to get him sacked. On the other hand, Arnold had gone off gallivanting without a backward glance.

'I'll talk to him and say you are much too ill to come in. Now go and sit down.'

'Actually, I was hoping to go out and do some shopping.' David had filled his pockets with the fifty-pence pieces and planned to buy the basic essentials on his list, and perhaps even some smoked salmon, if his hospital search proved fruitless.

Ingrid looked at him even more suspiciously, Arnold never shopped. 'Tell me what you want and I'll bring it home with me from the Co-op.'

David read out his list. 'Oh, and a cafetiere, I couldn't find one in the kitchen earlier.'

Ingrid had no idea what a cafetiere was, but more worrying, why did Arnold want one? Where was he getting these strange ideas from. He'd never shown any interest in muesli, Brazilian-blend ground coffee and avocados before. Was his fancy woman introducing him to exotic food stuff?

Ingrid didn't think Arnold had smuggled her in during the short time she'd been at the Co-op, but she thought she'd check the bedrooms, just in case. But first she went and put the kettle on. The kitchen looked immaculate. She peered into the bathroom on her way down the hall, again immaculate. She carefully opened her bedroom door and put her head round it and held her hand to her heart. Nothing was out of place.

Normally when Arnold was left to his own devices, he created so much mess the house looked as if a glue-sniffing teenager had exacted revenge on everything that had gone wrong in his life. On one occasion Ingrid had even called the police, convinced they had been burgled. The young officer said he had never seen such devastation, but as nothing had been stolen, he couldn't do much about it.

She checked the spare bedroom, perfect. Whoever this woman was she certainly tidied up behind her. As she was waiting for the tea to brew, she checked the shed in the back garden and felt a bit silly when she saw it was empty. Then she checked the garage, that too was empty - but it should have been housing an elderly Ford Escort.

She marched back into the house where David was sitting, staring into space. 'Arnold, what have you done with the car?'

Courtesy of Daddy's money – and a room becoming available, David had been moved into the adjoining private hospital. Suzie could now spend her time sitting looking at him in comfort. But the change of scenery had not improved his condition, which was still baffling the medical staff, who now had him hooked up to an even greater variety of machines, wires and tubing – it's surprising how many more electronic gadgets are available in the private sector.

A young consultant came in, looked at David's supine body, gave the gadgets attached to it the attention they deserved, and then checked the clipboard at the end of the bed. 'All his vital signs are good.'

'But when's he going to come round? The bump on his head is much smaller.' Suzie picked up David's hand and stared at his face, willing him to wake up.

'The honest answer is, I don't know. I mean there is no reason for him not to, it's just he…' The consultant looked around for a suitable medical term, couldn't find one, so said, 'he looks a bit vacant.'

David had no idea where Arnold's car was. He remembered Arnold asking him if he'd driven it home, but that was all. 'What make is it?'

'What make is it?' Ingrid was now getting seriously worried. It was one thing to forget his boss's name but to forget what car he owned. 'It's a red Ford Escort.'

'Are you sure?' David couldn't believe he drove a red Ford Escort.

Ingrid looked at him, wondering whether she should ring the doctor. Perhaps he'd hit his head while she was at work and was suffering from concussion. She held a finger in front of his face. 'How many fingers can you see?'

'One, why?'

'Can you remember your name?'

'No, and not for want of trying.' David then realised she was talking about Arnold. 'Hang on, I remember now it's Arnold…' he pulled Arnold's business card out of his pocket, '…Collins.'

Ingrid was about to say he should go back to bed when she remembered that it was dangerous for someone with concussion to go to sleep. 'I want you to stay awake Arnold, do you hear me? I'll pour your tea and then I'm going to phone Mr Britten to tell him you've had a knock on the head.'

After agreeing that the heating could be turned up a little more to keep the customers warm - but only if necessary - the last item on Margaret's list was Bernard's book 'Out of Body Experiences' by Zxama Zxaman. A firm believer in the importance of the free national lending library system, she had never allowed her books to become overdue. If she hadn't finished one, she took it back and renewed it.

She looked at her watch, it was ten-thirty and the desk diary showed there would be no clients for another two hours – plenty of time to visit the library and have a cup of tea and a toasted teacake in the new cafe, in the High Street 'Teacakes are Us'.

Bernard was less than enthusiastic. He was happy to go out for a teacake, but not about returning the book. In the event he was proved to be right.

The librarian checked the date the book had been taken out and then looked at Bernard over the top of her stern, horn-rimmed glasses. 'This book is two months and eighteen days overdue.'

Bernard was shocked at the fine, it was probably more than the book had originally cost. But he took out his wallet and handed over the money. 'I'd like to renew it,' he smiled at the librarian, 'and I promise to return it on time.' He held out his hand for the book.

The librarian did not smile back and firmly put the book on a shelf under her counter. 'I'm sorry that won't be possible, Mr Hornby, I saw from the date stamps that you have already had this book out three times, someone else may want it now.'

'Does someone else want it?' Bernard found it hard to believe that there would be much interest. Before he had borrowed it the last date stamp inside the front cover showed it hadn't been taken out since 1974.

'I will have to check if anyone has requested it, but in the meantime please feel free to borrow any of the other books on the shelves.' And she picked up a pile of books waiting to be put back in their allotted places and walked away.

'See Margaret, I knew it was a mistake to bring it back.' A disconsolate Bernard was not only out of pocket financially but had lost his book as well.

Margaret gently took his arm and steered him down the road to the tea rooms, 'But do you still need it? I mean you must know it off by heart now.'

Seated in front of a steaming cup of coffee, waiting for his teacake Bernard had to admit it wasn't the end of the world. And as Margaret had pointed out, if no one else borrowed it the library would lend it to him again in the not-too-distant future.

He looked round the small café, tastefully decorated with vases of dried flowers and pictures of kittens on the walls. 'I've never been in here before.'

'I think it's only recently opened.'

'It's certainly doing more business than I am.' Bernard felt a twinge of envy as he watched the tables filling up with elderly ladies and the odd office worker.

Unnoticed by Margaret and Bernard, Lettice Long was also in the library on Friday morning, killing time before her appointment with Astral Travel by browsing through the books on physics – she wanted to read up on Gluons which had been discovered ten years earlier.

Curious about the book they had returned, and for which Mr Hornby had paid a large fine, she waited until the librarian had put it back on the shelf in the non-fiction area and then pulled it out to see what it was.

'I've told Mr Britten that you won't be in today, Arnold, as you are suffering from severe concussion and memory loss.' Ingrid looked at David, 'Do you think I ought to call the doctor to come and take a look at you?'

David gave it some thought and decided that it was probably better not to involve Arnold's G.P. in case he insisted on calling an ambulance and carting him off to hospital - although he was tempted by the chance of looking for his body while he was in there. 'No Ingrid, I'm fine and I'm sure I haven't got concussion.'

Ingrid wasn't convinced, 'But you don't seem to be yourself Arnold.'

David was almost prepared to tell her why, but how would she cope knowing there was someone else in her husband's body – probably not well! What he really wanted was to start ringing the hospitals to find out where his body was. 'I'm fine, a nice quiet day at home will soon see me running about again.' As soon as he said the word running a vague memory flashed into his head of running after a ball and hitting it with a racket. Did he play tennis…or squash? He couldn't see Arnold playing either of those games but decided to check, just in case. 'I don't play tennis or squash, do I?'

'No, of course you don't Arnold, whatever gave you that idea.'

'Oh, I was just wondering whether to take them up.'

'I don't think you should at your age.'

But David wasn't really listening, he now had some more pieces of information about himself – he was younger than Arnold, he enjoyed tennis and squash and he definitely didn't drive a Ford Escort.

'Now, about the car, have you remembered where you left it Arnold?'

David took a wild guess, 'I left it at work. I wasn't feeling well so thought I'd walk home, you know, to clear my head.'

As Arnold never walked anywhere, and certainly not to clear his head, Ingrid felt another twinge of worry – on top of dieting he now seemed to be trying to get fit. Was this all part of the mid-life-crisis that Stella was on about? She picked up his hand and patted it. 'Well, we won't worry about the car now. You drink your tea and I'll phone the Co-op and say I won't be in for the rest of my shift.'

The last thing David wanted was Ingrid spending the rest of the day looking after him. He stood up and did a couple of star-jumps much to Ingrid's amazement, 'See I'm much better now. I insist you go back to work - I'll be fine here on my own.'

'Well, if you're sure you're okay...' Ingrid was torn, on the one hand she wanted to stay with Arnold and check he didn't have concussion – and another woman tucked away somewhere - on the other she was keen to get back to the Co-op. Not because she was worried about losing her job, but because she had so much to tell Stella, and desperately needed her advice. 'Shall I leave you something to eat for your dinner?'

'No, don't worry about that, but if you could just get those things on my list, that would be brilliant.'

Ingrid looked at him, that was the second time Arnold had turned down the offer of food. He normally ate like a horse. Something was seriously wrong, perhaps she should stay at home.

David saw her hesitating and quickly added he would get himself something when he felt able to eat, and on no account was she to worry. It took several more minutes to persuade her to go - and three more star-jumps.

As soon as she'd gone out the front door, David collapsed on the settee, gasping for air. He couldn't believe how unfit Arnold was.

CHAPTER 13

In Hawaii, Arnold was wondering how much longer he could bear to hang around watching a group of young women hang garlands of flowers round the necks of portly American tourists wobbling off yet another cruise ship. How did they manage to stay so cheerful. Okay, the weather was lovely, the scenery stunning, the sand was white and the sea was blue, but those grass skirts must be a bit itchy.

He was bored out of his mind and had no idea what the time was. He floated along the beach and watched some surfers riding the waves. It looked fun, so he stood on the back of one of the boards, but he chose the only surfer to fall off, and being flattened by a huge wave left a lot to be desired.

The problem for Arnold was he had a limited imagination. When he and Ingrid had their week's annual holiday at the seaside, all he wanted to do was enjoy a beer or three, eat fish and chips and play a round of crazy golf. Before coming back to Hawaii he'd made a quick trip to Bournemouth in an attempt to relive the giddy excitement of holidays past – Benidorm being his one and only trip abroad - but it was no fun watching other people drinking beer and eating fish and chips. And he couldn't even kick pebbles into the sea, another favourite pastime.

The thought of visiting museums and art galleries never entered his head. Neither the Mona Lisa in Paris nor Michelangelo's David in Florence would ever feel his gaze upon them. Rome's Coliseum or the Pyramids of Giza were safe from his attention.

The sight of smoke rising from a barbecue outside a beach café caught his eye – surely that must mean it was dinner time. The guy in his body had turned out to be a fair cook. That was it, he was going home.

'Yes, I am relative... yes a very close relative as it happens...just because I don't know his name doesn't mean I'm not a relative, I don't remember the names of any of my relatives... oh, she's gone.'
'What are you doing?'
David spun round and saw Arnold standing in the hall. 'You're back then, what happened didn't Hawaii come up to expectations?' David was feeling irritable. It seemed that hospitals wouldn't give out any information about patients unless you knew their name, shoe size and the colour of their eyes.
'Hawaii was brilliant, mate.' Arnold would die before admitting he was bored – but he still had to stay this way for at least another twenty-four hours if he was to see the football match. He wasn't sure he could do it.
Then it hit him. What was stopping him getting back in his body and then popping out again on Saturday afternoon for the match. All he would have to do was persuade Ingrid he was still seriously ill and had to stay in bed - and on no account was he to be disturbed. He didn't want her popping in every five minutes to take his temperature. Only one thing was standing in the way of his master plan – the interloper in his body. So, the sooner he helped the guy find his own body the better.
   He casually drifted round the hall and checked for dust on top of the curtain rail, then as nonchalantly as possible said, 'If you must know I didn't want to come home, but then I thought I'd better pop back, just see how things are going.'

'Yes, well things aren't going well if you must know. None of the hospitals in the area will give me any information about patients brought in yesterday.'

'Shall I go round them and have a look?'

David looked at Arnold suspiciously. Previously, he'd flatly refused to help so why the sudden change of heart. 'I guess you could, but as you were quick to point out earlier, you don't know what I look like?'

Arnold shrugged, 'There can't be many patients who look as if they've been mugged or involved in a car crash, assuming that's what's happened to you.'

'And then what, you'll come back and tell me?'

'Yes, then you can drive down and pretend you're a visitor.'

'And how am I going to do that? According to your wife your car is missing.'

Arnold was momentarily stopped in his tracks. 'Oh, she's noticed, has she?' He thought for a moment, 'Hang on a minute sunshine, what was she doing in the garage?'

'How should I know?'

Arnold was confused, Ingrid never went in the garage, that was Arnold's space, she had the shed. 'So, when did she tell you it wasn't there?'

'When she came back from work just now.'

Arnold was even more confused - Ingrid wasn't due back until after three-o-clock when her shift ended. If there was one thing he could rely on, it was having the house to himself if he sneaked home for forty winks after seeing a client over a liquid lunch. 'Okay, well, you'll have to go and get it.'

'Where from?'

'Gasworks Road, it's outside Astral Travel.'

'Ah, I told your wife I left it at work.'

'What the hell did you say that for?'

'Because that seemed the most logical place for you to leave it.'

Arnold conceded it probably didn't matter where Ingrid thought the car was, the main thing was to get it back. 'It shouldn't take you long to walk there.' Which was a bit rich coming from someone who never walked anywhere.

'How far is it?'

'I don't know...about a mile or so.'

'In your body!' David looked in the hall mirror, 'It nearly killed me walking from the pub to here yesterday.'

'So, you'll know the way, the pub is just down the road from where I parked it.'

David groaned and looked at his feet. 'Don't you have any comfortable pairs of shoes?'

'I never needed any.' Arnold floated towards the kitchen. 'But what you need is another nice fry-up to build up your strength. And if you don't need one, I certainly do.'

Ingrid walked to her till and sat down. The manager of the Co-op had been very understanding in his office, but said she had to work through her lunch hour to make up for the missing time.

Stella gave her customer the wrong change and then leaned across, 'So, did he have a woman in there?'

'No, but he said I've got to work through my lunch hour.'

'Not the manager, Arnold.'

Ingrid started scanning items. 'No, there was no one there. But the place was immaculate. Arnold never leaves anywhere immaculate.'

Stella was immediately on red alert. 'His fancy woman must have done it so that you wouldn't suspect she'd been there.'

'The car's missing as well.'

'It's probably at her house. She must have driven home in it.'

'He said he left it at work yesterday.'

'So, what's he doing walking in that direction?'

Ingrid swung round in time to see Arnold, if not exactly striding briskly, going past the shop door.

Stella was the first to react. 'You stay here and finish your shift, Ingrid.' In the flash of an eye, she'd told the rest of her queue to join Ingrid's, shut down her till and told the manager, who was wandering past the household cleaning products, that she was taking an early lunch. When Stella had the bit between her teeth there was no stopping her

An avid fan of crime series on the television, such as 'Juliet Bravo' and 'The Bill', Stella was convinced that her tracking skills were second to none. Arnold, who was about fifty yards in front of her, would never know he was being followed.

David of course wouldn't have known he was being followed even if she had tapped him on the shoulder. The only time he'd seen Stella was when she slapped him round the face, and the shock of that moment had erased her features from his memory - but not her shell suit.

Besides, he was trying to retrace the route he'd taken yesterday, and that needed all his concentration.

He still wasn't convinced his body was lying vacant in Gasworks Road. Logic told him that however weird Astral Travel was, the owner of the agency would have noticed it and done something about it, although what didn't readily spring to mind.

Stella, meanwhile was hiding behind lamp posts, darting into doorways, pretending to look in shop windows and generally causing concern to all the other shoppers in the High Street, who couldn't decide if she was eccentric or inebriated.

Arnold had gone ahead to Astral Travel to check whether there were any empty bodies in the separating room that he'd missed yesterday – there weren't, but that didn't mean one hadn't been moved to somewhere else for safe keeping overnight. He remembered Hornby wanted insurance to safeguard him against being sued if something happened to a body while the owner was off travelling. So where would he put an empty body?

He drifted through the office where Margaret and Bernard were eating sandwiches while waiting for their next group of clients. He couldn't see a body in there, empty or otherwise, and neither was there one in the other office.

He drifted back outside to check if his body and the interloper had arrived. It had been late setting off because Arnold couldn't remember where he'd left the car keys. They were eventually found in the lining of his suit jacket where they'd slipped through a hole.

He sat on his car bonnet and watched a small group of people go into the agency and wondered if he could trick the interloper into taking part. He only needed a fraction of a second for Hornby to work his magic and get him to come out and he would be back in like a shot.

But then another thought struck him – if he was going to come out to go to the football match tomorrow it would leave his body empty again. What was to stop the interloper getting back in? After all, he now knew where Arnold lived, and hiding his body in bed wouldn't be enough. The more he thought about it the more complicated it became. Either he had to hide himself somewhere really safe, where the interloper couldn't find him, or he'd have to miss the match.

He looked down the road and saw his body limping slowly along the pavement looking at all the cars. As it drew level with the Ford the door of the agency opened and Margaret came out.

'Ah Mr Collins, we thought this must be your car. It's been here all night you know.'

David looked round surprised. The woman seemed to know him. But he had no idea who she was. He was even more surprised when she took his arm and said, 'Quick come inside.'

And he nearly shot out of his skin when Arnold whispered in his ear, 'This is the woman who helps run Astral Travel. You need to go with her, mate, see if your body's in there, and if it isn't, try and borrow another one.'

From across the street Stella watched as a woman, who clearly knew Arnold, took his arm and pulled him inside. All her suspicions were confirmed, the only puzzle was the woman looked much older and plainer than she'd expected. But then where men were concerned there was no accounting for taste.

CHAPTER 14

Margaret pulled the reluctant David into her office.
'Now Mr Collins, I've been keeping an eye out for you...'
'Actually, I'm not Mr Colins.' David felt it necessary to correct that misapprehension before this strange woman went any further.
Margaret glared at him. She never forgot a face and as far as she was concerned the man standing in front of her desk was Arnold Collins. 'So, who do you claim you are?'
'That's the problem, I don't know who I am Mrs...?'
'Hamilton, and it's Miss. So, are you saying you've lost your memory?'
'In a manner of speaking...'
Margaret smiled triumphantly. 'Well, I can help you there.' She raised her voice and spoke very slowly as if he were slightly stupid and not a little hard of hearing. 'Your name is Arnold Collins and you are an insurance agent.' She watched him closely to check he understood and then added, 'Now, Mr Hornby wants you to help the next group of clients to come out of their bodies. You've been our only real success so far.'
Arnold snorted derisively in David's ear and muttered, 'Success my arse,' then he drifted to the window just a few seconds too late to see Stella hot-footing it back to the Co-op. After watching a cat washing itself, which was as interesting to Arnold as watching paint dry, he wandered off to mooch around the building.
'It's not just my memory I've lost, Miss Hamilton, it's my body as well. In fact, I was wondering whether it might be here.'

Margaret was pretty certain Mr Collins had got back into his body and left with it. She remembered seeing him dashing out of the door. Why did he think he'd left it here? She inched past him, 'I think Mr Hornby is better able to deal with this.' And she was out of the room like a shot.

Arnold drifted back 'If they have got your body, they've got it well hidden, I've had a good poke round.'

David looked round the unfamiliar room. 'I'm pretty certain I've never been here before, so let's go. The sooner I can start going round the hospitals the better.'

But he was too late, Bernard came into the room and viewed him warily. 'Ah, Mr Colins, how nice to see you again.'

David tried not to sound too exasperated, 'As I said to Miss Hamilton, I'm not Mr Collins, I just happen to be in his body.'

Bernard flashed a quick glance at Margaret who had followed him in, a glance which suggested that that they needed to treat Mr Collins with great caution. 'So, who are you?'

'As I also told Miss Hamilton, I don't know.'

Not unreasonably, Bernard suggested that if he had lost him memory, it was more than likely he actually was Mr Collins, but had temporarily forgotten.

David sighed 'No, you don't understand, Mr Collins is right here.'

Bernard looked round the room and then asked cautiously, 'Exactly where do you mean?'

Arnold had had enough of the conversation, 'Tell him, go on tell him this is all his fault.'

David sighed again, 'Mr Collins says to tell you this is all your fault.'

Margaret whispered in Bernard's ear that Mr Collins was obviously delusional and should be asked to leave immediately.

But Bernard was more curious. 'So, Mr Collins is talking to you.'

'Yes, and he is standing next to you, or rather his ghostly form is.'

'You mean he's dead!' Margaret looked as if she was going to faint.

'No, he's not dead, but according to him he came out of his body when he was here yesterday.'

'Yes, he did, he was my first proper success.' Bernard beamed at the memory and then suddenly became suspicious, 'But I still don't understand – if his astral body is standing next to me, what are *you* doing in his body?'

Arnold had adopted a fighting stance. 'Tell, him to come out and I'll make him understand.'

'Mr Collins says could you kindly come out of your body and he will explain precisely what has happened.'

Bernard was about to say of course when common sense prevailed. Perhaps he should find out more before leaving his body empty so-as-to speak. After all, when he was a bank manager, he would never have sanctioned a loan without going over every aspect with a fine-toothed-comb, no matter how honest the client might claim to be. 'So, if I could just clarify Mr ummm…you say Mr Collins came out of his body and you got in it. Am I right so far?'

'Yes.'

Bernard would have preferred to have been sitting behind his desk, then he could have steepled his fingers together, which he always believed gave him gravitas and helped him formulate his questions. 'Can I ask you why you did that?'

'Because along with my memory, I'd lost mine and I was fed up with wondering around bodiless.' David was also fed up with answering questions. 'So, can you come out and talk to Mr Collins yourself, which Mr Collins leads me to believe is possible. If not, we will be on our way.'

Bernard's fingers itched to steeple. 'So, am I right in saying you can both see and hear Mr Collins?'

'Yes.' Unfortunately, David added to himself because Arnold was keeping up a constant stream of invective against Bernard Hornby, Astral Travel and Margaret Thatcher's government - the last coming as a surprise to David as he had no idea who was running the country. 'I can also talk to him if that's of any help.'

Bernard took a few moments to digest the information. In his experience, which he knew to be limited, he thought it was only astral bodies who could see and talk to each other. Now it appeared that whoever was in Mr Collins body could also see, hear, and talk to Mr Collin's astral body.

'And can Mr Collins hear what I'm saying?' Bernard decided he'd better tread cautiously.

'Yes, he can.'

Margaret was less interested in who could talk to whom, and who could hear what, but whether Astral Travel could be held liable for, what she chose to think of as 'this mix-up' and she whispered her concerns in Bernard's ear.

Bernard suddenly felt a bit queasy. They still hadn't organised any insurance and now there was a strong possibility they could be sued. 'Before I take up Mr Collin's kind offer of an explanation, could I ask you Mr ummmm, did you enter his body on these premises?'

'No, it was in the pub along the road, I believe it's called the 'Rose and Crown'.'

Bernard's queasiness diminished slightly. If the alleged body takeover had happened somewhere else, he could hardly be held responsible. He had no idea where Arnold's astral body was at that moment so stared at a corner of the office and said, 'I'm sorry Mr Collins but if you leave your body in a pub and someone else comes along and gets in it then that has nothing to do with Astral Travel. We have no liability in this matter whatsoever.'

He had no idea whether Mr Collins had taken that on board because the sibilant mutterings, which had been pervading the room for a while, had now reached the same decibels as a pneumatic drill and the door was abruptly flung open to reveal an irate man with red hair and a face to match. He pointed to his watch and tapped it sharply, 'My session was booked for twelve-forty-five and it is now twelve-fifty-eight. Unless we can start the session immediately, I shall take my custom elsewhere.'

'I'm so sorry Mr Inglis, I'll be there straight away.' Bernard turned to Margaret, 'Perhaps you could see if anyone would like a cup of coffee first, and a biscuit.'

Margaret efficiently shepherded Mr Inglis and the rest of the group back into the separating room, where some of the cushions had already been bagged by clients by putting a jacket or handbag on them.

'Look, Mr ummmm, as you can see, I am very busy so perhaps you and Mr Collin's astral body could see yourselves out.'

'Only too happy to. To be honest I only came here to collect Mr Collin's car, it was your assistant who pulled me in here.'

Arnold could see his chances of getting back in his body diminishing by the second. He hovered in front of David. 'Tell him you want to take part.'

'But I don't.'

'You don't what?' Bernard really wanted them to go.

'I don't want to take part in your session or whatever it is.'

'Good because I've changed my mind about asking you to.' The last thing Bernard wanted was two astral bodies possibly fighting over one corporeal one. 'Goodbye.' And with that he went out of the office and into the separating room, firmly closing the door.

'So that's it, is it sunshine, you're refusing to come out.'

'Yes - until I find my body, I am staying in yours. So, the sooner you start checking the hospitals the quicker you will have it back.' And with that David walked out of Astral Travel and got in the Ford Escort. He was surprised to be so assertive - he had a feeling that normally he was far too nervous. Perhaps it was because he was in Arnold's body.

Arnold got in the other side. 'I suppose you know how to drive.'

David turned on the ignition and the car coughed and spluttered into life. He didn't know if he could, but his feet naturally put themselves on the pedals and his hand grasped the gear stick. He put it in first, checked in the rearview mirror, signalled he was pulling out and slowly drove away from the kerb. It looked as if he could.

Arnold was not a good passenger and issued a constant stream of instructions and criticisms which David tried to ignore. 'If you don't like my driving, why don't you go and start looking round the hospitals.'

'No, you're alright, I want a cup of tea first.'

David groaned, that meant drinking a mug of builders' brew, as Arnold like to call it, with three heaped teaspoons of sugar in it. But he knew better than to argue, Arnold's astral body was as assertive as his corporeal one.

Stella positively flew back to the Co-op. She still had a few minutes left of her lunch break and all that walking had given her an appetite, so after telling Ingrid she'd talk to her asap, she bought a sandwich and headed for the staff room where the manager pointed to his watch and said, 'You have ten minutes, Mrs Threadgold.' As soon as he walked out Stella pulled a face, but ate her sandwiches as quickly as she could.

As soon as they were sitting side by side on their tills, she leaned across to Ingrid and in a loud whisper, said, 'It's just as I thought, I followed him to this place in Gasworks Road and there was his car parked outside, as bold as brass.'

Ingrid tried not to get upset, after all there could be a reasonable explanation. 'But that doesn't mean…'

Stella, ignoring Ingrid, and her queue, continued, 'As soon as he arrived this woman opened the door and I heard her say "quick come inside", then she grabbed his arm and pulled him in.'

Ingrid couldn't think of a reasonable explanation for that. It was as Stella had said - Arnold was having an affair with another woman. And on their china anniversary as well. She choked back a sob and scanned an item.

'I don't think she lives there…it was some kind of travel agency. But yesterday she must have taken him back to her place, for some you know what, and then driven him home.'

Ingrid quickly clutched a passing straw, 'If it was a travel agency, perhaps he was booking a holiday.'

'Has Arnold ever booked a holiday before? No, you always have to do it.'

'But there's always a first time.'

'Yes, a first time for playing away from home.'

'Ask her what this woman was like.' By now both queues were listening closely and the woman at Ingrid's till couldn't wait to hear all the details.

Stella, looked round to make sure the manager wasn't about and then said, 'Well, I didn't get a good look, but she had shortish, permed brown hair with a lot grey in it. She was wearing an expensive suit, which I think she must have got from Sasha's Boutique, because I saw it in the window a few months ago, and she had on a cream blouse with a tie neck and sensible navy shoes. As I say it was only a quick glance.'

Another shopper further down the line, called out, 'How old?'

Stella thought for a moment, 'I would say she was in her fifties.'

Ingrid choked back another sob - Arnold's fancy woman was older than she was. She looked down at her pull-on crimplene trousers, with their front crease permanently machined in place, and her baggy nylon jumper. It was clear what had happened – she'd let herself go and now Arnold was attracted to someone who dressed in an expensive suit and a blouse with a tie neck, and had a neat perm, not like her straggly locks.

Stella could see the shoppers were hanging on her every word so added, 'I could see she was the bossy type, the way she pulled him in and shut the door, but then some men like that kind of thing.' Including, she suddenly remembered, her husband, who'd gone off with a whip-waving dominatrix.

'What am I going to do Stella?'

Ingrid's heartfelt question was immediately answered by the shoppers, who all had their own ideas of what to do with a philandering husband – some more painful than others.

The debate would have continued if the manager hadn't put a stop to it. He had caught the tail end of one of the suggestions and was feeling slightly nervous. 'Now, now ladies. Let's move along here.'

Stella called across to Ingrid that they would continue the conversation over a pot of tea in the 'Singing Kettle' café opposite as soon as they finished their shift.

Much to the café owner's delight half the shoppers went as well.

David carefully parked the car on the drive, thankful to be back home, but only for a nano-second. Then reality kicked in and he groaned, 'Noooo, this isn't where I live.'

'No, but it's where I live so go and put the kettle on.'

David glanced across, but Arnold had gone. As soon as he'd made the tea, he would insist that Arnold go round the hospitals. He had to have his own body and his own life back.

When he got in the kitchen, he realised he was feeling pretty hungry again, despite the recent fry-up. He had the feeling that Arnold never stopped eating, yet he still stayed so slim. 'I'm going to make myself a sandwich.'

'Good, I'm starving,' Arnold pointed at the fridge, 'and I fancy a cheese and pickle one with a bag of crisps and a can of beer.'

'I thought you wanted a cup of tea.'

'I'll have that afterwards with a wedge of cake. And don't go easy on the cheese.'

David opened the fridge door, but his hopes of finding French Brie or a delicate Gouda were soon dashed. Still, he reasoned, there was nothing wrong with Cheddar. But as he buttered the bread and cut thick slices of cheese under Arnold's watchful gaze, tiny memories of smoked salmon and dill or pâté with slivers of cornichon slid in. 'Don't you have any smoked salmon or pâté?'

'I'm not eating that muck.'

'Have you ever tried them?'

'Course I haven't, and I want more pickle than that.'

David sighed, spooned on more pickle and then tried to flatten the sandwich thin enough to actually be able to eat it. Pickle oozed out round the edges, 'Do you have any paper napkins?'

Arnold snorted, 'Yes, kitchen roll over there by the cooker. You're not one of them, are you?' and Arnold started mincing round the kitchen. 'Smoked salmon, paper napkins.'

'I'm trying not to get pickle over your clothes.' David looked down at the jumper he was wearing, which was a palimpsest of past meals, and decided not to worry about adding any more to it. 'And if you mean, am I gay, no I'm not.' But inwardly he started to worry, how did he know he wasn't - and did it matter?

The shoppers reached the café first and immediately pulled two tables together and commandeered extra chairs much to the annoyance of the mothers and babies who considered it was their prerogative to take up all the space. By the time Ingrid and Stella arrived they had all introduced themselves, discovered endless connections with friends and families and were getting along like a house, if not on fire, definitely smouldering. But as soon as they saw Ingrid and Stella arrive, they pointed to two empty chairs in the places of honour and one of them went and ordered tea and cakes for them on the proviso that nothing was said until she got back to her seat.

Stella was easily persuaded to repeat how she'd skilfully tracked Arnold to Gasworks Road, this time with additional embellishments such as how she pretended to tie up her shoe lace when he'd glanced sideways before crossing the road, and stared in a shop window when he slowed down. She could see they were hanging on every word so decided to tell them what had happened the previous day.

They all commiserated with Ingrid about the flowers – highly suspicious. Forgetting their anniversary – completely unforgivable. And having an affair – a hanging offence.

Stella also came in for concern about his unwarranted attack on her virtue, while wearing pyjamas, and she conceded that it had 'properly shaken her up.'

Their collective heads were then put together to agree what Ingrid should do next. Reaching a consensus was going to take time, several more pots of tea and numerous slices of chocolate cake. For once, Ingrid would not be getting home in time to make Arnold's tea.

David carefully washed up his plate, glass and tea cup while Arnold watched and burped. 'Why don't you start looking round the hospitals instead of hanging around here?'

'Because I'm letting my sandwich go down. I don't want to get indigestion.'

'It won't be you that has it, it'll be me.'

Arnold wasn't prepared to concede that David was right, so said, 'Alright, keep your hair on, sunshine.' But he still didn't move. 'So where am I supposed to be looking?'

'We've been through this. If I was involved in some kind of accident then my body will either be in intensive care or the orthopaedic ward - so start with those. I certainly won't be in the maternity unit.'

'How do you know?'

'Because I'm not...' David stopped, he'd assumed he was a man, but was he? Perhaps he was a woman. He mentally shook his head, no surely, he'd feel differently. Anyway, he wasn't prepared to go down that route, '...I'm not a woman.'

'And if I find someone, I think might be you, then what?'

'Come back here and tell me.'

'Then what?'

'I'll work out a plan while you're gone.'

CHAPTER 15

Suzie rushed into her mother's arms, tears steaking her mascara. 'The hospital doesn't think there is anything more they can do for David.' She had gone back to his private room after a late lunch and was told by the nurse that there had been no change in his condition and the consultant was completely baffled as to what treatment to suggest next.

Deirdre Baker-Brown, a fleshy-faced woman, with a high colour and the demeaner of a Rottweiler, had given up a bridge afternoon to visit her daughter's fiancé. While she made various soothing replies she was also wondering if it was too soon to invite Elliot round for tea - Elliot being the son of her best friend Fiona, and much more suitable husband material. She didn't actually dislike David, but she and Elliot's mother had been planning their offspring's wedding since they met at the age the age of eighteen when, as debutantes, they had both attended Queen Charlotte's Ball in nineteen-fifty-eight. It was the last one to be held – but no blame can be attached to them for the Queen putting an end to the 'season'.

Fiona had snagged a husband that night and Deirdre had been a bridesmaid at her society wedding a year later, where she managed to snag a husband in the shape of Cameron Baker-Brown. He might not have been a member of the landed gentry by birth, but with a sharp business mind combined with a willingness to take risks, he had amassed enough of a fortune to buy his own land and a mini manor house, which was 'landed gentry' enough for Deidre.

Fiona, carrying on the tradition of doing everything first, produced an heir, Elliot, and then a spare. Three years later Deidre was blessed with a daughter and nothing more. The two kept in touch by phone and letter, and met for luncheon in London once a month while their offspring were cared for by a succession of nannies and then au pairs, who were cheaper if less reliable.

Each summer both families met up for three glorious weeks, initially in Scotland – if it was good enough for the Queen it was good enough for them – and in later years on the continent, where the weather was more reliable, and finally, sans children, on cruises.

'Darling, that's terrible, what's going to happen?' and Deidre patted her daughter's back before gently pushing her away. A silk suit can only cope with a small amount of snot and tears.

'I don't know,' Suzie gave an un-lady-like sniff, 'but surely all the while Daddy is paying, they should keep him until they can find a cure?'

'Well, yes, darling, but how long would finding a cure take? And will he be the same person?'

Suzie suddenly brightened up, 'I read somewhere that it's possible to freeze people in case they can be cured in the future.'

'Where on earth did you read that?'

'At the shop. We were looking to see if it was possible to freeze flowers.'

'And is it?' Deidre asked.

'Well, no actually, but some people have already been frozen so it must work.'

Deirdre thought if it didn't work for flowers, it was highly unlikely to work for humans, but didn't think this was the moment to tell Suzie, who was already on the phone to her father, telling him to come to the hospital as quickly as possible.

As Ingrid and Stella turned into their road, they saw the Ford Escort parked in the drive.

'Oh, so he's decided to come home has he.' Stella was outraged.

Ingrid on the other hand was pleased to see it. 'Perhaps he's left her.'

'Now don't go all soft on him Ingrid, remember what we all agreed in the café, you are going to stay with your sister for a while until he comes to his senses.'

Ingrid had a horrible feeling that Arnold would be thrilled if she went and stayed with her sister for a while - and wouldn't come to his senses for quite some time. 'But if he says sorry...'

'He still needs to be punished.'

The man in question was floating near the hall window at that moment and saw Ingrid and Stella glaring at his car. And from the way Stella was gesticulating he could see trouble was brewing. Well, as the interloper had his body, *he* could deal with whatever mischief the harridan was putting into Ingrid's head.

'So, I'll just get off and start going round the hospitals, shall I?'

'About bloody time.' But Arnold had disappeared.

David was just wondering whether to snatch forty winks while he had the chance when he heard Ingrid's key in the door. His stomach immediately started churning and he hoped she wouldn't try anything amorous.

He jumped off the settee and was smoothing the cushions when Ingrid opened the door. 'Ah did you have a good day, Ingrid?' Although he could see from her face that she hadn't.

'I see you found the car Arnold.' Ingrid tried to speak severely.

'Yes, well, it wasn't lost. As I told you, I left it at work yesterday when I wasn't feeling well.'

'So, that's where you've been is it, back to the office?'

David wasn't brilliant at reading body language, but even he was picking up the fact that Ingrid was now carrying a lot of suppressed anger, but why? 'That's right, I went back to the office.'

'So, you saw Mr Britten?'

'Ummm yes, and he was very understanding.'

'And have you been anywhere else today, Arnold?'

David was wondering where this conversation was going – and how many lies he was going to have to tell, so he cautiously asked, 'Like where?'

'Like Gasworks Road to see your lady friend, the woman you're having an affair with.' And with that Ingrid swept out of the room in tears, slamming the door.

David stared at the door which was still quivering in its frame. So, was something going on between Arnold and the woman at Astral Travel? He hadn't got that impression while they were there, but his wife certainly seemed to think so - no wonder she was in a strop. And no wonder Arnold wanted his body back.

Even from the lounge he could hear doors banging and drawers being thrown about. He was just wondering what to do when Ingrid appeared carrying a holdall.

'Just tell me the truth Arnold, are you having an affair with the woman in Gasworks Road?'

David hesitated, did she really want the truth, and what was the truth? 'I can't say Ingrid.'
'Can't or won't.'
'Can't, because I don't know.'
'You don't know if you are having an affair?'
'Not really, no.'
This was not the answer Ingrid had been expecting. Stella was adamant that Arnold was having it off with that woman and probably had been for months, but perhaps he wasn't. She was about to relent when the phone rang. It was Stella.
'Has he confessed yet?'
'Not exactly, he says he doesn't know if he's having an affair or not.'
She could hear Stella spluttering down the line. 'Well now I've heard it all. You don't believe that rubbish, do you?'
'He did seem confused.'
'Confused! Of course, he's confused. He never thought you'd find out, did he?'
'So, what shall I do Stella?'
'Well leave of course. He'll soon come to heel when he has to cook his own food.'
But Ingrid was weakening, 'I'm not sure Stella, perhaps he really went there to book a surprise holiday.'
'Okay so ask him where's he's taking you.'
Ingrid replaced the phone, went back into the sitting room and took a deep breath. 'Arnold, have you booked a surprise holiday for me?'

CHAPTER 16

After leaving David to cope with Ingrid, Arnold headed to the main hospital in the area, The Northaven Infirmary. He wandered up and down the various wards, but while many of the patients looked comatose, none of them looked empty. Most had their eyes shut and those that were sitting up were unenthusiastically looking at their curling ham sandwiches and chocolate wafer biscuits. He was about to give up when he saw a sign pointing to the private wing.

Paying for treatment was such an anathema to his socialist beliefs he could barely force himself to go and have a look. He couldn't believe his eyes. No wards, just private, en-suite rooms with televisions and comfortable armchairs for visitors. The first dozen patients looked anything but comatose as they tucked into their smoked salmon sandwiches, tiny quiches and chocolate éclairs. So, this was how the other half lived!

The patient in the last but one room was not sitting up and taking notice. He was attached to various machines by various lengths of piping and electric wires. Monitors beeped, screens flashed several different coloured lines and three people were sitting watching silently.

Arnold looked at the name written about the bed: David Telford. Was this the interloper? There was only one way to tell and that was to try to get in, but something held him back.

It was difficult to see with bedclothes over him, but the guy looked on the short side and Arnold didn't think he would fit in. He also didn't think he could take off all the bits of wiring and piping to make a quick exit. Perhaps this wasn't the right body.

He checked the last room, which held an elderly woman who was watching television while constantly pressing a call button for a nurse. The nurse, who had been at the woman's beck and call all day, was in no hurry to answer it.

Cameron Baker-Brown had arrived at the hospital as soon as he could, but wasn't convinced about Suzie's freezer plan. But once Suzie got an idea in her head nothing would shift it, and long ago he found the best course was to let her run with her mad schemes until even she realised, they weren't going to work. In any event he certainly wasn't proposing to fork out millions of pounds to keep his unwanted future son-in-law on ice.

On the other hand, his wife might be more enthusiastic about the idea, she liked David well enough, but he knew her heart was set on Elliot and she would see this as a way of persuading Suzie to break off the engagement. After all it would be impossible to plan a wedding to someone in a freezer.

They sat round the bed, staring at the recumbent form lying on it, waiting for the consultant to arrive.

Suzie picked up David's hand. 'Don't worry darling, we've got a wonderful idea to save you.' At this, her parents looked at each other and discretely pulled disbelieving faces.

Cameron stood up and took a turn round the room to stretch his legs. He gazed down at the wan figure lying in the bed. It looked as if David had lost a bit of weight, which in Cameron's opinion wouldn't come amiss as David erred on the side of chubbiness despite all the gym workouts, tennis and pounding the streets for miles.

He looked at his watch, the consultant was taking his time. The consultant, who had to drive back twenty miles from his home to have this chat, came in at that moment and enthusiastically shook Cameron's hand. He then nodded his head to Deidre and laid a sympathetic hand on Suzie's shoulder. 'Now Suzie, what is it you want to talk about regarding David's treatment?' He gazed down at his patient and a look of bafflement crossed his face. 'We are doing all we can, but he isn't responding.'

'I know you are Mr Edwards,' Suzie gazed up at him, tears blurring her beautiful blue eyes, 'but he's not getting any better and we were wondering if freezing him would be the answer… just until someone comes up with a cure.'

The consultant looked at her. He'd heard of some quack theory called cryonics where people were stored in liquid nitrogen, but he wasn't aware that anyone had been successfully frozen and then defrosted as it were. He looked at Cameron, surely Suzie's father wasn't going to go along with this crazy idea. 'I can't stress too heavily Mr Baker-Brown that this is an unproven procedure. David is suffering from the trauma of a car crash not a currently incurable disease.'

Cameron pulled him to one side while Suzie explained to David how much she loved him and what they were planning to do.

Arnold, who had drifted back into the room as the consultant was talking about the interloper being in a car crash, listened with horror as Suzie outlined what was now in store for him.

'I know it's a crazy idea,' muttered Cameron, 'but she won't listen to me so I'm relying on you to put her right.'

Had Arnold waited around a little while longer he would have heard Suzie finally accept that she couldn't keep David in a frozen state - but as soon as he heard her talk about freezing her fiancé he'd instantly returned home in a panic. If the interloper's body was going to spend the rest of its life sitting on a shelf with a bag of frozen peas for company, he was never going to come out of Arnold's. He had to get him to go to the hospital immediately.

Ingrid repeated her question about the surprise holiday at the same moment Arnold returned and said, 'They are going to put your body in a deep freezer, sunshine.'

'What!' David shrieked. 'Why?'

Unsurprisingly, Ingrid, who could neither hear or see her husband's astral body, took exception to the answer.

'That's it, Arnold Collins, I'm going to stay with my sister, and I hope you're happy with your fancy woman.' And with her lips trembling, she picked up the holdall and walked out.

David and Arnold stared at the door which had been slammed behind her, again, and then at each other. Then they both tried to speak at the same time, which was never going to work.

Finally, David held up his hand, 'Shouting over each other is getting us nowhere.' His excitement that Arnold had found his body was overshadowed by what was being planned for it. 'So, where is it?'

'In a private ward at The Northaven Infirmary. You should see the rooms…'

David cut him off short. 'So, what's my name?'

'David Telford.'

'David Telford?' The name meant nothing to him, 'Are you sure?'

'That's what it said on your bed.'

'So, what happened to me?'

'You were in a car crash.'

David briefly thought about the loss of his no-claims bonus and hoped he wasn't the one to have caused it. 'Did you find out anything else?'

'You've got a girlfriend called Suzie.' And Arnold chuntered on about private healthcare and blue-eyed blondes.

But David had stopped listening, he'd hoped that once he knew his name, and what had happened, the rest of his memory would come back, but it didn't. Although he had the feeling that it was lurking tantalisingly close in his subconscious. 'And you're really sure it's me?'

'No, because I don't know what you look like, do I? You'll have to go and have a look. But I wouldn't hang about, like I said, they're planning to bung you in a freezer.'

'But why?'

'It's your girlfriend's idea she wants to keep you on ice until a cure can be found.'

David paced up and down the lounge. 'When? How long have we got?'

'How do I know? And now it's my turn to ask a few questions – like why has Ingrid stormed off to her sister's? Not that a few days peace and quiet wouldn't go amiss. And what's all this about a fancy woman?'

'You tell me, your wife seems to think you're having an affair.'

'Are you mad, the last thing I need in my life is another woman – one's enough.' Arnold bobbed about erratically. 'So, who told you I was?'

'Your wife.'

'What! Whatever gave her that idea?'

'How do I know?'

'It's you isn't it? As soon as you got in my body you've treated it like a plaything. I saw the way that woman at Astral Travel couldn't wait to get her hands on you, she practically dragged you in off the street.'

'Of course, she did, because that's who you're having an affair with.'

Arnold, shaken to his core, stopped bobbing up and down. 'No, I'm not.'

'Well, that's what your wife thinks. Now, how to I get to this hospital?'

Before going to her sister's, Ingrid popped in to see her neighbour to bring her up to date and have a good cry. 'He lied to me Stella…I asked him where he had to go to get the car and he said his office… and when I asked if he had booked a surprise holiday for me, he started staring at the fireplace and his eyes went weird and he shouted "What! Why?" as if that was the last thing on earth he'd do.'

Stella patted her hand and then put the kettle on. 'You're doing the right thing Ingrid. And don't you worry, I'll keep an eye on what goes on next door. As soon as he moves his fancy woman in, I'll let you know.'

Ingrid gulped a few times, dried her eyes and blew her nose. 'I suppose I'd better ring Greta and let her know I'm coming to stay for a while. Can I use your phone?'

'What do you mean you don't know the way to the hospital, you've just come back from there?'

'Yes, but I didn't drive there, did I? I just thought that's where I want to be and I was there.'

David pulled out the telephone directory and looked up the address. 'It's in Coronation Road, where ever that is.' He went into the spare room and found his street map pushed under the bed. 'You'll have to map read.'

'Shouldn't I go on ahead, see if the coast is clear, check you're still in your room?'

'No, I need you to direct me.'

David rushed out to the car and spread the map out on the passenger side of the dashboard so that Arnold could see it. They hadn't gone more than a hundred yards when the car hit a pothole. Arnold shot up in the air and the map slid off the dashboard into the well of the car. David took his eye off the road and asked, 'Can you read it down there?'

'No, I can't, I'm not a ruddy contortionist.'

Exasperated, David slammed on the brakes.

Arnold glared at him. 'Well, it's no use getting stroppy with me, sunshine, I could have told you it wouldn't stay there.'

'So why didn't you? Is there anything in the glove box to hold it down?' David leaned over and rummaged around, pulling out a box of matches, one glove and a small torch. He put the map under the torch, but it kept rolling on to the floor. 'This is ridiculous.'

'What you need is some sticky tape.' Arnold was sitting with his arms folded, looking smug.

'Do you have any?'

'No, but that's what you need isn't it.'

David took a deep breath and tried to remember his yoga exercises for relaxing. 'If I held it up for you, do you think you could memorise the way.' He picked up the map and held it in front of Arnold.

'I've got a better idea, just lay it on the front seat and I'll hover over it.'

David took another deep breath, but the yoga exercises were having less and less effect. He slammed the map down on the front seat. 'So, why didn't you say you could do that in the first place.'

'Well, I've said it now, alright. Okay take the next left and then left again.'

Muttering under his breath David did as he was told.

'Turn left again and then turn right.'

David followed the instructions and after five minutes, realised he was back where he started. 'What are you doing? We're going the wrong way.'

Arnold twisted round above the map. 'That's your fault, you put it on the seat upside down.'

After a diversion round some road works, three shouting matches and a long period of angry silence, they arrived at the hospital and parked in the car park.

Arnold said, 'I'll go and check that you're still in the ward and then you can come up and visit.'

'But we can't swap over while all those people are there.'

'We can if you're quick. Just make sure you're sitting down before you come out.'

He disappeared, leaving David drumming his fingers on the steering wheel. He tried his yoga exercises again and then it struck him that another piece of memory had come back without his realising – he knew yoga exercises. But the tension remained – he was so close to getting his body and his old life back that he just couldn't relax. Surely, once he was back in his body, all his memory would come back.

Arnold appeared in the passenger seat. 'Yes, you're still there and so are Suzie and her parents. So out you get.'

'I can't go in there while they're all there.'

'Well, you can't wait until they've gone. You could be whipped off to a freezer any minute.'

The more David thought about it the more implausible the idea of his being frozen seemed, but he couldn't take the risk. 'So, which room am I in again?'

'Last but one on the righthand side. Now go, I'll meet you up there.'

'And the private wing is easy to find?'

'Yes, it's all signposted, so get a move on.'

David's legs felt heavy. He cursed Arnold's unfitness, as he walked up the steps and along, what seemed to him, endless corridors. The adrenalin, sloshing around in his stomach, was giving him a nauseous feeling – Arnold was clearly feeling nervous as well.

When he reached the private wing, he tried to walk past the reception desk, but the receptionist called him back and asked who he was visiting. 'Would you sign in please – name and address,' and she held out a book. 'It's for security, in case there was a fire or something.'

David, hoping there wouldn't be a fire or something, scribbled something undecipherable and as much of Arnold's address as he could remember. The woman looked at it and then said, 'You haven't put in the patient's room number.'

'I don't know the room number.'

The receptionist looked at him more closely. 'Are you sure you're in the right part of the hospital? This is the private wing.'

David's nausea went up a notch. 'He's in the last but one room on the righthand side.'

The receptionist looked down at her paperwork. 'David Telford?'

'Yes, that's right'

'That's room thirteen. I'll fill it in for you.'

More adrenalin poured into his stomach, why did he have to be in room thirteen? He thanked the woman and walked towards the corridor.

When he reached his room, the door was open and he could see three people sitting round the bed chatting quietly, while his supine body lay surrounded by tubes, beeping machines and bags of fluid. He didn't recognise any of them, not even his own body. He hoped Arnold had picked the right one.

As he gingerly slipped inside the young woman, he assumed was his girlfriend, Suzie, looked round and smiled, but the man he assumed to be her father swung round and glared at him. 'Can I help you?'

David panicked, he couldn't see another chair to sit on and he'd promised Arnold he wouldn't come out standing up. 'I've come to visit the patient, is it all right if I sit down.'

Suzie's mother now turned and glared at him, taking in the scruffy clothes in a nanosecond. 'Who are you?' and her tone suggested she thought he was a particularly disgusting piece of roadkill which had been vomited up by the cat.

'David Telford.'

'Is this some kind of sick joke,' bellowed the man. 'Suzie, do you know this man?'

Suzie dragged her eyes away from David's body for a second, 'No of course not, Daddy.' And she went back to staring at David's body as if by the force of her will, she could wake him up.

'What do you think you're playing at, barging in here, pretending you're my daughter's fiancé?' Suzie's father was turning a nasty shade of red, 'This is a private room, and David Telford is a very sick man. Now get out.'

David panicked for the third time, 'No, sorry, sorry, a bit of confusion there. I meant I'm a, umm very close friend of David.' After a pause while Suzie's parents continued to glare at him, he added, 'A very close friend. We know each other really well.'

Suzie's mother turned to her daughter, 'You know all David's friends don't you darling, and this man's not one of them is he?' Her tone suggested she desperately didn't want him to be.

Suzie quickly glanced in his direction again and said, 'No, I've never seen him before in my life.'

'Right, that's it,' said her father, glowering at David and taking a threatening step forward, 'If you don't leave immediately, I shall have you thrown out.'

It was at this point that Arnold, who had taken up a position above the door, appeared in front of him demanding to know what the holdup was.

David panicked for the fourth time, 'Do you think I could sit down, just for a moment...I'm feeling a bit faint.'
'Absolutely not, there are chairs in reception, go and sit down there.' Suzie's father was even redder in the face. David gulped - the man looked as if he was about to resort to physical violence. 'But I'd really rather sit down here.'
'Out' The man pointed at the open door.
David backed out of the room, apologising profusely, and headed back the way he came. He could hear the man shouting behind him, 'And if you come back, I'll call the police.' David had a feeling this wasn't the first time Suzie's father had shouted at him.
Arnold bobbed along beside him. 'What are you playing at, where are you going?'
'You heard what he said, he'll call the police if I stay in there.'
'So, where are you going?'
'You said I had to be sitting down, so I'm looking for a chair.'
'Well, I suppose you don't have to be in the same room as your body when you come out,' Arnold conceded, 'Anywhere around here will do.'
When they arrived back at the reception area the few chairs available were now occupied by visitors waiting their turn to see their loved ones. After fidgeting for a while waiting for someone to get up and go, Arnold said, 'I know, we'll go back to the car, you can come out in there. You know how to get back to your body.'

Once he was safely sitting behind the steering wheel, David shut his eyes, took a deep breath, concentrated furiously, and thought about room thirteen. When he opened them again, he was still sitting behind the steering wheel and Arnold was glaring at him from the passenger seat.

'Well, come on then come out, I want to get home.'
David tried again – nothing. 'I don't know how to.'
'What! Just say the password.'
'I don't have a password.'
'Well, say mine – "What a load of rubbish".'

David repeated the process and shouted, 'What a load of rubbish.'

He opened his eyes – he was still sitting in Arnold's car. 'It's not working.' He covered his face with his hands. 'It's no use, I'm stuck in your body. Forever.'

CHAPTER 17

There was a long silence while they both tried to get their heads round the situation. It was finally broken by Arnold's, 'Nooooooo. You're not having my body. Try again.'

'It's no use,' David was close to tears. 'Do you think I'd stay in here one second longer if I could get out.' He looked out of the window at the hospital, 'My body's in there, it's so close, but it might as well be a million miles away.' He had convinced himself that once he was back in his body his memory was going to come back. He pulled out one of Arnold's grubby hankies and blew his nose loudly. 'And now I'm going to be like this for ever.'

Arnold on the other hand was not giving up. 'No way sunshine, no way, just give me a moment.' He snapped his fingers, not easy for an astral body, 'I've got it. You need to be right next to your body, then you'll be able to leap across.'

'But they won't let me back in the room, you heard what that man said, he'd call the police if I went back.'

'I know, but what if I brought your body down to the car, eh.' Arnold was so pleased with his brainwave he would have patted himself on the back if he'd been able.

David felt a slight twinge of hope. 'How are you going to do that?'

'I'll just pop into your body, get them to unplug me and then I'll say I've just got to pop down to the carpark for a minute or two, and we can swap bodies in here.'

The twinge of hope was deflating. 'Do you really think they'll let you do that?'

'Course they will. Your Suzie will be so pleased to have her beloved back she'll agree to anything.'

David wasn't as convinced as Arnold was – he couldn't see Suzie allowing him to run down to the carpark as soon as he came out of a coma. And from what he'd seen of Suzie's father, he couldn't see him agreeing to it either. Unfortunately, he couldn't come up with a better idea.

But before he could express any concerns, Arnold had disappeared. And once again he was left drumming his fingers on the steering wheel.

Up in the private room, Suzie's father was shouting down the phone at the receptionist for allowing a vagrant to get past her, but before he could add that her job would be on the line if it happened again, he heard a small scream from Suzie.

'I saw his eyelids flicker, Mummy, look, he's waking up.'

And it was true, Arnold had managed to get into David's body and after a lot of wriggling and shoving, trying to fit into someone much shorter than he was, he was now ready to face the world. His eyes snapped open and he found himself staring at three faces who were watching him intently. 'Alright then sweetheart?'

'David, darling, you're back with us.' Suzie would have thrown herself on him if it hadn't been for all the paraphernalia keeping him alive so she settled for holding tightly on to his hand.

Cameron heaved a sigh of relief - it looked as if he wouldn't be forking out shed loads of money for weeks to come. His wife looked less enthusiastic.

Arnold wanted to swap bodies as quickly as possible. 'Any chance of getting the quack back to unplug all this crap?'

At Stella's, Ingrid was waiting for her brother-in-law to come and pick her up. She'd told her sister she would catch a bus, but Greta wouldn't hear of it. Not as easy going as Ingrid, she thought men in general, and husbands, in particular, should be kept occupied at all times. That way they wouldn't have time for anything else. And under the heading 'anything else' she included extra-marital affairs.

In fact, Ingrid's head was still ringing from the torrent of advice which had poured down the phone, ending with, 'You brought this on yourself, you've been too lax.'

Stella and Greta had an uneasy alliance when it came down to what was best for Ingrid. Greta believed in keeping the marriage going, but making Arnold suffer while Stella favoured severing all relations with him. 'It would serve him right if you never went back. I'm sure your sister will let you stay until you've got yourself sorted out.'

Ingrid was horrified, she only intended to stay at Greta's for two or three days at the most, not until she sorted herself out – whatever that meant. 'Oh, I couldn't do that, Stella, they've only got one bathroom and Graham spends an awful lot of time in there. And when he does come out, he says, "better leave it for a few minutes".'

'Nonsense, you've got to give yourself time to get over this.' Stella was never happier than when sorting out other people's lives, 'And when you're ready you will be entitled to a share of the house and his pension so you could buy yourself a nice little flat.'

'But I don't want to live in a flat.' The thought of having to leave her cosy little home for ever was too awful to contemplate, but before she could tell Stella that there was a ring on the doorbell - Graham, looking as lugubrious as a bloodhound and as downtrodden as ever, had arrived. And although he didn't dare express an opinion, in his heart he was cheering Arnold on and hoped he would escape from the marital chains even if he couldn't.

After the calling consultant's pager to drag him back to the private wing – luckily, he was still in the building, Suzie's parents, guessing it would take some time to examine his patient and assess the situation, said they would go and have a coffee while they waited.

A surprised Mr Edwards rushed into the room and stared at Arnold with relief. He hadn't lost a patient yet and he didn't want to break his record. But he was in no hurry to uncouple all the equipment attached to David's body.

'I shall have to give you a thorough examination, we don't want you to have a relapse.'

'Look, mate, there's nothing wrong with me, just unplug it all.' Arnold tried to sit up, felt woozy and fell back on the pillows. 'I just need a couple of minutes to get used to being in here, alright, then I have to pop down to the carpark.'

'The carpark?' Suzie patted Arnold's hand, 'No darling, there's no rush to get home. You need to stay here and rest.' She looked the consultant, 'That's right, isn't it Mr Edwards.'

'Yes, at least another forty-eight hours just so that we can check there's been no brain damage.'

Arnold didn't like the sound of brain damage – the sooner he got back in his own body the better. 'Look, I won't be down there more than a minute and I'll come straight back, alright, that's a promise.'

Mr Edwards laid a restraining hand on Arnold's arm. 'Just try to relax and I'll start by asking you a few questions. So, what is your name?'

'Arnold Collins, now can I go.'

Suzie gasped, 'Your name isn't Arnold Collins, darling, it's David Telford.'

'Oh yeh, sorry sweetheart, I forgot. It's David Telford.'

'And where do you live?'

'Twenty-seven Whitehouse...' Arnold stopped, that was his address not the interloper's, 'No, sorry, mate, can't remember.'

The consultant turned to Suzie and whispered, 'Was that David's former address?'

'No, he wasn't living there when we first met.'

The consultant shrugged, 'Perhaps it's where he was born.' He turned back to Arnold, 'What's your date of birth?'

Arnold hesitated and wished he'd checked the chart hanging on the end of the bed, which would probably have told him. 'Can't remember.'

The consultant whispered to Suzie that he would try some general knowledge questions, 'What year is it?'

Arnold was on safer ground now. 'Nineteen-eighty-nine. Look can I go now?'

'Not yet, I've got a few more questions and then I must run some tests.'

Arnold sighed, 'Go on then, sunshine. Let's get it over with.'

'Who is the Prime Minister?'
'Margaret, bloody Thatcher.'
Suzie looked shocked. Her parents venerated Margaret and she'd never heard David call her 'bloody' before. Was the blow to the head showing his true colours. Surely, he wasn't going to vote Labour in the next election! She was certain her mother wouldn't approve of that. She might even insist the engagement was broken off.
The consultant was less shocked. 'Yes, good, good. So, who is the leader of the opposition?'
'Neil Kinnock.'
'Good. Can you remember what you do for a living?'
'Insurance.'
'No, you don't,' Suzie was getting seriously worried, knowing the leader of the Labour party was one thing, but forgetting what he did for a living was another!'
Arnold quickly agreed, 'No I don't.'
'So, what do you do?' asked the consultant
'He works in computers, he creates programmes.'
The consultant sighed. 'It's better if David answers the questions rather than you Suzie,'
Arnold was impressed, 'Blimey, does he?'
'Does who?'
'The interloper,' Arnold snapped. He was starting to feel a grudging admiration for David. He knew Mr Britten was having the office files put on a computer over the weekend and it was going to cost a fortune. The guy must be rolling in it.
'What interloper?' the consultant asked warily.
Thinking more about David's earning capacity than the question he said, 'The guy in my body.'
'Does he have a name?' whispered the consultant.
'Of course, he does, David.'

'And he's in your body?'

Arnold realised he was getting into deep waters and tried to back track. 'He could be.'

'So, who are you?'

'I'd rather not say if you don't mind, sunshine.'

'Earlier, you said your name was Arnold Collins. Are you in there with David?'

'Are you mad, there's only room for one of us.'

'So, there is an 'us'.'

Arnold was now completely confused – so were Suzie and the consultant, who pulled her away from the bed. 'I don't like the sound of this. It looks as if David has developed a multiple personality syndrome.'

Suzie didn't like the sound of it either. 'What do you mean?'

'He thinks he's two different people.'

Suzie looked back at Arnold, 'He certainly doesn't sound himself. David would never say Margaret bloody Thatcher – or call anyone sunshine.'

'So that's this Arnold personality saying that.'

'It must be.' Suzie's eyes start to tear up again.

'We need to get David back and hope this other personality disappears. The consultant approached the bed again. 'Ah Mr Collins…Arnold…can I speak to David please?'

Arnold looked at him, he could hardly say no he's sitting in my car in my body. On the other hand, until he could convince the guy he was David not Arnold, he wasn't getting out of this room any time soon.

He had no idea how David spoke, but from the way he cleaned the kitchen and bathroom and generally behaved, he guessed he was a bit prissy so he raised his voice up an octave and squeaked. 'I am definitely David, there's no one else in here with me, so can you unplug me...please. I need to go down to my car, it's very important.'

Suzie looked even more worried – if that were possible. 'That's not David, he doesn't talk like that.'

The consultant looked even more worried – if that were possible and pulled Suzie to one side. 'That means there's another personality in there as well. And it sounds as if it could be a woman!'

CHAPTER 18

In the carpark, David alternated drumming on the steering wheel with looking at Arnold's watch. Arnold had been gone nearly an hour. He was just about to get out of the car to go and see what was happening when he saw Suzie's parents parking two spaces along from him. He ducked down behind the steering wheel, hoping they hadn't seen him. They hadn't.

Rather than risk the beverages on offer in the hospital cafe, they had driven to a nearby bar and restaurant, which had taken longer than they had anticipated. Although neither of them said anything, privately they each had mixed feelings about David's apparent recovery. But now they were back.

As they entered the private room Suzie rushed into her mother's arms. 'David had gone doolally.'

'I wouldn't put it quite like that,' said the consultant, 'but there does seem to be a problem.'

Cameron sighed, in his experience 'a problem' meant money. 'What sort of problem? He's conscious, isn't he? And I've paid for the best of care. If you're telling me something has gone wrong, I shall sue you for negligence.'

The consultant blanched. He didn't see how he could be blamed for David having multiple personalities – he might have always been like that – but Suzie's father looked like the sort of person who sued first and asked questions afterwards.

'It's difficult to explain to a lay-person, Mr Baker-Brown, but I think David should be moved to a psychiatric hospital.'

'Oh, my goodness,' gasped Deidre, desperately trying to think how this could be kept a secret from the neighbours, her bridge club and the butcher who was the biggest gossip of all. 'What has happened?'

'We think he hit his head in the car crash,' sobbed Suzie, 'and now he thinks he's three different people.'

'Three different people!' Cameron was rapidly coming to the conclusion that one of David was more than enough of a problem, he certainly didn't want to deal with two more – and he certainly wasn't paying for two more. 'What the hell's going on here, Mr Edwards?'

'Well, as I said, it's difficult for a lay-person to understand, but it seems that, as I explained to your daughter earlier, David is suffering from a split personality syndrome or DID.'

'So, he doesn't anymore?'

'Yes, he does, that's the problem.'

Cameron took a deep breath, 'You just said "or did". In my book that means he doesn't.'

'Ah, yes, sorry Mr Baker-Brown, DID stands for Dissociative Identity Disorder – it's the same thing really.'

'Yes, you see Daddy, as well as himself, he thinks he's some guy called Arnold Collins, who...' Suzie could hardly bear to say the words, '...who hates Margaret Thatcher.'

There was a sharp intake of breath by her parents. 'He what!' gasped Deidre.

Suzie ploughed on, 'And then there's someone else who talks in a high squeaky voice.'

'Don't tell me,' roared Cameron, 'I suppose that one wants to wipe out the entire royal family.'

Arnold was outraged, as a child he'd once waved a flag as the Queen Mother drove past his school. 'Oy, I can hear what you lot are saying about me you know.'

'Oh, so you're not deaf then.' Cameron glared at him, 'Thank god for that.'

'No, I'm bloody not. I just want the quack here to take off all these bits and pieces,' Arnold waved an arm at the various tubes and wires, 'and let me go down to the carpark for a couple of minutes.'

The consultant pulled Cameron away from the bed and whispered. 'There's no way he can be allowed to leave this room unless it's to go straight to a place where he will get specialist attention.' And Derek Edwards had just the person, and place, in mind to do this. 'My cousin is an eminent psychiatrist and has a discreet private clinic.'

'How discreet?' Deirdre whispered, hoping that perhaps all was not lost.

'I can't name names,' Mr Edwards whispered, 'but he has helped several footballers, a well-known soap star and one or two politicians.'

Cameron was less interested in the clientele than the price. 'I suppose this is going to cost me an arm and a leg.' He didn't bother to whisper which made Arnold worry about what they were planning.

Deidre was still struggling to understand why anyone would hate Margaret Thatcher. 'So how can we get rid of this Arnold person?'

Mr Edwards shrugged 'It will take a lot of psychological help.'

Cameron glared at the consultant, 'If you'd been here, keeping an eye on him instead of clearing off home none of this would have happened.'

Mr Edwards was affronted, after all, he had come rushing back, leaving a delicious lasagne steaming on the dining room table. 'I really don't see how I can be held to blame, he could have been like this for years, but the condition hadn't manifested itself before.' He could see Cameron was about to start shouting again, so he quickly added, 'But the sooner we can get him into the clinic, the sooner my cousin can start the treatment.'

Suzie looked imploringly at her father. 'Daddy?'

Grudgingly he agreed, 'Alright get on the phone to him, I want this sorted as quickly as possible.'

Arnold didn't like the sound of being sent to a clinic, which was only marginally better than being frozen, and decided that perhaps now was the time to explain what had really happened. 'Look sunshine, I don't want to you to lay out shed loads of money. I'll tell you what's happened, alright. I'm not David, I'm Arnold Collins and I'm in David's body. And David is sitting in the carpark in my body. And he's waiting for me to pop down there and swap over.'

The consultant looked at him and then at Cameron and whispered, 'It's worse than I thought. Arnold has taken over, and he's completely delusional.'

Susan burst into tears and her mother sat down heavily on one of the chairs and wished she had some smelling salts.

CHAPTER 19

David decided he couldn't wait in the car for ever so he gave the couple, he assumed to be Suzie's parents, ten minutes and then went back into the hospital. Fortunately, the receptionist was on the phone so he pointed to the pad on her desk and mouthed 'I've already signed in.' And legged it.

He reached the door of number thirteen in time to hear a man's voice saying 'thanks for taking him in straight away Alistair, I think you are going to find this patient a fascinating case...yes, there might even be a paper in it for you...see you soon, bye.'

He peered round the door frame and saw the man put down the phone and turn to Suzie and her parents, who were standing well away from the bed. 'Right, a private ambulance will be here in about twenty minutes so I will just make sure David is ready to travel.'

Suzie grasped the man's hand. 'Can I go with him Mr Edwards?'

'No, I don't think that will be advisable, Suzie.'

'But I will be able to visit him, won't I?'

'Of course, once his medical condition has been stabilised. Now, I would like you all to leave while I check him over.'

David quickly backed into the room next door to avoid being seen. A voice behind him made him jump, 'Hello dear, I don't think I've seen you before. Could I have a bed bath?'

He glanced over his shoulder at the frail, elderly woman sitting up in bed with a gleam in her eye. 'What?' he whispered.

'I'll ring the bell for the nurse to bring the hot water and sponge, shall I?' And she started pulling her buzzer towards her. David didn't think Arnold's body could move that fast, but he managed to grab the flex the buzzer was attached to and pull it away from her. 'Not yet, I'll come back later.' He peered round the door and saw Suzie and her parents heading towards reception. He was about to head into room thirteen again when the other man came out.

Behind him he heard the sound of a buzzer being pressed – the old lady was stronger and quicker than he'd realized.

Arnold was in a dilemma. The consultant had rung for a nurse to come and remove the various tubes and monitors while he went to fill in the paper work and meet the ambulance. Should he wait and let her do it or should he try to remove them himself and leg it. He looked under the bedclothes, felt squeamish, and decided to wait. Pulling off a piece of sticky tape holding a wire in place was one thing, removing a catheter was another.

He looked up as the door opened and saw not the nurse but David come into the room. 'Well done sunshine, we've only a minute to do the changeover, sit down there as close as possible.' He decided against telling David where he would be going, once he was back in his own body David would find out soon enough.

'I hope this is going to work,' David whispered.

'You and me both mate, now concentrate.'

They both shut their eyes and intoned 'What a load of rubbish.'

They both opened their eyes.

'It hasn't worked,' gasped David.

'Perhaps we shouldn't try and do it at the same time, I'll go first.' Arnold whispered his password, nothing. He said it louder, nothing. He was still shouting it when the nurse came in, carrying a small tray.

'What are you shouting about Mr Telford, everything is going to be fine.' The nurse turned to David, 'Are you from the clinic?'

'What clinic?'

'The psychiatric clinic.' She looked at him suspiciously. 'I don't think you should be in here upsetting my patient.'

'He's not upsetting me, it's you lot that's doing that,' shouted Arnold, trying to get out of bed.

'Now calm yourself Mr Telford,' she picked up a syringe off the tray and sprayed a small amount of liquid into the air. 'Mr Edwards said I'm to give you a sedative for the journey. Now, just a little scratch…,' and with practiced efficiently she jabbed the needle into Arnold's arm. '…and you'll soon feel relaxed.'

Arnold, who hated injections and avoided them like the plague, nearly shot off the bed with the shock of it. 'Little scratch! That bloody hurt.'

'Oh, don't be such a baby,' she said jovially. 'Now lay back down the ambulance will be here soon.'

David was also shocked, but this was due to his body's immediate departure to a psychiatric clinic. 'Where are you taking him?'

The nurse took his arm, 'I think we should discuss this outside.' She looked back at Arnold, who had subsided onto his pillows and had a vacant look on his face. 'There look, he's relaxed now bless him.'

David didn't want to bless him. Back in the corridor he asked again where Arnold was being taken.

'That is confidential information, but he's going to a private psychiatric clinic.'

'What! Why?

She lowered her voice, 'Because he has multiple personality syndrome.'

'What does that mean?'

'He thinks he has two other people in there with him.'

David was horrified. No wonder they couldn't swap over - his body now had three astral spirits in it. Even if Arnold came out, what about the other two? And who the hell were they?

'So where is this clinic?'

At that moment his elderly nemesis from the adjacent room came out into the corridor. 'Oh, there you are, dear, my nurse had brought the hot water and look, I've got the sponge,' and she smile impishly at him.

The nurse looked at him and back at the elderly woman. 'Oh look, your mother is waiting for you. You were in the wrong room.' She leaned closer and whispered, 'But we don't encourage visitors to wash the patients.'

David was relieved to hear that, but before he could ask any more questions two burly men appeared and the nurse accompanied them into Arnold's room and firmly shut the door. It looked as if the only way he was going to find out where his body was being taken was to follow the ambulance.

Telling the elderly woman, he would be back in a second, he headed down to the carpark, then it struck him he had no idea where the ambulance was waiting. He took a deep breath and tried to think logically. He wished he had a pen and piece of paper, he always felt more in control if he could write a list.

He assumed the private wing probably had its own entrance for stretchers, so he started walking round the outside of the hospital. He finally found a set of double doors with the words St Hilda's Suite above them and sat on a nearby bench to wait. After about twenty minutes the burly men appeared wheeling a trolley and took it across to an anonymous grey van. One of them opened the van doors to reveal a stretcher inside. He watched as his body was lifted onto the stretcher and the van drive off.

It was then David realised there was a flaw in his plan – his car was a good five-minute's walk away and the anonymous grey van had already disappeared into the traffic.

CHAPTER 20

David rushed back to the Escort just in time to see Suzie and her parents get in their car and drive off. Without giving much thought to the situation, he quickly backed out of his parking space and followed them.

Suzie's father drove fast with the expectation that most motorists would get out of his way so David struggled to keep him in sight. But even Cameron didn't dare jump the lights at the road works, which gave David a chance to catch up. Eventually shops and houses gave way to green fields and expensive properties – and finally the Bentley stopped outside the gates of one of the largest. David slowed down and saw the gates opening as if by magic. Inside was a circular drive, surrounding a smooth green lawn, and a substantial house with a columned portico. Then he was past and wondering what to do next.

Just beyond the gates was a passing space. David forced himself to pull in and ignore the 'no parking' sign – he really hated breaking the law, but desperate situations called for desperate measures.

He walked back to the house. The gates were closed but next to them was a side gate and on one of the pillars was a box and a notice saying, press the buzzer. He did so, expecting the side gate to open and nearly jumped out of his skin when a man's voice said 'Yes.'

'Ah, I wondered if I could come in and see you.'
'And you are?'

David was in a dilemma – if he said Arnold Collins, they might remember him from the hospital and if he said David Telford, they would think he was lying again. Finally, he said they didn't know him, but he'd run out of petrol and could he please use their phone.

The voice said, 'You're the third person this week,' there was a long pause and then a grudging, 'Oh well I guess you'd better come in.'

The side gate squeaked open and David crunched across the gravel to the front door, which opened as soon as he got there. Suzie's father pointed to an alcove in the hallway and said, 'The sooner you people get yourselves mobile phones the better instead of keep disturbing us. The house phone is there.' He started to walk away and then stopped abruptly, turned round and glared. 'You again! What the hell are you doing here?'

Arnold had vague memories of being wheeled along a corridor and then a ride in some kind of ambulance, but now he was in a comfortable bed and loath to wake up.

His dreams however were interrupted by a voice saying, 'Hello…so, what would you like me to call you David or Arnold?'

Arnold kept his eyes shut tight – there was no good answer to that question.

'Okay,' said the voice, 'I know this must be difficult for you.'

You don't know the half Arnold thought.

'Perhaps I could talk to the other person. Does he…or she' (Alastair remembered being told the third personality had a high-pitched voice so possibly a woman) 'have a name?'

Arnold's eyes snapped open. 'No, she doesn't, there is no she.'

'Ahh, good, we have established a line of communication. Now, my name is Alastair.'

'I don't care what your name is sunshine, where am I?' Arnold quickly looked round the room and didn't like the look of the bars across the window – surely, he hadn't been taken to prison.

'You are in my private clinic.'

Memories of a muffled conversation in the hospital started coming back, something about cousins, psychiatrists and footballers. He briefly wondered if any of the footballers had played for Manchester City, and would it be worthwhile staying here so that he could have a chat with them about tomorrow's needle match. He decided against it and swung his legs out of bed.

'Okay, sunshine, I'm out of here.' Then he realised he was only wearing a hospital gown, precariously tied at the back, and swung his legs back under the covers. 'Where are my clothes?'

'To be honest I don't know. I expect your fiancée took them home after the accident?'

'What accident?'

'You were in a car crash. I take it you still don't remember it, Arnold.' Alastair thought he'd slip in a name to see the reaction.

'No, that wasn't me mate, I've never been in car crash in me life.' Arnold was wriggling around in the bed, fretting about his near nudity rather than concentrating on what Alastair was saying.

Alastair felt the excitement rising. 'So, who did have the accident...was it, David?'

'Yes, I think so.' Arnold fidgeted some more. 'Look, could you go and find me something to wear, I'm feeling a north wind blowing round me privates.'

'Yes, in a minute.' Alistair paused. 'Could I talk to David?'

'If you can find him, yes. I'd quite like to talk to him meself.'

Alastair's excitement rose another notch. 'So, where is David at the moment?'

'How should I know?'

'Isn't he in there with you?'

Arnold stopped pulling at the gown and stared at him. 'Look, like I told the other bloke in the hospital, we are not in this body together,' he went to throw the covers back to prove it, remembered the gown, and quickly changed his mind. 'I'm in here on me own right, but I'm in the wrong body.'

Alistair paused, perhaps the guy wasn't suffering from multiple personalities after all, he just didn't feel at home in his body. In his experience quite a lot of people didn't. 'Is there anything in particular that you don't like about your body?'

'I don't like anything about it, mate.'

'Why is that?'

Arnold was getting exasperated, 'because it isn't mine.'

'So, whose is it?'

'David Telford's.'

Alastair sighed, they seemed to be going round in circles.

Ingrid sighed as she unpacked her bag in Greta and Graham's guest room. Like the rest of the house, it reflected Greta's taste – in other words every surface was covered in porcelain crinoline ladies, glass dishes full of trinkets picked up on holidays, crochet covered boxes of tissues, lacey doilies and room fresheners.

Despite this, the room felt plain and unwelcoming with its pink fitted carpet and magnolia-emulsioned walls. Ingrid really missed flowery wallpaper.

Greta called up the stairs that she had made a cup of tea and to hurry up and unpack. Ingrid heard Graham head into the bathroom and lock the door. He'd obviously been told to make himself scarce while Greta rearranged Ingrid's life.

Graham was more than happy to shut himself in there. He really didn't want to hear what Greta had in mind for Arnold. Escape while you have the chance he thought as he flushed the loo and then sat on the edge of the bath to wait.

As usual, when he was banned to the bathroom, he thought about his marriage. Even though they had plighted their troth thirty-one years ago it still came as a surprise to him. He had been happily helping to run his parents' shop 'Hodges Hardware' when his mother announced one day that she was having an affair with the kitchen implement salesman and would be setting up home with him in Broadstairs.

His father had taken the news in his stride and told Graham not to worry they would get an assistant to help serve the customers.

The assistant was Greta, a bonny sixteen-year-old who set her cap at him. Two years later, much to his surprise, he found himself walking down the aisle in a tight-fitting suit to await his blushing bride – who had never blushed in her life.

According to custom, their first, and as it turned out, only child, Jonathan, was born two years later and Graham, who had never figured largely in Greta's life after their marriage, now didn't figure at all. But he didn't mind, he adored the new baby, and when Greta was feeling tired which was quite often, he was allowed to wheel Jonathan's pram round the park, teach him to ride a two-wheeler bike and take him to football matches.

Sadly, this was not enough to keep Jonathan in England and when he was eighteen, he told his parents he was emigrating to New Zealand to work on a sheep farm. When they said goodbye to him at Heathrow Airport, Jonathan had whispered in Graham's ear, 'Sorry Dad.' And Graham had whispered back, 'You've nothing to be sorry about, son, have a wonderful life.' And Jonathan had.

Surprisingly Jonathan's departure hadn't upset Greta as much as might have been thought. She could now boast to her friends about how well he was doing without having the bother of doing his washing or cleaning his bedroom.

Graham looked at his watch and wondered how much longer he had to stay out of the way. Knowing what Greta was like he felt sorry for Ingrid.

Cameron walked towards David in a threatening manner. 'Are you stalking us?'

'No. Well, yes, I admit I followed your car, but...'
Before David could complete his sentence, the man had snatched up the phone, dialled nine, nine, nine and asked for the police.

At that moment Deidre came into the hall to see what all the shouting was about. As soon as she saw David she started shouting as well. This brought Suzie into the hall, but she just stared at David sadly.

Although David still didn't recognise her, he knew she was supposed to be his fiancée and he stared sadly back at her. If he could just get back into his own body, he was sure his memory would come back and they could carry on with their lives together – and seeing her standing there looking so pretty, he really wanted that.

Up until that moment he had been prepared to rush out of the front door and escape before the police arrived, and he knew they would be here any minute because Suzie's father was now explaining just how well he knew the Chief Constable. But the sight of Suzie invigorated him – faint heart never won fair lady and all that. He walked up to Cameron and said, 'If you would just give me a chance to explain, all this could be sorted out.'

Cameron put the phone back on its cradle. 'You have precisely seven minutes. And it had better be good.'

'I just need to see David - it would only be for a few minutes and I promise I wouldn't upset him or anything.'

'I should hope not,' said Cameron threateningly, 'And why is it so important that you see him?'

David wondered how much to tell them, but decided a body swap wouldn't be believed. 'I've lost my memory and I think he could help me get it back.'

'I don't see how as my daughter says you don't even know each other.'
'But I do know him, I know him very well.'
'If you've lost your memory, how do you know that. No, this sounds very fishy to me.'
'I agree,' said Deidre, 'This is some sort of scam.'
'No, honestly, I was in a car crash.'
Suzie gasped, 'So, was David.'
'Yes, I was in the same one.'
Cameron glared at him. 'Now I know you're lying, the police said no one else was injured. Right, I've heard enough, I'm holding you here until the police arrive.'
But Suzie clutched his arm. 'Daddy, you can't have him arrested, he hasn't done anything,' she turned back to David, 'Would you promise never to come here again if Daddy changes his mind?'
David thought it was safe to make that promise because when he did come back, he would be in his own body. 'Absolutely, and thank you.' And then he fell in love with Suzie all over again.
Deidre put her arm round Suzie and took her back into the inner hall. 'You are too soft-hearted, darling, the man is a menace.'
Cameron opened the front door, 'Well, you heard what my daughter said so against my better judgement I'll tell the police when they get here it's all been a misunderstanding.'
David started to thank him, but he could hear a siren in the distance, which was getting louder by the second, so he rushed out of the front door. As it slammed shut behind him, he heard Suzie's father shouting, 'And don't let me ever see you again.'

David fervently hoped the same as he rushed towards his car, but not before seeing over his shoulder a police car pulling up outside the front gates. He flung open the car door and hunched down in the driver's seat. There was no guarantee that Suzie's father wouldn't change his mind about what he told the police – and then he would become a wanted man!

Stella, armed with a thermos flask of tea and a plate of ham sandwiches, settled herself in the armchair by the window. A pair of binoculars, hurriedly left behind by her husband many years ago, were handily placed on an adjacent coffee table.

Stella was on a stake out and nothing was going to happen next door without her noting it.

CHAPTER 21

Rather than continue going round in circles, Alastair decided to fill in the file he had started on David Telford. Some of the information had already been given to him by Mr Edwards, who got it from the Baker-Browns, such as date of birth, home address, where he worked and religious inclinations, but he thought he'd ask the questions again – just to check. 'So…David where do you live?'

'I'm not telling you anything until you find me some clothes.'

Alistair, convinced he had the upper hand in this situation said, 'As soon as you answer my questions, I'll ask the Baker-Browns to drop some off for you.'

The impasse lasted three-and-a-quarter-minutes with Arnold sulking the whole time. Finally, he agreed to co-operate. Needless-to-say, the information given by Arnold didn't tally with the information given by Suzie and her family, and he completely refused to give his address.

Alistair decided not to say anything about the discrepancies as it was more important to the keep lines of communication open. 'Well, that was all very helpful David or should I call you Arnold. You don't mind me calling you Arnold, do you?'

Arnold didn't bother to reply.

'Just a couple more things, you said you didn't like your body,'

'No, I keep telling you it's not mine.'

Alistair ignored that and said, 'Can you explain exactly what it is you don't like about it.'

'Everything, it doesn't fit properly and it's the wrong shape.'

Alastair's ears pricked up at those words, was the patient trying to tell him he was a woman trapped in a man's body?

'And have you always felt like this?'

'No, only the last hour or so.'

'The last hour or so?' Alistair was surprised, people who thought their bodies were the wrong shape had usually had these feelings for years. 'So, you haven't *always* felt like a woman trapped in a man's body for instance.'

'Are you raving mad?' Arnold couldn't have been more affronted.

But before Alistair could probe Arnold's psyche any further a nursing assistant came into the room bearing a tray loaded with soup, sandwiches, a banana and an individual trifle – in other words all the food Arnold normally avoided like the plague. But he was starving so he screwed up his face, and started tucking in.

Alastair watched him slurping the soup and decided to come back again later. He also decided not to ring the Baker-Browns to bring in some more clothes. He had no authority to keep the man under lock and key, but reasoned he was unlikely to walk out wearing nothing but a skimpy hospital gown.

He went back to his office and started pulling out text books.

David waited until the police car had disappeared through the gates then hurriedly executed a nine-point turn in the narrow lane and started back the way he'd come. He was tempted to put his foot down and get away from the place as quickly as possible, but he didn't want to get stopped for speeding.

Once his panic about being arrested had subsided another panic took its place – where was he, and how was he going to get home? The incongruity of calling Arnold's house home, also struck him. But he had nowhere else to go and he needed the bathroom, a stiff drink and some paper and a pen to make a list of what had to be done.

As he drove along the winding country lanes, he had time to think about the other astral bodies in with Arnold. He hadn't given them a thought as he struggled to keep the Baker-Brown's car in sight, but now they were all he could think about.

Had Arnold, somehow, smuggled them in with him – but why? Had some floating astral bodies from the travel agency followed them and taken the opportunity to try out someone else's body – but again, why? Had someone accidently come out in the hospital, got lost and pitched up in his room. He fervently hoped it wasn't the elderly lady, armed with a sponge and a determined look in her eye. He didn't think he could cope with that.

At last, he reached suburbia, where roads once more had names, so stopping well away from the yellow lines he consulted the street map. After a few wrong turnings he finally pulled into Arnold's drive.

His rapid exit from the car and into the house was duly noted by Stella, who wrote down the time and the fact that Arnold was on his own and in a rush. She wondered whether to add this must be because he is in a hurry to get back out to see his fancy woman – or would that be considered speculation?

Ingrid sat in Greta's front room, nervously tearing a flower-patterned paper serviette into shreds and wishing she hadn't left home. The room was normally only used for special occasions or important visitors. Ingrid's visit didn't fall into either category, but Greta felt the gravitas of the situation deserved special treatment. To this end the special bone china tea service and three-tiered cake stand had been placed on a heavily embroidered table cloth laid over a gate-legged occasional table, and Graham had been banished to the bathroom again.

Greta passed a cup of tea to Ingrid and then held out the cake stand for Ingrid to choose one from a selection of home-made cakes. But while the room was well furnished with bookcases, pouffes, flowering ferns in copper pots and over-stuffed chairs, it lacked side tables or any uncovered space at all. Ingrid could see no way of handling a fragile tea cup and a plate without putting down one or the other – so she passed on the cake, although she would have loved a slice of coffee and walnut sponge.

Greta had no such problem, there was room for her to put her cup back on the tray so she was able to select a large slice of lemon drizzle cake.

Ingrid waited in misery for the inevitable conversation, without the consolation of something sweet to chew on. Greta was four years older than her and took her elder sister responsibilities seriously – in other words she had relentlessly bossed Ingrid from the day she was born.

Arnold worked his way through the soup, sandwiches and trifle, but eating fruit definitely went against his principles so he threw the banana in the wastepaper basket.

Feeling fortified, he started planning his escape. He had no idea of the time, but there was still some daylight so couldn't be too late. He just needed to get to phone. He slid out of bed and peered out into a corridor. He could hear a hum of voices coming from a room at the far end which started to get louder. A nurse came out and rushed towards him so he hurriedly ducked back. She went straight past and he heard her telling someone next door he needed to come quickly as an argument had broken out between a footballer and a minor celebrity.

Arnold recognised the man following her as the guy who'd just given him the third degree. As soon as they had disappeared, he shot into the corridor. The door was still open to the room the man had exited and he could see it appeared to be an office so he guessed it must have a phone. There were books all over the desk and as he rummaged around under them, sending several sliding to the floor, he finally found it. He pulled it free and almost dropped it in his eagerness to ring home.

David finally found a bottle of whiskey at the back of the sideboard and poured himself a large measure. He sat down on the settee knocked it back and then poured another one. Slowly he started to relax. He now felt able to get paper and pen and start planning what to do next. Just the thought of writing a list made him feel more in charge of events.

He felt his pulse, yes it was much slower. It was safe to think about the extra astral spirits in his body and what had happened at Suzie's home.

As he was remembering how pretty his fiancée looked, a stray thought slipped into his mind - mobile phones, or rather one mobile phone, his. When her father had shouted 'The sooner you people get yourselves mobile phones the better,' he knew he had one, or something similar, but where was it?

The strident ringing of the hall phone pushed the memory back out of his mind and sent his pulse rate back up again. He sat fidgeting nervously wondering whether to answer it. He decided to ignore it, but it went on and on. He crept into the hall and quietly lifted the receiver, 'Hello,' he whispered.

'About bloody time.'

'Arnold?'

'Of course, it's me. Now pack a bag of clothes and meet me outside asap.'

'Outside where?'

'This clinic place, hang on,' Arnold rummaged around some more, and more books slid to the floor, but he finally found a brochure in a drawer. 'It's called 'Safe Haven.'

David interrupted, 'I can't come this evening, I've just had two large glasses of whiskey, I'm not fit to drive.'

'I don't care if you're paralytic, you've got to come and get me, now.'

'But…'

'May I remind you sunshine that this is your body here and I don't mind telling you the guy running this place thinks there's a woman trapped in it.'

'What!' So, it was true there were others in with Arnold.

'And I wouldn't put it past him if he didn't find a way of giving you a change of sex.'

David felt decidedly ill. 'I'll make some black coffee. Give me the address.'

'And bring some clothes with you.'

Twenty minutes later Stella's patience was rewarded by the sight of Arnold's car reversing out of the drive, hitting the curb opposite, and then staggering down the road. The time was duly noted, plus the direction taken - and the erratic way it was being driven.

While tucking into her tea and cake, Greta gave Ingrid exact instructions on what she was to do next. 'Men like Arnold are incapable of managing on their own. Mark my words, after three days he will be begging you to come back.' She broke off a small piece of lemon drizzle and popped in her mouth. Ingrid watched enviously as it disappeared, and waited nervously.

After a quick dab of her lips with a paper serviette, Greta continued, 'But you are not going back until you have made it quite clear to him that things are going to be different.' Another piece of cake followed the first. Greta didn't often have a captive audience to dispense advice to and she wasn't going to hurry. 'Naturally, he must give this woman up, although I find it hard to believe he found one in the first place. Mark my words, this whole affair is in his head.'

Ingrid was inclined to agree, Stella must have got it wrong. But she knew better than to interrupt her sister.

Greta ate another piece of cake. 'However, it wouldn't hurt to play along with this charade because it gives you, as the innocent party, considerable leverage.' Greta gave a discreet burp, and then continued, 'If he wants you to return to the marital home, he must treat you with a lot more consideration. And that means remembering wedding anniversaries and birthdays.'

As soon as she'd finished her cake, she took Ingrid's cup, which was still half full, and said she was off to prepare supper. Greta had read that the upper classes didn't have tea in the evening, or even dinner, but a two or three course meal, served at eight-o-clock.

Ingrid who never ate any later than six-thirty wondered how her digestive system would cope. And that set her thinking of Arnold's digestion and his gastric imbalance, and she wondered how he was coping, cooking for himself.

It was dusk by the time David found 'Safe Haven'. He parked a little way away and flashed the headlight once as agreed. A ghostly figure slid out of the hedge in front of the clinic and flapped towards him. He was about to drive off in terror when he realized the apparition was wearing a white hospital gown. Assuming it wasn't a patient who'd come back to haunt the place, he drove towards it and the next minute Arnold was in the car.

'Quick, drive off. I think they're looking for me.'

The shock of seeing his body sitting next to him, practically nude, sobered David up quicker than any amount of black coffee. 'Can't you cover yourself up a bit? It's very distracting trying to drive.'

Arnold attempted to straighten the gown and pull it over his knees. 'It's your body, surely you've seen it all before.'

'Yes, but not from this angle…it's weird.'

'Yes, well, pull up in the next layby and I'll change into my clothes.'

A few minutes later Arnold was standing at the side of the road wriggling into a pair of trousers and a jumper, neither of which fitted him. He looked down at David's, now his, tiny paunch. 'Bloody marvellous! You are the weirdest shape. Look at me! I look ridiculous.'

'It doesn't matter, get back in the car.'

'This jumper is strangling me and my trousers are too long but won't do up round the waist.' Arnold had another unsuccessful go at pulling up the zip.

David was in terror of a police car coming along and being asked to explain what he was doing in the layby with Arnold, who was half undressed, and then, even worse being breathalyzed. 'Please just get back in the car, no one is going to see you.'

Of course, he was wrong. Stella, alerted by the headlights sweeping up Arnold's drive had the binoculars glued to her eyes. The light from the street lamp showed Arnold going into his house accompanied by a short plump man whose trousers fell down before he reached the front door.

Alastair had sorted out the argument, which was, for the hundredth time, about the off-side rule, which the celebrity understood and the footballer didn't. Which was why he was in the clinic. Then he rushed back to his office to start reading up on people who believed they were in the wrong bodies. He was so absorbed that he completely forgot about Arnold. It was only when the assistant told him that the new patient had eaten all his tea - apart from the banana which she had rescued from the bin - but was now missing.

He went back with her to Arnold's now empty room, to check for himself, but despite searching under the bed, in the wardrobe and finally the whole clinic he had to accept she was right, his patient had disappeared. He didn't immediately panic, reasoning that the man couldn't have got far wearing only a hospital gown and was probably outside sitting on a bench.

But after searching the gardens, panic did start to set in. He rang Derek Edwards, who rang the Baker-Browns. Cameron's response was to call his lawyer to check what grounds he had for suing, and then to ring Alastair to threaten legal action if his daughter's fiancé wasn't found, unharmed, immediately. It was a bluff of course - he was in no hurry for David to be found, the longer he was missing the more chance there was of Suzie forgetting all about him. But suing people was his default mode.

Once inside the front door, David waited until Arnold had hitched up his trousers before turning on the hall light. He was desperate to see what he looked like. All he'd seen of his body so far in the hospital was part of a face - the rest of him had been under a sheet and covered with tubes and wires. And then in the car it was just a sideways view.

He now saw a plumpish, round-faced young man in his late twenties with curly hair, sticking up on end, blue eyes and a wispy moustache staring back at him.

'What?' Arnold was cold, tired and despite the sandwiches, hungry.

'I wanted to see if I recognised myself.'

'And do you?'

'No.' And David turned sadly towards the kitchen.

PART THREE – SATURDAY

CHAPTER 22

Stella woke early with a stiff neck and a bruised toe from the binoculars slipping out of her unconscious hands and landing, heavily, on her left foot. She was mortified to find she had drifted off during a stake-out and had been asleep in the armchair all night. Then it all came flooding back along with the vision of Arnold's 'friend' losing his trousers, tripping over them and falling in the front door.

She didn't dare phone Ingrid at her sister's. Not many people were able to deflate Stella, but Greta was one of them. Fortunately, she remembered Ingrid was on the Saturday morning rota with her this week, so Stella would be able to tell her, plus their now regular gang of customers, about the latest development. A development which was far worse than they could ever have imagined.

Arnold also woke with a stiff neck. He was back in his own bed, but it didn't feel as comfortable as it usually did. As the sun edged through a gap in the curtains and into his eyes, he fidgeted around, turned over, pulled his legs up, pushed them back down again, plumped the pillow, threw back the eiderdown, got cold so pulled it back over him and then turned over again. It took him several minutes to work out that all the bumps and hollows in the mattress, which perfectly accommodated his long skinny body, no longer fitted his short plump one. He could now add this to his list of grievances, along with the severe bout of indigestion, after cooking himself a fry-up, which had kept him up half the night. The interloper's digestive system left a lot to be desired in Arnold's opinion. Then it struck him that he was now an interloper too.

The sound of Arnold crashing along the hallway, kick-started David's headache and dragged him out of a nightmare where he was being pursued by a policeman wearing a backless white gown and carrying a truncheon. The relief at waking up was immediately knocked sideways by his hangover. Groaning faintly, he staggered along the hall in search of painkillers and black coffee.

They met in the kitchen and glared at each other.

The previous evening, they had tried several times, unsuccessfully, to swap bodies. David was convinced it was because Arnold had other astral spirits in with him, which Arnold vehemently denied.

'But you told me that there was a woman in there with you and that the consultant was talking about a sex change.'

'Ah, I may have exaggerated a bit there, sunshine.'

'So, there is no woman, it's just you!' David didn't know whether to be relieved or hopping mad that Arnold had conned him. Unable to decide, he finished off the bottle of whiskey while watching in horror as Arnold burned, and then ate, a pound of sausages, eight beef burgers and a packet of potato waffles. He could see his body expanding before his eyes and changing from plump to obese.

Then there had been an argument about who was going in the bathroom first – Arnold maintained that it was still his bathroom, so he would, while David maintained that technically it belonged to Arnold's body and he should have first dibs. There had been an embarrassing scuffle outside the bathroom door. Eventually they'd tossed a coin for it and David had won.

Unable to stand the headache any longer, David spoke first 'Where do you keep the painkillers?'

'Got a hangover, have you?' Arnold was less than sympathetic.

'Could you please not shout.' David groaned and held his head.

'I'm not surprised mate, the way you were knocking back my whiskey.' Arnold carried on muttering as he felt around the fridge for something, anything to fry for breakfast. But having eaten everything the previous evening, all he came up with was a wrinkled carrot which he threw in the bin.

As David had won the toss the night before he decided to be conciliatory. 'Look, I'm sorry about the whiskey, I don't normally drink that much, but this situation…well, it just got to me last night…I am finding it very disconcerting seeing my body doing things I would never do.'

'You and me both sunshine, and I've had to put up with you wrecking my body for more than two days now, you've only just started suffering.' Arnold was having better luck in the larder where he found some eggs.

David was about to remonstrate that he wasn't wrecking Arnold's body when the noise of Arnold beating the eggs with a metal whisk in a metal bowl went through his head. 'Please can you stop that, just for a moment.'

Arnold continued for another few seconds and then tipped the frothy mixture into a frying pan where he attempted to make an omelet.

David couldn't bear to watch so took over from him and produced two perfectly folded masterpieces. But as he couldn't face his Arnold ate them both. Having satisfied his hunger, Arnold magnanimously opened a kitchen drawer, pulled out a packet of aspirin and tossed them to David.

Two strong cups of coffee and two aspirins later David felt well enough to contemplate the future and formulate a plan of action. He was itching to get his hands on a pen and some paper. 'We need an action plan.'

'We need our own bodies back, that's what we need, mate.'

'I know, but until that can be actioned, we have to work out how we are going to live like this and what steps we need to take...' He looked at Arnold's face, 'Am I boring you?'

'In a word...yes. We don't need no action plan - we just need to go round to the guy at Astral Travel asap, and throttle him until he does something. Oh, and I'm going in the bathroom first this morning, and we're not tossing for it.'

'That's what I mean,' said David, 'To avoid arguments and coin-tossing we need a rota for using the bathroom and another one for household chores.'

'You won't catch me doing housework, that's Ingrid's job.'

'In case you hadn't noticed your wife has left home.'

Arnold looked round the kitchen as if checking that she wasn't there. He wasn't yet ready to concede that David might be right.

David continued, 'So, are we agreed that you can use the bathroom first in the morning and I will have it first at night.'

Arnold shrugged morosely which David accepted as agreement. 'I would also like to add a rider to that. The bathroom must be left clean and tidy after use.' Without waiting for a response, David ploughed on. 'Until we can get to Astral Travel, which I do agree should come up high on our agenda, we need to go shopping as you have eaten all the food.'

Arnold scowled, 'Well, we can't go to the Co-op that's where Ingrid and the harridan from hell work.'

'I'm sure there's a Waitrose somewhere.'

Arnold nearly fell off his chair, 'Waitrose! Well, I hope you've got plenty of money sunshine.'

'I don't have any money.'

'Exactly, but you're quite happy spending mine.' Arnold continued muttering Waitrose under his breath.

'If it makes you happy, I will keep a running total and I will pay you back as soon as I'm back in my body.' David really wanted to go to a Waitrose, he had a strong feeling that was where he regularly shopped and where he could get all the food that was dear to his heart.'

Arnold stood up, 'Is that it then? Because I need the bathroom.'

David looked across at his body wearing a pair of pyjamas which were too tight round the middle and too long in the leg. 'You also need some new clothes, yours don't fit my body.'

'I am not spending money on new clothes. Why can't you go home and get some of yours for me?'

'You know why, I can't remember where I live, but if you want to go round losing your trousers every five minutes...' David hadn't forgotten the sight of a trouser-less Arnold falling through the front door and exposing his backside to the whole road illuminated by a street lamp.

Arnold didn't want to repeat the experience again either, so grudgingly agreed that David could buy him a new pair of trousers, the cheapest he could find, he would make do with the rest of what was in his wardrobe. There had to be a baggy jumper somewhere which would fit his new rotund state. 'And then we'll go to Astral Travel,' he stipulated.

'Yes, then we'll go to Astral Travel.' David looked at the kitchen clock, it was only five-past eight. 'But they probably won't be open yet.'

He thought it best not to insist they do a housework rota before they went to the travel agency, as with a bit of luck they wouldn't need one.

'So, while you're in the bathroom, I'll write a list of what food I think we need and then while I am taking my ablutions you can add what you want to it.'

As Arnold shuffled out of the kitchen, holding up his pyjama trousers, David called after him, 'Don't forget to leave it tidy.' And received the age-old two finger reply.

Suzie woke up and for a few happy moments let her eyes wander over her rosettes hanging on the wall opposite her bed. Then she remembered David was missing and burst into tears.

Cameron was up early and on the phone to a private investigator. Suzie had insisted that something had to be done to find her fiancé and Cameron didn't want to disappoint her even though he would have preferred David to stay missing. So, he picked Sidney Spraggs, who had been recommended by a golfing buddy, and was so incompetent that it took him six weeks to find the buddy's wife in bed with her lover in the next village. Cameron neither wanted or expected any results.

Alastair Grey had contacted the police the previous evening to report David missing, but was told as he was an adult, they wouldn't start a full-scale search for a day or two. So, he'd rung Cameron and asked him to drop a photo of David into the police station. Cameron agreed and was looking for one in which David wouldn't be easily recognised.

Deidre walked into her daughter's bedroom carrying a breakfast tray loaded with all Suzie's favourite food, including golden fried bread. She had decided the best way to treat her was as if she was an invalid. 'Here you are darling, you've got to keep your strength up.'

Suzie stared sadly at the tray, which Deidre had laid across her knees. 'Oh, Mummy, I don't think I can eat a thing.' But as soon as Deidre had gone out, the smell of crispy bacon, mushrooms and a perfectly fried egg quickly changed her mind. Deidre certainly knew how to get their cook to make a delicious breakfast.

CHAPTER 23

When David managed to get into the bathroom, he could see that his and Arnold's idea of leaving it clean and tidy were poles apart. With a sigh he rehung the towels on the towel rail, fished the soap out of the wash basin where it was fast turning into a gooey mess and picked Arnold's pyjamas up off the floor and put them in the laundry basket.

He then noticed that Arnold had used the electric razor, leaving it covered in hair – fine hair. He stared at it for a moment before realising what Arnold had done. He mentally added disposable razors to his shopping list and walked out unshaven and angry.

Back in the kitchen he glared at Arnold. 'You shaved off my moustache!'

'Have I? Yes, well, I didn't like it…it was all itchy.'

'But it's my body, you can't make changes like that without asking first.'

'Oh, keep your hair on, it'll grow again.'

'I grew it to make me look older, now you've made me look like a twelve-year-old.'

'No, you don't.' Arnold, in truth, had no idea what David looked like as he couldn't bear to look in the mirror and see a face which wasn't his, so had shaved with his eyes shut. A somewhat dangerous practice as he'd shaved the moustache off by mistake. 'Look, we've more important things to think about like this shopping list.' And he thrust the piece of paper at David.

David found half his shopping list had been scribbled out and a whole load of junk food had been added. He couldn't believe Waitrose even sold half the stuff Arnold wanted.

Arnold, meanwhile, was sitting with his arms folded and a defiant look on his face. 'I like oven chips and burgers and I don't want humous.'

David sighed, - he realised he'd been doing a lot of sighing lately. 'Do you know what it is?'

'No, and I don't want to. And I'm not eating ratatouille either or bean sprouts.'

If Arnold was allowed to eat all the fattening food now on the list David knew his body would end up looking like a barrel. It was only a combination of a strict diet and regular exercise that kept it looking merely plump. 'My metabolism is different to yours. Your body can eat what it wants and mine can't.'

'Well, aren't you the lucky one, sunshine, being in a body that can eat what it wants.'

'Not really because I don't enjoy all that fatty food, even if your body does.'

Arnold glared, 'Look, if I'm going to have to eat healthy food while I'm in your body, you are going to have to eat what I like, while you're in mine. It's only fair. My body is used to sausage, chips and baked beans and beef burgers and fish fingers, and it will deteriorate without them.'

David doubted that, but agreed it was only fair to keep to each other's diets. But he wondered if he could slip something into their agreement regarding exercise, although he couldn't see the pair of them jogging down the road anytime soon – or visiting a gym.

Having agreed a final version of the shopping list, Arnold reluctantly handed over his debit card and PIN. 'I ought to charge you for board and lodging, mate.' He then wandered back to his bedroom muttering, Waitrose and humous under his breath.

In the Co-op Stella was beside herself with excitement as Ingrid took her seat at the next till. Because Greta lived on the other side of town, Ingrid hadn't been able to pop in for coffee before their walk to the High Street together, so this was the first chance she'd had.

They opened their tills and then Stella leant across and hissed, 'It's worse than we thought.' But before she could say any more the manager walked towards them. 'I hope neither of you are planning to suddenly dash off today, or change your hours or keep your customers waiting while you chat.'

Ingrid shook her head, silently, she had slept badly and was feeling terrible. At that moment she didn't really care if Arnold had gone off with another woman, she just wanted to go home.

Stella on the other hand was feeling great. 'We don't keep our customers waiting, the queues are getting longer because there are more shoppers, and I think that's down to us and the service we give, so don't give me any hassle.'

The manager would have liked to have given Stella some hassle, but it was true, word had got around that there was some delicious gossip going round the Co-op and no one wanted to miss out on it. In fact, they were pouring in the door and he found himself pushed out of the way as the first shoppers started to unload their baskets on the conveyor belts. Leaving him with nothing to say but, 'I'll be keeping an eye on this area, Mrs Threadgold.'

Like Stella, the customers were also beside themselves with excitement. It really was worth getting up early to be first in the queue – and the first to get the latest news. None of them had ever met Arnold, but they now felt as if they knew him personally and were therefore entitled to give their opinion.

Stella scanned the first item, a tin of chopped tomatoes, 'Well,' she said, and after a dramatic pause, she started to give a blow-by-blow account of how she had set up a command post in the bay window of her sitting room where she could observe all the comings and goings next door.

Then surreptitiously pulling her log out of her handbag, as an aide memoire, she continued. 'At six-fifty-six, the suspect pulled into his drive in a tearing hurry. He appeared to be on his own. He entered the front door and disappeared from view.' She looked up, 'I haven't added this to my log, but I suspected he was in a hurry to get back out and see his fancy woman.'

There was a collective intake of breath from the shoppers.

She scanned a few more items, while her queue waited impatiently. One customer could stand the suspense no longer, 'Don't worry about the shopping, then what happened?'

Stella looked around, 'I have to keep scanning or the manager will be down on me like a ton of bricks.' This was nonsense of course, she just wanted to drag out the story. Stella wasn't often in a position where her every utterance was received in awe, and she was determined to enjoy it to the full.

The queue looked across at Ingrid slumped sadly over her till and someone asked her if she was infuriated by her husband's behaviour. 'Not really,' she sighed, 'I just want to go home.'

The queue looked back at Stella in excited anticipation of the next instalment. Stella had a quick check to see that the manager wasn't in sight and another quick check at her log. 'At seven-twenty-three the suspect came back out and got into his car. He then proceeded to back out of the drive so fast that he hit the pavement on the other side of the road. He then drove off in a very erratic fashion, leading me to believe that he was drunk. I was certain he wasn't going to see his wife as he was heading in the opposite direction.'

The queue turned back to Ingrid to see if she wanted to add anything, but she didn't. Ingrid was remembering how she and Arnold had first met.

It was at a jazz club she'd reluctantly gone to with a couple of friends. They were soon jiving away, leaving her sitting alone and lonely when Arnold had sat down next to her. Over the noise of the jazz band, he asked if she wanted a drink and they had headed to a pub across the road. It turned out he'd come with some mates as well, but they had disappeared. He asked her to go to the pictures with him the following evening and they began dating.

Following the customs of the time, she had knitted him a brightly striped jumper, which was still stuffed at the back of one of his drawers, and he'd bought her a locket with his photo in it.

This was followed by an engagement ring and then a wedding ring.

Two lonely people would never be lonely again. Ingrid would have liked a bit more romance, but she was mostly content with her life. But now it turned out that Arnold wasn't content with his – why else was he chasing other women?

Her queue turned back to Stella, who told her first customer that her bill had come to twelve pounds and fifteen pence, but the woman was loth to miss anything so packed her shopping as slowly as possible. And for once no one complained when she couldn't find her debit card and had to count out the cash in small change.

Adroitly putting the money in her till, Stella prepared herself for her big reveal. 'At eight-forty-seven, the suspect returned and entered the house. He was followed by a second person,' again she paused for dramatic effect, 'a man, whose trousers fell down as he entered the house, exposing himself for all to see.'

Sir John Gielgud, probably never had such a moment of awed silence at the end of one of his Shakespearean performances as Stella did at that moment. It was finally broken by the queue drawing synchronised breaths and then all talking at once.

Stella looked across at Ingrid, but she appeared not to have heard. 'It's worse than we thought Ingrid, Arnold brought home a man last night.'

Ingrid shrugged listlessly, 'He was probably a work colleague.'

'I don't think so,' said Stella, 'work colleagues don't drop their trousers when they walk in the front door.'

'Well, I'm sure there is a reasonable explanation,' Ingrid's mind was back in the past when Arnold used to hold her hand, and she slowly scanned a few items without seeing them.

Luckily, the shoppers didn't agree with her. The story of Arnold's behaviour was passed along the lengthening queues, and like Chinese Whispers, gained embellishments and misunderstandings on the way.

Although Stella and Ingrid couldn't go, the queue was ready to head to the café opposite for coffee, cakes and a full dissection of events. It was also agreed that a table would be booked for lunch so that Stella and Ingrid could join them, and then an even fuller dissection of events could take place.

Stella didn't think it was necessary to say she'd fallen asleep on her stake-out so might have missed an important development.

David decided to buy the trousers for Arnold first and then dash into Waitrose for the emergency ration.

He selected a pair of cheap beige chinos from a men's shop just off the high street. It was either those or workmen's dungarees. He was almost tempted to buy a pair for himself as Arnold's jeans really needed to go in the wash, but decided it wasn't worth the argument about the cost when he got home.

Finally, he made it to Waitrose. As he wandered round the supermarket's shelves, he felt very much at home.

Another vague memory came back of buying ingredients for Duck a l'orange for a dinner party.

He toyed with the idea of getting some duck breasts, but Arnold's body practically walked him past the meat counter and up to the deep freezers, where he was surprised to find that Waitrose did sell most of Arnold's favourite foods.

Perhaps gourmet burgers wouldn't be so bad after all.

As soon as he got home, Arnold insisted on inspecting every item and grudgingly accepted that the food he'd demanded for his body had been purchased and that what David had bought for him to eat actually looked quite tasty. He then tried on his new trousers which, although wouldn't have been his choice, were a comfortable fit.

David checked the kitchen clock, 'Right, it's nearly eleven-o-clock, let's get round to Astral Travel.

Neither spoke on the journey, there was too much riding on the visit for casual conversation.

CHAPTER 24

A soon as they pushed open the door to 17 Gasworks Road they were met by Margaret. 'Oh, it's you again Mr Collins, what do you want this time?'

David smiled politely, 'As I told you yesterday, Miss Hamilton, I am not Mr Collins,' he turned to Arnold, 'this gentleman is.'

Margaret glanced at Arnold and then back at David, 'If you say so, but we have a busy morning so...' and Margaret started to usher them back out.

David stood his ground, 'No, you don't understand, Mr Collins is in my body and I'm in his.'

Margaret continued to usher them towards the front door. 'And as I said yesterday this has nothing to do with Astral Travel.'

Arnold decided a firmer line needed to be taken, 'Look where's Hornby? He's responsible for what's happened and he needs to sort it out.'

Hearing raised voices Bernard came out of his office. When he saw David his face fell, 'Oh, it's you again Mr Collins.

David sighed then pointed to Arnold, 'No, this is Mr Collins, but he's in my body.'

'Yesterday you said he was floating around in the air.'

'Yes, he was, but then he found my body and got in it.'

'So, who are you?'

'David Telford.'

It was now Bernard's turn to sigh, 'This is all most irregular Mr Telford. My clients are only supposed to go astral travelling not body swapping.'

'We have not been body swapping,' Arnold was getting more and more annoyed, 'He got into mine, so I had to get into his, and now we are stuck like this.'

'I'm sorry, but I'm not sure what it is that you want me to do.'

'We want you to get us out, sunshine, and then we can get back into our own bodies.'

Bernard sighed again, 'Well I suppose I could try.'

'That's more like it.' Arnold pushed past him into the separating room, 'So let's get started.'

Bernard ushered David in after him. 'We'll have to be quick - my other clients will be here soon.'

'Don't worry about that mate, you can be as quick as you like,' and Arnold settled himself on the floor with his head on a cushion. David laid down cautiously alongside him

Bernard told Arnold to use the same password and told David he would need to think of one for himself, and then he started to intone. 'Focus on a small pinpoint of light, feel your body getting heavier as your astral spirit gets lighter.'

When nothing happened after ten minutes of Bernard intoning, they swapped passwords. After fifteen minutes, with Bernard's intoning becoming more desperate, it was clear that nothing was going to happen. Apart that is from Arnold getting cramp in his feet and David getting a crick in his neck and wishing he'd grabbed a cushion.

Arnold sat up. 'That's it, I'm suing you for every penny you've got.'

'I don't understand it Mr Collins,' said Bernard, 'when you were here on Thursday you came out straight away. In fact, you were my first success.'

'I don't think you can call it a success,' said David also sitting up, 'when we are left like this.'

Bernard looked at him baffled. 'As a matter of interest, how did you come out of your body in the first place?'

'I was in a car crash.'

Bernard felt a surge of relief, he definitely couldn't be held responsible for what happened in car crashes. 'In that case I don't see how I am able to help you.'

Margaret came into the room to tell Bernard Miss Long and two new clients had arrived and could they come in.

'Yes, send them through, these gentlemen are just leaving.'

Arnold had no intention of leaving. 'You're not getting rid of us that easily. So, what do you intend to now, sunshine?' And he took up a threatening stance.

Margaret quickly assessed the situation and said she would take the clients into her office and make them some coffee.

When she'd gone, David adopted a more conciliatory tone. 'Mr Collins told me that you're able to leave your body at will. How did you learn how to do that?'

Bernard didn't really want to reveal that he'd learned how to from a book, but it looked as if it was the only way to get rid of them. 'If you must know I got the idea from a book I borrowed from the library.'

Arnold was incredulous. 'You taught yourself from a library book! No wonder you're bloody useless.'

He stormed up and down the room, kicking any cushions unfortunate enough to be in his path. 'You, mate, are a crook.' More cushions went flying as he got into his stride. 'I'm reporting you to the police.'

David pointed out that they didn't really have any grounds for involving the law. He was still feeling nervous about his close encounter with the boys in blue yesterday. He turned to Bernard, 'What's the name of this book?'

'Why do you want to know that?' Arnold kicked another cushion for good measure.

'Because we might be able to teach ourselves how to come out like Mr Hornby did.'

Bernard, seeing a way to get rid of them, said he'd write down the title and the author if they would come into his office.

Five minutes later they were back in the car and heading for the library.

In the Safe Haven clinic Sidney Spraggs, the private investigator hired by the Baker-Browns, was interrogating Alastair Grey who told him that David Telford had Dissociative Identity Disorder. 'Or as you would probably say he has multiple personalities.'

Sidney had seen the film 'The Three Faces of Eve' starring Joanne Woodward and remembered that one of Eve's personalities had tried to strangle the daughter of the other personality.

'So, is this chap dangerous, Dr Grey?' Sidney was starting to feel concerned for his safety.

'I don't think so, but I never really got the chance to examine him properly before he disappeared.'

'If he's as mad as a hatter, shouldn't he have been locked in his room?'

Alastair frowned, 'This is a private clinic, people come here voluntarily, we can't lock them up. The bars over the some of the windows are to stop people getting in not getting out.'

'Okay, if you say so.' Sidney wasn't convinced, but it wasn't his job to tell the guy how to run the place. 'Now, I'm being paid to find David Telford, but who are the other people in with him as well.' Sidney wondered if he could charge extra for finding more than one personality.

'The dominant person at the moment is an Arnold Collins and I think there is a woman in there as well, although she has had very little to say so far.'

Sidney made a note. 'And you've searched the grounds?'

'Of course, it's only a small garden, he's definitely not here.'

As he was leaving Sidney said, 'As a matter of interest how do you cure someone like this?'

'Oh, we can't cure them, we just have to help each personality to live in harmony with the others.'

As he got into his car Sidney wondered which of the personalities was wearing the hospital gown, and whether the other personalities were in harmony with it.

Although Arnold had never been into the library, he knew where it was because he sometimes dropped Ingrid off there so that she could indulge her passion for sloppy romances.

He marched in followed by David and glared round for the librarian, who was finding places for returned books and studiously ignoring them.

Eventually his loud banging on the counter forced her to put the books down and go across to where they were standing. 'Stop that noise at once, this is a library.'

'Good,' said Arnold, 'because I want to borrow a book.'

The librarian, who knew most of her readers by sight, viewed him suspiciously, 'Are you a member?'

'No, but my wife is.'

'Well, you can borrow books for your wife, but I would need to see her membership card.'

'I don't have it on me, but her name is Ingrid Collins...you must know her she's in here all the time.'

'I'm sure I do know her, Mr Collins, but I only have your word for it that you are her husband.'

'Of course, I'm her husband, you must have seen me dropping her off.'

The librarian looked him over, shook her head and made to move back to replacing books.

David put a hand out to detain her. 'What if we joined the library, could we borrow a book then?'

The librarian sighed and pulled out two forms. 'Fill these in and bring them back to me.' She handed David a pen and pointed to a low table with a couple of even lower chairs.

Perching uncomfortably on what was clearly a child's seat, David said it would make more sense for Arnold to fill in the form as he lived in the town and David didn't.

Arnold knelt down and scribbled in his details. 'Come on let's get this over with.'

They headed back to the counter, but before Arnold could start banging on it again the librarian hurried over and took the form from him and frowned over his handwriting.

Eventually she said. 'I shall need to see some form of identification Mr Collins, such as a driver's licence or a passport, and a utility bill in your name.'

'That's ridiculous, I don't carry those things around with me.'

'That's fine, just drop them in next time you're passing,' she put the form under the counter, 'I'll hang on to this for you.' She looked at David, 'Didn't you want to join?'

'No, not today, but Mr Collins can borrow a book now, can't he?'

'No.'

'What!' Arnold desperately wanted to bang on the counter again, but there was now a short queue behind him and he could hear very, very quiet mutterings. Even angry queues stuck to the library rules of maintaining silence. 'Why not, I've filled in the form?'

'Yes, but you haven't got a card yet, and you can't have a card until you've proved who you are.'

David could feel the tension rising, 'Can we just sit and read one of the books?'

The librarian wasn't happy, but she didn't have any grounds for refusing. 'I suppose so. Now if you'll just move aside, I have to see to these people.' She would have liked to have added people who are bona fide library members.

David pulled a seething Arnold away and pulled out the piece of paper Bernard had given him. 'It will be in the non-fiction section.'

They headed to the far side of the room and started looking along the shelves.

There were books on every conceivable subject from pruning bonsai, which David was tempted to pull out, making him think perhaps he owned one, to home brewing beer for beginners, which tempted Arnold, who hadn't realised that a library could open up all kinds of possibilities. But there was nothing on how to get out of your body.

'We'll have to go and ask her where it is,' and David pulled a reluctant Arnold away from the Do Your Own Plumbing shelf. Not that Arnold intended doing any, but he thought Ingrid could.

The queue had reduced to one and when that person had been dealt with, the librarian no longer had a reason to ignore them.

'We can't find this book on the shelves,' and Arnold read off the title and author from the piece of paper David passed to him.

'No, we don't have that book in this library.' She turned to walk off.

'But you must have, someone we know borrowed it from here.' And Arnold passed the piece of paper to her.

The librarian looked at it and then at Arnold. 'Why didn't you say you were looking for Zxama Zxaman's book.'

'I did.'

'No, you didn't you gabbled something about bodies by Xmas Eczema.'

'Same difference.'

'No, it's not, I was about to point you to the medical section.'

David decided to intervene as, again, he could feel the tension rising. 'So, you do have it in this library.'

'Yes, it was recently returned, after several months I might add. There was a hefty fine to pay on it.'

'Can you point it out so that we can read it,' David could feel a glimmer of hope.

'No.'

'Why not?' shouted Arnold, completely forgetting the silence rule.

The librarian played her trump card. 'Because someone else has borrowed it.'

CHAPTER 25

Despite their pleas she refused to tell them who had borrowed the book, but said Arnold could request it be saved for him when it was returned. 'You should have your library ticket by then Mr Collins.'

David's glimmer of hope was dissipating fast when a thought struck him, 'Can you tell me who published it please?'

The librarian looked as if she was about to refuse, but couldn't find a good enough excuse, like a queue of customers or children pulling books of the shelves, so she started to flick through the index cards in a metal filing cabinet behind her. After a lot of muttering, she pulled one out. 'Yes, it's not printed by a well-known publisher,' she frowned, 'In fact I think they were based here in the town.' She turned back and showed them the card. 'They've probably gone bankrupt by now if this was the sort of book they churned out.'

David wrote the name Hazelwood Publishing down on the unused library application form, earning the disapproval of the librarian who pointed out that it wasn't to be used for notes and should have been returned.

As David was giving back her pen, Arnold muttered, 'You should have kept that, miserable old…' he didn't complete the sentence as the librarian was leaning over her desk in a threatening manner. 'I am going to tear up your application form Mr Collins, we don't allow bad language in the library.'

David could see Arnold was about to answer back, so quickly pulled him out of the door and into the high street. 'We need to find a telephone box so we can look up the publisher's phone number and ring them.'

'We also need something to eat.' As usual Arnold was hungry and David knew this didn't bode well for his body.

'There's a Wimpy Bar over there.' And Arnold marched across the road, regardless of traffic, which also did not bode well for David's body. He followed as fast as he could, apologising to the irate drivers forced to stamp on their brakes.

'We're closing,' the young lad behind the counter looked morose.

'What! Right this minute?' Arnold looked around the room which was full of happy diners.

'No, not this minute, at the end of the month. A Macdonald's is opening further up the road. So, what do you want?'

After ordering a Mega Size Burger with chips for himself and the smallest plain burger for David they found a table and waited.

David fidgeted with his cutlery. 'We need to get home to try to get hold of this publisher.

'When we've had our lunch, alright mate?' Arnold looked at his watch, the football match wouldn't be starting for a while, but now he was stuck in David's body there was no chance of seeing it from the stands, so, he'd have to watch it on the telly. 'Course, if you had one of them fancy mobile phones you could ring from here.'

'I have got one.'

Arnold was consumed with envy. 'So where is it?'

'Ah that's the problem, I can't remember.'

'How come you've never mentioned this before?'

'Because it wasn't until yesterday when I was at Suzie's house that it came back to me and ....'

'Hang on a minute sunshine, what were you doing at your girlfriend's house while I was trapped in that madhouse.'

'I followed their car.'

'What did you do that for? That's my petrol you're burning up on your joyrides.' Arnold felt righteously aggrieved.

'I followed them because I wanted to find out where you'd been taken.'

Arnold was slightly mollified. 'So where do you think your phone is now?'

David frowned as he tried to pin down the memory, and this time he was successful, 'It's in my car, it's a car phone.'

Arnold was impressed. 'And where's your car?'

'I've no idea, but let's use a bit of logic. We now know I was in a car crash, and it must have been around here somewhere because I was taken to the local hospital. So, what happens to vehicles damaged in crashes?'

He waited for an input from Arnold, but none was forthcoming. 'I would have thought they get taken somewhere.' David started to feel excited, 'My car could be in a garage somewhere nearby, I've got to find it.'

'Back up a minute, sunshine - you think your accident was near here?'

'Yes, quite likely.'

Arnold glared at him, while trying to work out the ramifications.

The reason he was late arriving at Astral Travel and got caught up in Hornby's astral travelling session - and lost his body - was because of an accident which caused a tailback. An accident, he now knew was caused by the berk sitting opposite him. 'You bloody imbecile this is whole thing is all your fault.'

The young lad, who brought over their lunch at that moment, took offence at the remark which he wrongly thought was aimed at him and refused to get the tomato ketchup.

David and Arnold were barely speaking on the way home. David could see the sense of returning to Arnold's house where there was a telephone directory and a phone. He was less pleased that Arnold intended spending the afternoon lolling on the sofa, watching football rather than trying to track down the author of 'Out of Body Experiences'.

'I told you,' Arnold said, 'this is a needle match and for once I won't have the wife wittering on the whole time. So, I intend to sit down with several cans of beer, several packets of crisps and as many pork pies as I can eat. You can do what you want. After all this whole mess is your fault.' And with that he paid a quick trip to the bathroom, collected up his iron rations. which he had insisted on buying on their way home, and settled down in front of the television.

David stared at him for a few moments, worried as much about his poor body's digestive system as finding the publisher.

But despite his pointed glare, it soon became clear that Arnold was not going to budge. He looked at the television where some men holding microphones were standing talking at each other. 'But the match hasn't even started yet.'

'I like to hear what the pundits have to say.'

'But you said on the way home they don't know what they're talking about?'

'No, they don't, but I still want to hear it.' Arnold still refused to drag his eyes away from the screen.

David waited a couple more minutes to see if Arnold would change his mind – he didn't. So, he went into the hall and pulled out the telephone directory. Hazelwood Publishers was listed and it looked as if the librarian was right, it was a local business.

He dialled the number, hoping that the company would be open on a Saturday afternoon. It was.

'Hazelwood,' snapped a military sounding voice.

'Hello, yes…is that Hazelwood Publishers?'

'Yes, how can I help you?'

David thought the man sounded a bit brusque. 'You published a book called 'Out of Body Experiences', is that right?'

'Yes, but it's out of print now.'

'I don't want to buy a copy Mr Hazelwood…'

'So why the blazes are you ringing me?'

David, fearful the man was going to hang up on him quickly said, 'I just want the author's address.'

'Why?'

David didn't feel up to explaining the complications of his situation so after a moment's hesitation, said 'I want to interview him…for a paper…I'm a reporter.'

'And your name is?'

'David Telford.'

'I'm sorry Mr Telford, but you can't expect me to give out the addresses of my authors to some guy who rings up out of the blue.'

That was exactly what David had expected Mr Hazelwood to do, but clearly, he wasn't. 'No, no I quite understand…but could you ask him if I could have his address.'

'A reporter you say. What paper?'

David crossed his fingers, '*The Telegraph.*'

'*The Telegraph.*' David detected a softening of tone. 'I take it you will want to interview me as well…as his publisher?'

'Absolutely.' David was crossing his fingers so tightly they were in danger of losing all sensation,

'Alright, I'll ring him and get back to you, give me your phone number.'

David panicked - he had no idea what Arnold's phone number was. 'Hang on a minute and I'll just get it.' Leaving the receiver dangling he rushed into the sitting room. 'What's your phone number?'

Arnold kept his eyes on the screen and mumbled under his breath.

'Say it again.'

Arnold mumbled louder and David rushed back into the hall and gave it to Mr Hazelwood, who promptly said suspiciously, 'That's a local number, I thought you'd be ringing from London.'

'Ah, yes, but as it's the weekend I'm working from home.'

'So how come you don't know your own phone number?'

David gulped - would these questions never end. 'I...I've been given a new phone line...the old one broke.'
'Alright, I'll ring you back.'
'As quickly as possible please, I'm working to a deadline.' David heard the line go dead and hoped Mr Hazelwood was already ringing Zxama Zxaman. He could hear Arnold alternately screaming or cheering at the television, interspersed with loud gulps of beer, followed by even louder belches. He hoped that when he got back into his body it would immediately return to normal.

After a couple of worrying minutes, the phone rang.

'Hazelwood here. Zxama Zxaman says he's happy to talk to you, in fact you can go round to his house now.'

David wrote down the address on the back of a flyer, which had been poked through the front door, and was pleased to see it was also local. 'Thank you so much Mr Hazelwood, I'll jump in the car and go round straight away.'

'And I will see you at ten-o-clock tomorrow, Mr Telford. You've got my address haven't you.'

'Tomorrow?'

'Yes, for my interview.

'I...yes...but it's Sunday tomorrow.'

'Is that a problem?'

'I...no... okay...tomorrow.' And David quickly put the phone down before the man could ask any more questions.

He went outside and got his, now somewhat tattered, street map from the car and pushed it in front of Arnold. 'Look this Zxaman guy lives locally, we could drive over there in ten minutes.'

Arnold pushed the map aside and swore at the referee. 'So, I'll go on my own then, shall I?' But David was talking to himself, Arnold was in another world as well as another body. 'So, can I borrow the car?' Arnold shrugged and flapped his hands about, which David took to be a yes.

Sidney Spraggs drove back into town. His next port of call was the St Hilda's Suite at the Northaven Infirmary, but he fancied some lunch first, which he intended charging to expenses. The first café he came to was a Wimpy Bar and he really fancied a beef burger. Had he arrived ten minutes sooner he would have seen the person he was being paid to find just leaving.

While he was waiting for his food, he pulled out David Telford's photo which Cameron Baker-Brown and sent over by fax. The blurry image of a skier could have been anyone.

On the pretext of visiting the loo, Ingrid managed to slip out of the café unnoticed after a lengthy lunch and hurried home. She told herself that Greta and Stella had her best interests at heart, even if they couldn't agree on what those best interests were, but she really missed her cosy bungalow.

There was no car in the drive so Ingrid assumed Arnold and his man friend had gone out. She opened the front door, expecting the worst. The hall looked the same, tidier perhaps and with a faint lavender smell to it. To her surprise, she could hear the sounds of a football match on the television. Had the man friend borrowed the car and gone off somewhere or had Arnold left him watching the television?

She crept into the kitchen expecting to see all the work tops and the sink full of dirty greasy crockery, and empty takeaway boxes spilling out of the bin, but the worktops were clear and clean, the sink gleamed and even the cooker sparkled. For a moment she wondered if she'd come into the wrong house by mistake.

She opened the fridge – it was full of speciality cheeses, smoked salmon, pate and fancy salads. This was definitely the wrong house. She opened the freezer and sighed with relief, at least that was full of Arnold's favourites.

The noise from the television masked her footsteps going past the sitting room to her bedroom. Again, that room looked immaculate. She went in the bathroom, surely there would be a mess in there – nothing was out of place. Someone was tidying up after Arnold.

With her heart thudding in her ears, she opened the sitting room door and peered in. A man was sitting on the settee, holding a beer can in one hand and a bag of crisps in another. The way he was slumped reminded her of Arnold, but he was younger and plumper.

Unsure of the etiquette for addressing one's husband's lover she said, 'Hello, I'm Ingrid…Arnold's wife.'

'I know that,' Arnold never took his eyes of the screen. 'Go back to your sister's and leave me in peace to watch the football.'

Ingrid was shocked, but determined. 'I suppose Arnold's told you all about me.' When there was no answer she tried again, 'I would like you to leave now and not come back.' Still nothing apart from a cheer as an overpaid player finally managed to get the ball into the back of the net. 'He's my husband and I want him back.'

Arnold was used to blanking out Ingrid's voice and even in a different body he still had the knack. He knew she was wittering on, but it wasn't until a player fell over and was rolling in agony on the ground that he heard her say, 'So where is he? What have you done with my husband?'

'What are you on about? I'm your husband.' Arnold had completely forgotten he was in David's body - the match had suddenly reached a critical point and he could only concentrate on one thing at a time.

Ingrid rushed out of the bungalow in tears and met Stella who had followed her home. 'Arnold's gone missing and there's a strange man in my house who says he's my husband.'

Stella, took her arm, 'Come on in and you can tell me all about it over a cuppa.'

It took David about twenty-five minutes to find where Zxama Zxaman lived. The house was not what he expected. It was in the middle of an Edwardian terrace, which had seen better days.

The author himself was even more unexpected. He opened the front door wearing old khaki shorts, a grubby T-shirt and brandishing a trowel. 'Come in, come in, I was just doing some weeding. That pesky bindweed gets everywhere.'

David wondered briefly if he had a garden, but he couldn't visualise himself mowing lawns or pruning roses so perhaps not. 'Good afternoon, Mr Zxaman, it's good of you to see me at short notice.'

'That's not my actual name you know, I'm Bert Herbert. As I say to everyone, my parents had a strange sense of humour. In you go.'

David squeezed past Bert and into the long, narrow hall, which like its owner was slightly grubby.

'Keep going and at the end turn right into the kitchen and then we can have a cup of tea.'

CHAPTER 26

David found himself in a room, which although clean and tidy, hadn't been updated since the nineteen-forties. Bert Herbert followed him in and after telling him to sit down, filled up the kettle and set it on the ancient gas cooker.

'It won't take a minute to boil,' he said as he rummaged around in a Welsh dresser for some biscuits. When they were both seated at a scrubbed deal table, with a cup of tea and a biscuit each, he said, 'I've never been interviewed by a reporter before. Fancy you coming all the way down from *The Telegraph* to talk to me about my book.' And in his excitement, he dunked his biscuit for far too long and it disappeared in a gooey mess.

David felt terrible, both about the biscuit and for deceiving him. 'I have a confession to make Mr Herbert, but I don't work for *The Telegraph*.'

'But you are a reporter.'

'No, I'm...a... bus driver.' David couldn't think of anything else on the spur of the moment, and he could see Mr Herbert was less than impressed.

'So why do you want to see me.'

'I desperately need your help, well we both do.' David then launched into a long and complicated explanation of what had happened to him, to Arnold and how Astral Travel was involved.

Finally, Bert shook his head in wonderment, 'You mean this Bernard Hornby bloke is using my book to teach people how to come out of their bodies.'

'Yes, but not very successfully I might add, I think Mr Collin is the only one - apart from Mr Hornby - who has managed it so far.'

Bert roared with laughter, 'I'm not surprised, I made the whole thing up.'

David stared at him with growing concern. 'What do you mean you made the whole thing up?'

'What I say. Oh, the chapters on real life experiences of people coming out of their bodies by accident are true, but they always popped back in again. As far as I know they didn't go off round the world. But Mr Hazelwood wanted the book to have a bit more zip before he would publish it, so I invented the last chapter on how to do it on command as it were.'

David had a sinking feeling. 'So, all that bit about small points of light and bodies getting heavier and passwords and being able to go where you want is all rubbish?'

Bert laughed even harder, 'Well, I guess not, if your friend managed it. But no, the last chapter is pure fiction. Not that I told Mr Hazelwood that, so I'd appreciate it if you didn't tell him either. It was also him who suggested I use the name Zxama Zxaman to make it sound mysterious and oriental.'

David's feelings had sunk so low he was hardly able to summons up the energy to say, 'So you can't help us.'

'Sadly not. But don't let your tea get cold. I'll top it up for you, shall I?'

Not wanting to go back to Arnold's and be forced to sit through the rest of the football match, David unfolded the street map and looked for the police station. He was still feeling nervous about actually talking to a policeman, but reasoned not everyone in the local force would recognise him – and it really was important to find where his car had been taken. Surely if he could find that a whole load more memories would be triggered.

After struggling to find somewhere to park Arnold's car, he nervously presented himself to the sergeant, manning the front desk, who said, 'How can I help you, sir?'

'I'm hoping you can tell me where my car is, officer.'

'Where do you think you left it?'

'That's the problem, I can't remember.'

The sergeant was used to little old ladies coming in to say they couldn't find their car, even when they no longer owned one, but it was rare for middle-aged men to forget where their pride and joy was. They were more likely to forget where their wives were than their cars. 'So, let's go back a bit, sir… now, you definitely drove it into town?'

'Yes.' David couldn't remember driving into town, but logic told him that he must have done.

'Can you remember what time this was?'

'Not exactly, but it was on Thursday.'

The sergeant frowned. 'You've been looking for it since Thursday?'

'Not exactly, officer. You see I think I was involved in a car crash.'

'People usually know if they've been in a car crash. Was it your fault?' The sergeant was no longer being pleasantly condescending.

David could feel a tide of panic rising, surely he couldn't be arrested for causing an accident that he couldn't even remember. 'I'm sure I wasn't to blame, officer. But I do need to know where my car was taken to.'

The sergeant pulled out a pad. 'I think I'd better take down some details. Now what is your full name?'

'David Telford.'

The sergeant looked up, that name rang a bell. So, this was the driver of the Vauxhall Astra, which had hit a lorry in the high street on Thursday morning. He knew the driver had been taken to hospital unconscious so was unable to answer any questions at the time. Then last night he had been reported missing from a psychiatric clinic and his details had even been put on the police's new-fangled HOLMES computer, although no one knew how that would help. 'Will you excuse me a moment sir.' And turning his back on David he whispered into his phone that someone needed to come to the front desk, pronto. 'No, he's not wearing a hospital gown, but it must be him.'

After finishing the call, he turned back to David and tried to smile in a calming way. The guy didn't look dangerous, but the sergeant thought you could never be too careful. 'Someone will be through any second, sir, and they will be able to help you.'

David wasn't calmed by the sergeant's smile, but he didn't know what else he could do but wait. After a couple of minutes, a young man appeared through a side door and introduced himself as Detective Constable Radcliffe. 'You told the sergeant here, that you're David Telford.'

'Yes…that's right…that's who I am.'

DC Radcliffe looked at David closely, the man didn't fit the description they had been given, 'Are you absolutely sure about that?'

David's panic started to rise again, but he nodded vigorously. 'Yes, I'm definitely sure.'

'In that case, perhaps you would come with me, sir.' And DC Radcliffe opened the door he'd come in by and escorted David through it. 'This way.' And he led David along a corridor and down a short flight of stairs, stopping in front of a door with a small window in it. 'Would you mind waiting in here while we get everything sorted out.'

He then went back to his desk and phoned Mr Baker-Brown. 'I have Mr Telford here at the station, sir. Will you come and pick him up or shall I ring the clinic?... No, he's quite safe - I've put him in a cell and locked the door.'

After several of Stella's fortifying cups of tea, Ingrid was finally persuaded to ring the police. 'They need to know that Arnold is missing, probably dead, and that that man is pretending to be him.'

They watched out of the window and as soon as the police car arrived, they rushed outside. Before Ingrid could say a word, Stella had given the two constables the whole story, or rather her lurid version of it.

One of them turned to Ingrid, 'So a man claiming to be your husband is sitting in there on your settee, drinking beer and watching football. Are you sure he's not your old man, luv?'

'Of course, I'm sure, he doesn't look anything like him.' Ingrid started to get tearful. 'I just want my Arnold back.'

The two constables looked at each other, shrugged and one of them said, 'You'd better let us in then luv, and we'll see what this is all about.'

They found Arnold watching replays of the goals with a happy smile on his face. Even the sudden appearance of two policeman couldn't dent his good humour. 'Afternoon officers, do you want to know the score?'

Before they could answer, Stella, who had followed them in, pointed at him and shouted, 'There he is, there's the imposter.'

Arnold looked at her. 'What you banging on about?'

Ingrid managed to push herself into the room and also pointed at Arnold. 'That man is not my husband. What have you done with him?' and she promptly burst into tears.

The older of the two constables suggested Stella take Ingrid into the kitchen and make her a cup of tea. When they had reluctantly gone out, after all, they were awash with tea, he said to Arnold, 'Are you Arnold Collins?'

'Of course, I am.'

'Can you prove it?'

Arnold suddenly remembered the police might be looking for him if the guy at the clinic had given them his name as well as David Telford's, and he certainly didn't intend going back there. He looked round the room for inspiration. 'Ah, that might be difficult,' he muttered

David had given up banging on the cell door. No one came and all he'd achieved was a bruised hand. He sat on the thin plastic mattress laid on a concrete shelf at the back of the claustrophobic room and wondered what was going to happen next. Surely, he was entitled to some kind of legal representation.

After what seemed like hours, but was only twelve and a half minutes, the door opened slightly and a cup of tea was pushed in. David jumped up hopefully, but the door was slammed shut again. He picked up the cup, the tea looked worse than the builder's brew Arnold favoured and tasted even viler. How he longed for a cup of Earl Grey and a Garibaldi biscuit.

After another long wait, this time really long, he heard Suzie's voice calling. 'Don't worry, darling, we've come to rescue you.'

The door was flung open and Suzie rushed into the cell and then stopped dead. She was closely followed by her father whose eyes bulged as he managed to shout, 'You again!'

CHAPTER 27

Before Arnold could come up with a way of proving his identity, Ingrid, closely followed by Stella, burst back into the sitting room brandishing a photograph album. She thrust it into the older constable's hands and said, 'See, he looks nothing like my Arnold.'

The constable slowly turned over the pages which started with photos of a wedding, followed by trips to a seaside, a barbecue in a garden and a visit to a zoo. He recognised Ingrid, but the man standing next to her in most of them looked nothing like the man in front of him. He passed the book to his colleague, who quickly flipped through it and came to the same conclusion. 'I have to agree, luv, he doesn't look like the bloke in the photos,' he looked at Arnold, 'I mean look, he's much shorter.'

'Yes, well that's old age mate, you shrink.'

'You might shrink, but you don't start looking younger, why, you look like a teenager.'

Arnold shrugged, 'That's because I've looked after meself, but I'm forty-seven.'

'You never are?' the constable looked disbelieving.

'See, he's lying, so, aren't you going to arrest him?' Stella could contain herself no longer.

'What for telling lies? We'd have to arrest half the population if we did that luv.'

'No because he's a murderer, that's what he is.'

Now Arnold could contain himself no longer. 'What you on about? Who have I murdered?'

Now Ingrid could contain herself no longer. 'My Arnold, that's who.'

Arnold glared at her 'But I'm your Arnold.' He turned to the two constables. 'Look, you don't want to listen to these two, officers, I'm Arnold Collins, and I've lived in this bungalow for years,' he gritted his teeth, 'with my darling wife.'

Stella pounced, 'There, see he's telling lies again, he never calls her his darling wife. He even forgot their twentieth wedding anniversary on Thursday.' She drew herself up to her full height to deliver the killer blow. 'And it was their china one.'

Ingrid nodded her head vigorously - but was too upset to add anything.

Arnold shrugged. 'Okay so I forgot our anniversary, but that's not a criminal offence is it officers?' He stretched out his legs and tried to make himself look thoroughly at home. 'I mean what would I be doing sitting here with a can of beer watching telly if I wasn't her old man.' He tried to think of something which would really clinch the matter. 'I know, what about that time I took you on the dodgems in Bognor and your gobstopper shot right out of your mouth when we hit the side.'

Ingrid immediately refuted any such unseemly memory even if it did ring a faint bell.

The two constables glanced at each other. It looked as if they were wasting their time here.

But Stella wasn't giving up and collared the older constable. 'He's just making things up. Last night I saw him and Mr Collins come home together,' she lowered her voice, 'we think they are having an affair.' She lowered her voice even more and nodded her head at Arnold, 'And his trousers fell down on the doorstep.'

The constable scratched his head, 'But if he isn't Mr Collins, why does he keep claiming he is?'

'It's obvious, isn't it?' said Stella, 'he's trying to create an alibi.'

'What alibi?' The constable looked bemused.

But Stella hadn't watched all the episodes of Juliet Bravo and several Bergeracs for nothing. 'If you believe he's Arnold - then he can't have murdered him can he, don't you see.'

The constable didn't see, but was prepared to have another go at sorting out the situation. He turned to Ingrid, 'Do you know this man, Mrs Collins?'

'No, I've never seen him before in my life.'

He turned back to Arnold, 'So if you're not Mr Collins, who are you?'

Arnold wanted to scream he really was Mr Collins, but it was obvious they weren't going to believe him, and he didn't think they'd believe him if he said he was in the wrong body either. And if he said he was David Telford, he'd be back in that hospital gown before he could blink. So, there was only one answer, 'No comment.' Arnold also had watched quite a few detective series.

'Okay, so have I got this right? You and Mr Collins came home together yesterday and now Mr Collins has disappeared.'

'No, he hasn't.'

'So, you know where Mr Collins is?'

'Yes, he's gone out somewhere.'

'Do you know where?'

'To see some bloke called Xmas Eczema, and before you ask, no, I don't know where he lives.' Arnold was starting to wish he'd gone with David to see Xmas, instead of staying at home watching the football.

'But he doesn't know anyone called that,' Ingrid was adamant.

'And that's not even a real name, he just made it up,' added Stella.

The constable privately agreed with Stella, but needed to keep control of the situation. 'Ladies, please, if I could just continue asking the questions.' The constable turned back to Arnold, 'Do you know why he is visiting this person?' the constable wasn't going to risk mispronouncing the name.

'Yes, it's about a book he wrote.'

'What book?'

Arnold was starting to feel the pressure, but before he could think of a suitable answer Ingrid said, 'Arnold doesn't even read books.'

And Stella added, 'See he's lying.' She paused, this was her big moment. 'I'll tell you where poor dear Arnold went, before he was done away with…17 Gasworks Road.'

Arnold stared at her in surprise – how did she know about Astral Travel? Not only that, but she'd called him poor dear Arnold when he knew for a fact she couldn't stand him - a feeling he reciprocated.

The older constable also looked surprised at this new piece of information. 'How do you know this?'

'Because I followed Arnold yesterday.' And Stella gave a minute-by-minute account of how she'd tracked him using all her skills to avoid detection. And how this woman had pulled him in the door. 'She's probably behind all this.' Stella hadn't forgiven Margaret for having an expensive suit and a blouse with a tie-neck. 'They're in it together,' and she gave Arnold another glare.

Arnold was shocked that she'd tracked his body that far, and he couldn't believe he'd missed spotting her, but guessed he was floating about, looking for David's body at the time.

The constable turned to his colleague, 'What do you think Brian?'

'I think it's above our pay grade mate.'

The older constable agreed. 'I think we will deal with this down at the station. Now, I don't want to cuff you, sir, so I hope you'll come quietly.' He turned to Ingrid and Stella, 'Someone will come and take statements from you both as soon as possible.'

As he was led out, Arnold made several attempts at protesting his innocence all of which were ignored by the officers. At the station he was put in an interview room and left to contemplate his future while the officers went in search of DC Radcliffe. His only hope was that David and the Xmas bloke could sort everything out and he'd soon be back in his own body.

David and Suzie had stared at each sadly. She because she felt sorry for him and he because he couldn't tell her he really was her fiancé.

Behind them her father berated the unfortunate DC Radcliffe. 'I don't care what this man told you, but he is not David Telford.' He brandished a photo of David and Suzie taken a few months earlier on a skiing holiday. 'Look, does that man look anything like my daughter's fiancé?'

The skier was wearing sun goggles and a woolly hat pulled down over his eyebrows, which made identification impossible, but DC Radcliffe was forced to agree that the guy in the photo was not only shorter and fatter, but he was dressed in expensive clothes compared to the scruffy bloke in the cell.

Pointing at David, Cameron continued, 'Yesterday he turned up at the hospital and then he followed us to my house. He has been hounding us. I want him arrested for stalking and impersonating my daughter's fiancé.' And with one last glare at David, he strode out of the cell. 'Come along Suzie.' But while Cameron had been venting his anger at the unfortunate Detective Constable, inside he was secretly relieved that David Telford was still missing.

Suzie gave David a wan little smile and followed her father out. The door banged behind them and David was once again locked in.

As he stared at the door he pondered the absurdity of the situation – it looked as if he was going to be arrested for impersonating himself.

DC Radcliffe headed towards his locker. It was the end of his shift and he intended rushing home to watch the highlights of the Manchester City versus Bournemouth game and forget all about missing persons. Whoever was on the night shift could sort out the stalker.

His hope of watching the football disappeared when the two constables walked in with a garbled story about a possible murder, a missing body and a suspect being held in the interview room.

'He claims to be someone called Arnold Collins, but his wife says he isn't and the neighbour is convinced he's murdered Mr Collins and is trying to take his place.'

Along the corridor, Arnold sat drumming his fingers on a scruffy desk, covered with cigarette burns. The whole situation was ridiculous. Surely there had to be a body before you could be charged with murder but he was starting to worry that perhaps there didn't. Was he really going to be charged with murdering himself?

CHAPTER 28

As soon as Arnold had been taken away in the police car, Ingrid rang her sister and told her what had happened. Greta immediately said she and Graham would come over straight away.

This was the first murder in the family and she had visions of herself as the family spokeswoman giving interviews outside on the steps of the Crown Court after the killer had been found guilty, and asking for the press to respect their privacy at this sad time.

The moment they walked in the door, Greta made it clear to Stella that this was a family matter and didn't concern her anymore. Stella hid her annoyance, but consoled herself with the knowledge that the police would be wanting to interview her. So, she went home and started making notes, she didn't want to forget any tiny detail to give the police when they came to take her statement.

Then, feeling peckish after all the excitement, she made herself some cheese on toast and settled down in her bay window with her binoculars and a fresh page in her notebook at hand. She had a feeling that there was more to see.

Next door, Ingrid had to go over the whole affair, from walking in the door and finding a strange man sitting on her settee to him being arrested and taken to the police station.

'It was terrible, Greta, he just sat there as cool as a cucumber and insisting he was my husband,' She blew her nose, 'and now Arnold's dead and I was so horrible to him.' This thought brought on another tsunami of tears.

Greta was equally shocked and said Ingrid had done the right thing phoning the police. Graham said nothing - not that he didn't have his own thoughts on what was going on, but he knew better than express them.

When Ingrid had recovered somewhat Greta said she must go back with them and not spend another moment in the bungalow. 'I don't think it's safe for you to stay here. Supposing that murderer is released on bail - he could come straight back here and murder you as well.'

But Ingrid was adamant she wasn't going to budge. 'The police could ring with news any minute, and they are coming back to take a statement.'

Greta was equally adamant that the police could ring Ingrid at her house. She didn't want to spend another minute sitting looking at empty crisp packets and scattered beer cans. But for once Ingrid wouldn't back down so Graham was dispatched to get a fish and chip take-away as neither woman felt up to cooking.

DC Radcliffe stared through a small window in the door of the interview room. The man's face looked vaguely familiar - he couldn't remember where he'd last seen him, but it was quite recently. He decided it was probably on a poster of a well-known criminal.

He walked into the room and sat opposite Arnold, followed by one of the constables, who leaned against the wall in what he hoped was a menacing manner.

DC Radcliffe opened a folder containing the notes he'd made. 'You claimed to my colleagues that you are Arnold Collins, is that right?'

Arnold decided his safest bet was to continue saying no comment, which he did.

'So are you now saying you're not Arnold Collins.'

'No comment.'

'Do you know an Arnold Collins?'

'No comment.'

'Did you murder Arnold Collins?'

'No.' Arnold was starting to get worried. 'Shouldn't I have a lawyer?'

'Do you need a lawyer?'

Arnold didn't know whether he needed one or not, but on the telly the baddie always asked for a lawyer – and got one. He decided to stick to no comment.

DC Radcliffe scribbled a note and then asked, 'Where do you live?'

'No comment.'

DC Radcliffe pulled a form out of a folder and looked at it. 'You were arrested at 27 Whitehouse Road and you claimed that was where you lived, but that's where Mr Arnold Collins lives. Are you claiming you live there with him?'

'No comment.'

And so it went on – DC Radcliffe asking questions and Arnold saying no comment. The young officer was getting desperate, he needed a confession because without a body and no evidence it was going to be difficult to arrest the prisoner for murder. He would have liked to charge him with breaking into a property, but there was no evidence that he had done that either.

He took the constable outside. 'He's not cracking is he.'

'Why not put him in the cell for a while see if that has any effect.'

'Good idea.' Then DC Radcliffe remembered the stalker was still in there. 'I just have to sort something out and then we'll take him down.'

David looked up hopefully as his door opened again. He wondered if it might be food as he was starving. Arnold's body was once again demanding sustenance.

DC Radcliffe stood in the doorway. 'I'm giving you a verbal warning. Do not pretend to be David Telford and do not go anywhere near the Baker-Brown family. If you do there will be serious consequences. Do you understand.'

David jumped up and promised faithfully to do neither of those things. But he kept his fingers crossed because, in the crazy world he was currently living in, he couldn't guarantee he wouldn't do one or the other - or even both.

'Give your name and full address to the sergeant at the front desk.' DC Radcliffe stood to one side to let David pass and then added, 'and I don't want to see you here again.'

As soon as the sergeant had taken his, or rather Arnold's details – he was starting to get confused himself - he rushed out, found Arnold's car, and headed for 27 Whitehouse Road. He wondered how he was going to tell Arnold the bad news about Zxama Zxaman.

Ingrid, Greta and Graham sat round the dining table staring at their fish and chips. Ingrid declared she was too upset to eat and Greta decided she didn't like the look of the fish. Graham would have liked to have eaten his, but knew that would be frowned on if the others weren't eating.

The silence was suddenly shattered by the phone ringing. Ingrid said she couldn't answer it as she'd come over faint, but Greta was more than happy to. When she came back into the room Ingrid grabbed her arm and said, 'Have they found his body, where is it, I want to see him. How did he die?' and then burst into tears again.

'No, it was some guy selling double glazing. I told him where he could put his Georgian triple-locked windows.'

As he wasn't allowed to eat. Graham asked if he could watch the television. It was the finals of the Eurovision Song Contest coming from Switzerland and he didn't want to miss it.

'Of course, you can't, have some consideration for Ingrid's feelings.'

The room lapsed once more into a morose silence, broken only by Ingrid's sniffs.

Margaret and Bernard locked up Astral Travel after another disappointing day. By unspoken mutual consent they headed to the pub for their evening meal together. Margaret, desperate to cheer Bernard up suggested they splash out, as it was Saturday, and have Chicken Kiev with a shared bowl of chips, instead of a Ploughman's. 'I'll pay, it is my turn, you've paid the last two times.'

Bernard didn't think chicken oozing with cheese and garlic would be enough to lift his depression, but didn't want to disappoint her. Why could he come out of his body, but no one else could? Apart from Arnold Collins of course, and look at the trouble he was causing, leaving his body lying around for someone else to get it. He might even try to sue them, and Bernard still didn't have any insurance.

'I think I'm going to close Astral Travel, Margaret, it's just not working out.'

Margaret's heart sank – not only was she about to lose her job, but she was about to lose Bernard as well.

The Baker-Browns were enjoying the supper prepared by the cook before she left for the day. Or rather Cameron was. There was nothing like tearing a strip off someone to give him an appetite. And the visit to the police station had done just that.

Deidre toyed with the stuffed seabass in a prawn sauce. but her mind was on the supper party she was planning to give the following weekend. It would be a small, intimate affair, just ten people, but amongst those ten would be Elliot and his parents, who would all be invited to stay overnight. Even if David were found, it must now be obvious to Suzie that he was no longer suitable fiancé material. All her daughter needed was a little nudge.

Suzie's mind was on the poor man in the prison cell. Although his clothes looked scruffy, and he hadn't shaved, there was something about his expression which reminded her of David. She worried that her fiancé was out there somewhere, lost, cold and hungry. Where are you, she called out in her mind. Where are you?

David, at that moment had just arrived at Arnold's house, where he was surprised to see a strange car parked in the drive. He sat looking at it for a few minutes, wondering whether he should go in or not. But finally, his protesting bladder forced him to head for the front door. There was a stainless-steel toilet in the prison cell, but he had been too embarrassed to use it.

He rushed to the bathroom, used the facilities, heaved a sigh of relief, and opened the door into the hall to find three people staring at him. He recognised Ingrid, but the other two were strangers.

To his amazement, Ingrid threw herself at him, in floods of tears and crying, 'Arnold you're alive, you're alive,' over and over again. The two strangers just stared at him and the woman looked distinctly annoyed.

Ingrid pulled him into the sitting room and sat holding his hand as if she would never let it go. 'We thought you'd been murdered.'

'Murdered! Whatever gave you that idea?'

'When I came home there was a strange man sitting on the settee and we thought he'd done away with you.'

David had an uneasy feeling. 'Where's this man now?'

The strange woman answered. 'The police arrested him and took him to the police station.'

David's feeling grew uneasier. 'On what grounds?'

'On the grounds that he's a murderer, what do you think, Arnold?' the woman snapped. 'I really think it's most inconsiderate of you to disappear, leaving that man in your house to frighten the daylights out of poor Ingrid.'

David jumped up, 'I have to go to the police station straightaway.' The thought of his body sitting in that wretched police cell was more than he could bear. And he did have a sneaking sympathy for Arnold as well.

Ingrid jumped up and held on to him. 'Why Arnold, why?'

'Because he's innocent.'

The strange woman snorted. 'Technically yes, but it wouldn't hurt him to spend the night locked up, considering the shock he's given us all.'

David looked at her, 'Sorry, but who are you?'

'Who am I? Is this some sort of sick joke Arnold Collins?'

All three of them stared at him as if he was mad.

Then Ingrid remembered Arnold had forgotten the name of his boss and several other things recently, such as where the bathroom was. 'He's not been well, Greta, his memory is all over the place.' She patted David's arm, 'This is my sister, Greta, and that's her husband Graham. I expect you remember them now.'

David nodded in their direction. 'But I still have to go to the police station, I can't leave him there.'

Graham spoke for the first time. 'Leave who there? What's this man's name?'

He hesitated for a moment and then said, 'David, David Telford.'

'You do realise that if you bring that man back here my sister will be suing you for divorce.'

Ingrid gasped and looked at Greta in horror, she only intended staying away for a few days to bring Arnold to his senses, not divorce him. 'I don't want to do that Greta.'

'Yes, you do Ingrid.' Greta had had enough of Ingrid's insubordination. And anyway, she didn't really intend that Ingrid would divorce Arnold, oh no he needed to suffer for many more years yet, but now was not the time to say that. 'You have to choose between your wife or your friend, Arnold.'

David was torn, he didn't want to cause a rift between husband and wife, but he couldn't leave his body where it was either. 'I'm so sorry Ingrid, I really am. I wish I could tell you what's happened and why I have to go, but I can't.'

As he walked out of the door he heard Greta shouting, 'Can't or won't.'

CHAPTER 29

Sitting up in her little bed, Lettice Long re-read, for the third time, the book she'd borrowed from the library. She'd been curious about the book that Bernard Hornby had returned, and paid a large fine on, so she had waited for the librarian to put it back on its shelf and then she'd pounced.

'Out of Body Experiences' by Zxama Zxaman, was quite a short book so it didn't take her long to whiz through it. But it was the final chapter, where it said that the connection between the astral body and the corporeal body was quite weak and could easily be broken - it just needed concentration and belief - which interested her most.

Well, thought Lettice, I've been concentrating and believing, but I still can't do it. So, she put the book down and picked up a copy of The New Scientist instead – she liked to keep up with the latest theories on quantum physics.

Stella's stakeout had turned out to be more rewarding than she could possibly have expected. First Arnold's car pulled up outside and after a few moments, much to her amazement, and, it has to be said, a little disappointment that he hadn't been murdered, Arnold had jumped out and run up his garden path.

A little while later he had come running out again and driven off in a tearing hurry. Five minutes later a tearful Ingrid was half led, half pulled by Greta and Graham to their car and they had driven off. As fast as she could she wrote it all down on her notepad.

David drove as fast as he could to the police station, playing over in his mind what he was going to say. He tapped on the counter to attract the sergeant's attention.

'Oh, it's you again. You made me look a right fool pretending you was that bloke that's gone missing.' The sergeant was not impressed. 'You're lucky you haven't been banged up.'

'Yes, I'm sorry about that officer, but....'

'No, don't tell me...you're Lord Lucan come to hand yourself in. Well, tough luck, I don't want to know.'

'No, no, it's about the guy you've got locked up in the cell.'

The sergeant glared at David. 'What about him?'

'You think he's murdered Arnold Collins, don't you? Well, I'm Arnold Collins so he can't have murdered me. Look, I'm standing right here.'

'Last time you were standing right there you claimed you was David Telford, so why should I believe you this time?'

David groaned this wasn't proving to be as easy as he thought it would be. 'Why would I pretend to be Arnold Collins if I wasn't?'

The sergeant turned away, 'Because you're a time waster, now clear off.'

David, risking the sergeant's wrath, tapped on the counter again. 'No, really, I'm not. My wife, Ingrid Collins told me what happened, so now do you believe me?'

The sergeant turned back. 'Okay, if you're Arnold Collins perhaps you could tell us what the alleged murder's name is because as I understand it all he's saying at the moment is "no comment".'

David wasn't surprised, Arnold could hardly say he was David Telford, he'd be sent straight back to the clinic. 'Yes, it's... Gerald Seymour.' For a moment he couldn't think why he'd picked that name then he remembered it was his cousin's name, so another little piece of memory had come drifting back.

'Gerald Seymour,' repeated sergeant and made a note of it. 'But you still haven't proved you're Arnold Collins.'

Fortunately, David didn't have to because at that moment one of the constables who had brought Arnold in, walked through past the counter on his way home at the end of his shift. He glanced briefly at David and then did a double take. 'You're the guy in the photos, the one what's been murdered.'

David wondered briefly what photos and then quickly said, 'Yes, that's me, except I haven't been murdered, look I'm alive.'

The sergeant looked up. 'Are you sure constable?'

'Yes, pretty sure.' The constable looked at David again, but more closely this time, 'It's definitely you, isn't? You was having a barbecue in the garden, and there was another one of you at the zoo.'

'Yes, yes that's right,' David turned to the sergeant. 'Now do you believe me?'

The constable looked back at the sergeant, 'You'd better break the sad news to DC Radcliffe. Tell him his body's turned up, but it's very much alive.' And with that he walked out of the door, whistling happily.

Within a couple of minutes DC Radcliffe was by the front desk. He took one look at David and shouted, 'You again!' then swore under his breath.

It didn't make sense - how did the guy he'd just released for stalking turn out to be the alleged murder victim. Just to be on the safe side he went back and collared the second constable to get him to confirm that David really was Arnold Collins. The constable had a quick look and was only too happy to.

DC Radcliffe came back and through gritted teeth asked David if he knew the name of the man arrested for his murder.

'Yes... it's Gerald Seymour... he's my cousin.'

'Your cousin. Not a friend.' And DC Radcliff, italicised the word friend. 'So why didn't your wife recognise him if he's a relative?'

In a panic, David started to embellish the story. 'Ah...he's come over from Australia, my wife has never met him.'

'So, he's here on a visit?'

'Yes, that's right, he's here on a visit.'

DC Radcliffe leaned in closer. 'On a visit your wife apparently knew nothing about.'

David leaned back a bit. 'It was a surprise for her.'

'You can say that again. She was so surprised she thought he'd murdered you.' DC Radcliffe leaned in even closer. 'So, you expect me to believe you just left him sitting... on his own... in your house. So, where were you?'

'I'd just popped out to buy some of his favourite Australian food.'

'What like termites' testicles and wallaby steak.'

'Something like that.'

'So how come he doesn't have an Australian accent.'

'He hasn't been out there long.'

'So where was he living, before he went to Australia?'

David leaned back a bit more. 'Up north…Northumberland.'

DC Radcliffe took a step back, 'Northumberland, how convenient.'

David smiled at DC Radcliffe, 'It's all been a terrible misunderstanding officer, but if you could just release him now, that would be wonderful.'

DC Radcliffe didn't see anything wonderful about it, but he couldn't think of a reason to keep this Gerald Seymour detained any longer, although he would have dearly loved to have locked them both up.

Before releasing Arnold, he asked him what his name was and where he was really from, but fortunately, Arnold continued to say no comment.

The journey home from the police station was subdued. Arnold's elation at being freed from the cell and allowed to go home without a stain on David's character was quickly flattened by the revelation that Bert Herbert couldn't help them. Even worse, he was now an Australian called Gerald Seymour over on a visit. 'Why the hell did you pick such a posh name. I can't go round telling people I'm called that.'

'You won't have to - it was just to get you out of the police station. I could have left you there you know.'

'Yeah, I suppose,' Arnold grudging acknowledged, 'thanks Davey-boy.'

David realised that was the first time that Arnold had used his name, or rather his version of it. 'That's okay…Arnold.' If he expected a response, he was going to be disappointed because Arnold had lapsed into silence again.

But not for long - as soon as David told him Ingrid was back with Greta and Graham in tow, he started muttering about interfering in-laws and hoped they be gone before he got home.

When they arrived back the house both he and David were relieved to find it was empty. There would be some explaining to do, but not for a day or so. From habit David tidied up the sitting room, removing all the detritus from the settee to the waste bin. He then prepared a late snack for them both.

Arnold was too depressed to notice he was eating healthy food and then stomped off to his bedroom, with the passing shot that he was going in the bathroom first and stuff the rota.

David washed up, leaving the kitchen tidy and then slumped on the settee. Was this his life from now on, living with a slob and watching his body deteriorate before his eyes.

In the bathroom Arnold splashed water about and contemplated his future - living with a prissy hygiene fanatic, bent on healthy eating and exercise.

They both went to their separate beds in a state of deep melancholy.

PART FOUR – SUNDAY

CHAPTER 30

David woke up and discovered it wasn't a dream – he really was stuck in someone else's body. He knew he should get up - he had a vague feeling that he used to go out for a run on Sunday mornings. And even when rain curtailed his exercise he still liked to bounce out of bed, ready for anything the day could throw at him.

He looked around the dreary room and decided to stay put. What was there to get up for? His body felt lazy so he turned over and went back to sleep.

Five minutes later the door flew open and Arnold stood glaring at him. 'Why are you still in bed?'

'Because I don't feel like getting up. Leave me alone.'

'You're wasting the best part of the day.'

David pulled the covers over him. 'Why are you up so early?'

Arnold looked round bewildered. 'I don't know, I just got this urge to go for a run.'

They both looked at each other and the realisation struck them at the same time. They were starting to turn into each other.

Arnold moved first. 'I'm going back to bed it's only seven-thirty.'

David jumped out of bed and shouted after him, 'I'm going to have a bath.'

Ingrid and Greta sat side by side on stools at the breakfast bar. Ingrid hated breakfast bars, she much preferred to sit at a proper table on a proper chair with her feet firmly on the floor instead of dangling uncomfortably in mid-air.

The bar had been installed the year before when the kitchen was completely renewed. Greta insisted it was an important part of the scheme and hated it as much as Ingrid did, but would have died before admitting it.

They were waiting for Graham to vacate the bathroom – and had been waiting for some time.

'This is why I want my own en suite, Ingrid. It's ridiculous the amount of time he spends in the bathroom.'

Ingrid would have liked to have said that's because you keep telling him to go in there out of the way, but old habits die hard so she bit her tongue and made a noncommittal, 'Mmmmm.'

'So, I'm planning to knock through into Jonathan's bedroom and turn it into a walk-in dressing room and shower room, just for me.'

'But won't Jonathan want his room when he comes home?'

'That's what Graham says, but I can't see him coming back for good, and if he comes over for a holiday, he can use the guest room like you. It's not like you are going to be using it for ever. As soon as Arnold comes to his senses and treats you properly you can go back home.'

Ingrid wasn't optimistic about Arnold changing his habits, but she did want to go back home.

David was wallowing in the bath when the door was flung open and Arnold walked in. David immediately grabbed a flannel to cover his modesty and slid under the bubbles.

'Oh for goodness sake, it's my body, it's not like I haven't seen it all before.'

'Not while I'm in it you haven't, so I'd appreciate a bit of privacy.' But he eased himself up feeling a bit embarrassed.

'Well, hurry up you've been in here ages.'

David stood up, grabbed a towel to wrap around himself and looked at the overflowing laundry basket. 'We need some clean clothes.'

'Well, don't look at me sunshine, I'm not fussed what I wear, so you're the one who'll have to sort it out.'

'I take it you have a washing machine.'

'Yeh, somewhere...but I don't know how it works, that's Ingrid's job.' But Arnold had a sudden urge to tidy up and take the laundry into the kitchen - an urge which he fought to stop himself turning into David.

David sighed. 'I'll sort it out after breakfast. Now go away.'

The Baker-Brown family were all sitting up in their separate beds, breakfast trays balanced on their knees and the Sunday papers strewn across the duvets. They had to pay the cook four times the hourly rate to get her to come in and make it, but that was a small price to pay for the luxury.

As well as skimming the colour supplements, Deidre was making notes about the supper party she was planning, and trying to shut out the sound of Cameron on the phone berating the private investigator.

'Right, I want a report first thing Monday morning.' He slammed down the receiver and tucked into his bacon, sausage and egg with renewed enthusiasm.

The guy was hopeless of course, which was why he was employing him. Yesterday he'd started legal action against the Safe Haven private clinic for allowing David to wander off, even though he didn't want him to be found.

Deirdre also would prefer it if David remained lost – unharmed, but somewhere else to give her chance to dangle Elliot under Suzie's nose again, or any other suitable husband material.

In her own room Suzie was wondering how David was managing. He'd now been missing for two days and she really missed him. She knew her mother was planning some kind of dinner party at the weekend and there was bound to be at least one eligible bachelor present. But Suzie didn't like the men her mother considered suitable. As far as she could see they were only interested in killing helpless animals. And when they weren't hunting, shooting or fishing, they were trying to kill themselves with too much rich food, hard drink and fast cars.

When she met David at the tennis club and watched him carefully lift a hedgehog off the court, and put it somewhere safe, she knew straight away they were soulmates. He loved animals as much as she did and they planned to own lots when they got married.

She had got her hopes up that he'd been found when the police had rung yesterday, but it was a false alarm. She thought about the poor guy sitting in the prison cell who had been mistaken for David and hoped he'd been released by now. He had such a sad look.

Lettice was also having breakfast in bed, but she had to get up and cook it herself. Every Sunday, as soon as she heard the heavy thud of the Sunday paper landing on her door mat, she shot into the kitchen where her tray was already laid. It was only a matter of moments to make her coffee and toast before she slid back into bed while it was still warm.

She glanced briefly at a news story from China where students, demanding political freedom, had taken over Tiananmen Square, before turning to the science section where there was a follow-up about the launch of a space probe to Venus and something called the World Wide Web, which had been launched by CERN scientist Tim Berners-Lee. She thought it looked interesting, but who would use it?

But what really piqued her interest was a piece in one of the supplements about ley-lines. She had heard of them, but as a scientist herself she had always dismissed them. However, the author was pretty persuasive that these energy pathways really existed and he invited his readers to prove this for themselves by using a pendulum to dowse for them.

Having nothing better to do, as soon as she was dressed, Lettice rummaged through her jewellery box looking for something she could use as a pendulum and found a pearl droplet on a chain which had been her grandmother's. Perfect.

Margaret, her mother and the cat were having breakfast together in Margaret's dining room. It was a Sunday morning tradition, followed by Sunday lunch cooked by Margaret. Afterwards the cat went out to annoy the neighbours, Margaret's mother went upstairs to her flatlet for a snooze and Margaret went for a walk.

Until today, the arrangement had suited Margaret perfectly, a peaceful haven at the end of each busy week, but now she felt irritable and twitchy – in a 'surely there is more to life than this' kind of mood. And then the phone rang.

The phone also rang at number 27 Whitehouse Road. David was loading the washing machine so Arnold answered it. 'What.'

'Mr Telford?'

'No.'

'Is he there?'

'Who wants to know?'

'It's Charles Hazelwood here, we had an appointment at ten-o-clock and it is now...let me see...ten thirteen.'

'Hold on.' Arnold left the receiver dangling and stomped into the kitchen. 'Some bloke called Hazelwood says you had an appointment with him.'

David put soap powder in the tray and started the machine. 'Oh damn, I'd forgotten I said that.'

'Who is he?'

David explained how he had obtained Bert Herbert's address by promising to interview the publisher.

'You idiot, why didn't you give him a false number.'

'I couldn't do that it would be lying.'

Arnold muttered something about if he told the truth all the time his life wouldn't be worth living.

'And anyway, he had to ring me back, so I couldn't give him the wrong number, could I?' David fidgeted about, but couldn't avoid the phone call for ever. 'I'd better go and talk to him.' He could hear heavy breathing when he picked up the receiver, had Arnold got this wrong? 'Hello... Mr Hazelwood? David Telford here.'

When David returned to the kitchen, he looked a shade paler. 'He's going to ring *The Telegraph* and complain about me.'

'So what, you don't actually work for them, sunshine, so what are you worrying about?'

'I don't know that I don't work for them, do I? I might really be one of their reporters, I can't remember.'

'But you said you made it all up when you told him who you were. I mean, fair do's mate you're good at making stuff up.' Arnold sat on the washing machine, a favourite seat of his, although until this morning he'd never realised what it was used for. 'I mean look at the story about me being your cousin Gerald Seymour.'

'Yes, but I do have a cousin called Gerald Seymour, I remembered that.'

'Ah, but is he Australian?'

'Not as far as I know.'

'See, so you lied.'

David couldn't exactly explain why that was different to giving Hazelwood a false phone number, but in his book it was.

'And anyway,' Arnold added, 'You're not a reporter, you work with computers.'

'What!' David couldn't believe his ears, 'How long have you known that?'

Arnold shrugged, 'I don't know, Friday? Yeah, Friday.'

'And you've only just thought to tell me.' David didn't know whether to be angry that Arnold hadn't bothered to tell him before, or pleased that he eventually had. 'But how do you know that?'

'Your Suzie said so.'

'She did! What else did she say?'

'I can't remember.' And Arnold jumped off the washing machine and made to walk off.

But David grabbed him. 'You must be able to remember something,' David was desperate to learn anything about himself and Arnold could be withholding vital information. 'What do I do with computers, make them, repair them, sell them what?'

'I don't know, she didn't say. Look, it's Sunday, I always go up the pub on Sunday, while Ingrid cooks the dinner. Perhaps some more will come back to me over a pint.'

When David looked less than convinced, he added, 'Come on Davey-boy, I'll treat you, but we'll have to go to the cash machine first.'

'But what if the police are still looking for me, they'll take you back to the clinic?'

'No, they won't they're convinced I'm your Aussie cousin, Gerald.'

David had misgivings, but was glad to get out of the house even if it meant wearing another pair of Arnold's scruffy trousers. He also wanted time to think about Suzie and the fact that he worked with computers.

CHAPTER 31

Stella was dying to ring Ingrid to find out what was happening, but didn't want to have to talk to Greta who was bound to answer the phone. The humiliation of being sent home by Greta the previous day, when she was the one who had called the police, and given them all the information they needed to catch Arnold's killer, still bruised her. And it still annoyed her that, after all that, Arnold had turned up alive.

She sat in her bay window with a cup of tea and a bowl of cornflakes, determined not to miss anything happening next door. She was soon rewarded by Arnold and his 'friend' getting in the car with the friend driving. She made a note of which direction they took, which was the same one Arnold took every Sunday to get to the pub.

Margaret replaced the phone and walked into the dining room with a spring in her step – all her gloom dispelled. 'That was Bernard,' she told her mother, 'He's invited us out to lunch.'

Her mother looked less pleased about the change in the routine, but guessed, correctly, she wouldn't get any Sunday roast if she didn't accept the invitation. 'Where's he taking us?'

'It's a surprise. He's booked a table and he'll pick us up at twelve-fifteen.' Margaret was already thinking about what she would wear.

After drawing out twenty pounds from the cash machine, Arnold and David walked into Arnold's local, 'The Dog and Duck', nodded at the other regulars and headed to the bar where Arnold said, 'He'll have a half pint shandy and I'll have my usual, mine host.'

Mine host continued polishing a glass and said, 'No you won't.'

Arnold glared at the man, 'Why not?'

'Why not! Because you're under age, sonny, that's why not.' He polished the glass a bit harder. 'You cheeky young brat coming in here as large as life and calling me "mine host".' He turned to David. 'You ought to know better than to try that on Arnold. I've a good mind not to serve you either. I could lose my license over this.'

'But he is over eighteen,' David couldn't remember exactly how old he was, but he had to be much more than eighteen.

'Well, he doesn't look it. If he wants a drink, he'll have to show some identification proving his age.'

Arnold could see his Sunday pint disappearing fast. 'What if I just have a lemonade and *he* has the pint of Bass?'

'But I don't like Bass.'

'It's not for you,' hissed Arnold, 'we'll swap over when we get to our table.'

'If you want a lemonade sonny, you'll have to sit outside with it.'

Arnold glowered for a few seconds and then agreed.

David resisted saying it was all Arnold's fault for shaving off his moustache and ordered their drinks.

As they sat in the sun enjoying their drinks, or rather as Arnold was - David would have preferred a sherry to the lemonade – he noticed Arnold was covertly staring at him.
'Why do you keep looking at me? I've noticed it before.'
'I'm just checking you aren't damaging my body.'
'Well, I'm not, I'm being really careful with it.'
'Oh yeah. So, who was it drank a bottle of whisky and had a hangover yesterday?'

While they continued to bicker, Sidney Spraggs was on his way to Arnold's house. His visit to the St Hilda's Suite the day before had paid dividends. A friendly nurse told him that Mr Telford had had a visitor who had annoyed the Baker-Browns and been thrown out of the private room.

'And does this visitor have a name sweetheart?'

'Course he has a name,' the nurse, who had seen too many 'Carry On' films than was good for her, giggled like Barbara Windsor.

'And what would that name be, darlin?'

'I don't know, but he would have had to sign in so it will be in the visitors' book.'

'So, are you going to show me the visitors' book?'

'I might.'

Sidney thought it would be easier to extract his own teeth, but he persevered. 'Good girl, and then I'll buy you a coffee…you can have a cake as well.'

When he eventually got his hands on the visitors' book, he was surprised that the name the nurse was pointing to was Arnold Collins, the same name as one of the personalities living in David Telford's body, but not being au fait with the multiple personality disorder he didn't know whether that was significant.

He was also pleased to see there was the first part of an address. 'I'm surprised they have to give their address as well when they sign in.'

The nurse gave another of her Barbara Windsor giggles. 'We tell them it's so we can inform their next of kin, but really it's so the company can send out brochures.'

He and the nurse then spent a pleasant half hour in the hospital restaurant while she was on a break, to be followed up by a visit to the flicks to see '*Nightmare on Elm Street 4*' that evening. Specially chosen by Sidney as the nurse was bound to be terrified and need a comforting arm round her. And after that it was too late to go round and check on this Arnold Collins bloke, so after seeing the nurse back to her flat he went home.

Normally he would have waited until Monday before visiting Whitehouse Road, but with Mr Baker-Brown's threats still ringing in his ears, and the thought he could charge double for working on a Sunday, he headed for number 27 and pulled up outside a nondescript bungalow.

There was no answer when he banged on the door, but he caught the movement of a curtain in the window of the adjacent property. And in Sidney's world you couldn't beat a nosy neighbour for getting information.

He handed Stella his card and was welcomed in with open arms.

Lettice set off from her flat, holding her pendulum lightly between her thumb and finger as prescribed in the article. She wasn't expecting anything to happen and was starting to feel a bit self-conscious walking down the street with a pearl droplet on a chain dangling from her hand. She was about to put it in her pocket when it started to oscillate.

She stared at it, convinced she was inadvertently moving it herself, but even when she held her hand as still as possible the pearl continued to move in a small circle. She took a step forward and it stopped. So, she took a step back did a quarter turn to the left and stepped forward. The pearl immediately began oscillating again. Slowly she found she was walking along a specific route. If she took the wrong direction the pearl stopped swinging and as soon as she was back on the ley line, which is what she became convinced she was following, the swinging restarted.

Sometimes she had to make a detour round a block of buildings, but was able to pick up the ley line on the other side. Eventually she found herself in the High Street. As she was crossing the road the pendulum swung even more violently. She took a step to the side, and the oscillating continued, she took a step to the other side, the same thing happened. By moving in different directions, she realised that she was on a junction of two lines – one going across the High Street and the other going up and down it. Luckily there was little traffic about so she was able to conduct her experiments without getting run over.

Arnold couldn't settle. Although there was nothing wrong with the 'Dog and Duck's' garden, it wasn't the same as being inside, trading jokes with the other drinkers - and he was still fighting the urge to go for a run. He drained his glass and stood up, 'Come on we're going home.'

To his surprise David found he was quite happy sitting in the sun, doing nothing, but then he remembered the washing machine cycle would be finished and he had to hang out their clothes, so, reluctantly he followed Arnold back to the car.

Their return was noted by Stella and Sidney Spraggs. Stella had given Sidney a blow-by-blow account of everything that had happened during the past few days, especially how she had followed Arnold to Gasworks Road - she thought he would be impressed by her tracking skills.

But Sidney wasn't really listening, he was more interested in the man who had fallen over the step next door. Was he the missing David Telford? The time between him being reported missing and arriving at number 27 tallied, plus the fact that he'd arrived with Arnold Collins who had visited him in hospital. Bingo.

But he decided not to tell Stella he believed the man was a missing patient from a private mental clinic, you could never tell how women would react to that kind of situation.

He and Stella waited for the two men to get indoors and then went round and knocked on the door. He had hoped to go round alone, but found it difficult to shake Stella off. For her part, Stella wasn't going to miss one single moment – after all she had the Co-op queue to think about, they would be expecting the next instalment on Monday.

As Arnold had gone off in a huff to his bedroom David answered the door. He recognised Stella, but not the man with her. 'Can I help you?'

The man handed him a card. 'I'm Sidney Spraggs, a Private Investigator, and I've been retained by the Baker-Brown family to find David Telford.'

David was overcome with mixed emotions. Suzie's family cared enough about him to pay a private investigator. But at the same time, he didn't want the guy to find him yet, not until he was back in his own body. 'I'm not sure how I can help you,' and he started to close the door.

Sidney leaned on it, being well practiced in the art of getting into houses when the occupant didn't want him to. 'Perhaps if I could come inside, we could have a chat.' And with another little push he was in, closely followed by Stella.

David quickly showed them into the sitting room and prayed Arnold would stay in his bedroom and that the visit wouldn't take more than a minute of two. But Sidney and Stella sat on the settee, showing every intention of staying put for some time.

Before Sidney could speak, Stella said, 'We know there's something going on here Arnold, so don't try to wriggle out of it.'

Sidney laid a restraining hand on her arm, 'It's probably best if I ask the questions.' He turned to David and said, 'You do know Mr Telford, don't you?'

David had to admit he did, but not very well.

'But well enough to visit him in hospital, Mr Collins.'

David agreed yes, well enough to visit him in hospital.

'So do you know where he is right now?'

David looked at them both and they stared back at him. This was going to involve more lies. 'No, I don't…sorry.'

At that moment Arnold walked in asking what they were going to have for dinner.

Sidney jumped up. 'Mr Telford, I've been looking for you. Your fiancé and her family have been worried sick.' The last part of that sentence was untrue of course, Mr and Mrs Baker-Brown were sick, but not with worry, but about the money it was costing them.

David reacted quickest. Pointing at Arnold he said, 'This isn't David Telford.'

Sidney pulled out his faxed photo and brandished it. 'Well, it looks like him.'

They all peered at the blurred image. This time Arnold reacted first, 'That looks nothing like him…me.'

Stella glared at Arnold, 'So, who are you?'

Arnold hesitated, he was so shocked that the Baker-Browns were looking for him, that he forgot what his name was supposed to be.

'His name is Gerald, Gerald Seymour.' David crossed his fingers - all these lies were going to catch up with him.

'That's right, I'm Gerald Seymour, from Australia…I'm his cousin.'

'Can you prove that?' Sidney was beginning to think Gerald Seymour was yet another personality living in with David Telford that the guy at the clinic didn't know about - and who had now taken over from the other personalities.

CHAPTER 32

DC Radcliffe was working the weekend shift, but Sunday was slow, just a drunk in the cell sleeping off a hangover. He was still fed up about the murder which never happened, and the sniggers behind hands when he went out of the locker room, so he decided to go and have a sharp word with Mrs Collin's and her neighbour Mrs Threadgold for wasting police time.

After finding no one in at Stella's he knocked on number 27. In the sitting room David, Arnold, Stella and Sidney, looked at each other, wondering who was going to answer the door.

Finally, Arnold nodded at David and said, 'I think you'd better go…cobber.'

As soon as David opened the door, DC Radcliffe could not stop himself saying, 'You again!' even though he knew Arnold Collins lived there.

David automatically took a step back. 'Good morning officer.'

'I want to have a word with your wife, Mr Collins.'

'She's not here at the moment, I'm afraid.' And David started shutting the door.

But DC Radcliffe was equally practiced in gaining access. He had recognised the car parked in the road as Sidney Spraggs' and, like all right-minded police officers, he had scant respect for private investigators. At best they got in the way, at worst they solved a crime before the police could.

He pushed against the door and said, 'I'd like a word with Mr Spraggs instead then, if you don't mind.'

David did mind, the whole situation was getting very complicated, but he couldn't very well refuse access to a police officer.

As they walked into the sitting room three pairs of eyes focused on them. DC Radcliffe focused on Arnold. 'Hello again Mr Seymour, are you still enjoying your stay in this country?' He didn't wait for an answer, it had been a rhetorical question and he couldn't have cared less whether the Aussie was having a good time or not. He turned to Sidney. 'And Mr Spraggs, you're here as well.' Again, he wasn't expecting an answer. Finally, he spoke to Stella, 'And you are?'

'Stella Threadgold, I live next door.'

'How very convenient because I want a word with you Mrs Threadgold. It's about wasting police time.' He could see Stella was about to speak so held up his hand, authoritatively. 'You caused my officers to spend time on a cock-and-bull story about a non-existent murder - time they could have been better employed using elsewhere.' Again, it looked as if Stella was going to say something and again up went the authoritative hand. 'If it happens again there will be serious consequences.'

He turned to David. 'When are you expecting your wife to return Mr Collins?'

David looked at Arnold for help, but none was forthcoming. 'I'm not sure, she's gone to stay with her sister for a few days.'

'How strange,' said DC Radcliffe, 'when you have gone to all this trouble to invite your cousin from Australia as a surprise for her.'

Sidney pricked up his ears – had he got it wrong. Was this guy really Gerald Seymour and not David Telford - or had DC Radcliffe got it wrong?

Stella's ears pricked up as well, this was the first she'd heard of Arnold having a cousin, let alone one from Australia.

As DC Radcliffe turned to go, he said, 'I shall still want to speak to your wife Mr Collins, please ask her to come into the police station on Monday.'

After the front door shut behind him there was a strong sense of relief in the sitting room. Sidney spoke first. 'So, are you really Mr Collins' cousin?'

Arnold snapped, 'I told you I was. So, unless you have anything else to say I suggest you sling your hook... cobber.' He turned to Stella, 'And you can go as well.'

But Stella had got her fighting spirit back. 'This isn't your house.' She glared at David, 'Go on tell him Arnold.'

But David was developing a splitting headache and wanted nothing more than to sit on the settee all the afternoon watching telly and drinking beer. 'I think it would be better if you went. And you as well Mr Spraggs or whatever your name is.'

Once outside Stella suggested Sidney want back with her for another cup of coffee and a sandwich. 'I don't believe that story about Arnold's cousin for one minute, there's definitely something funny going on there.'

Sidney was inclined to agree with her, but he wasn't being paid to investigate Australian cousins.

Back in number 27 Arnold was once again asking what they were going to have for dinner and David was reluctantly looking in the fridge for something to eat.

Margaret and Bernard were walking arm in arm round the grounds of a National Trust property. They had had lunch at the Golf Club, where Bernard was a member, and afterwards Margaret's mother said she was tired after eating all that rich food. So, they had taken her home and then driven out into the countryside.

'I was wondering, Bernard, if you'd had second thoughts about closing down Astral Travel?'

'I want to, Margaret, but I don't know what to do about the building. I've signed a ten-year lease.'

'I hope you won't think I'm being forward, but I've had an idea.' And Margaret launched into her plans for starting a coach holiday company – plans she had thought through in detail during a long, sleepless night. She explained that they could hire the coaches and drivers when they needed them and that all they had to do was plan the itineraries and where necessary, book meals. 'We could do day trips to start with and then weekend trips when it takes off and, at some time in the future, we could do five-day tours.'

Bernard was impressed. 'But what about Gasworks Road?'

'We shall need that to set up our offices to run the company, and if we spruce up the main room, we could let it out to Yoga groups or gardening clubs.'

'You are a genius.' Bernard pulled her closer to him, 'We'll start on Monday.' Then he stopped walking, 'But I've had that sign made for Astral Travel.'

'We can still use the same name - it'll just be a different way of travelling.'

She wanted to add the word, normal, but thought Bernard might be offended. So, instead she said, 'But would you promise not to do anymore astral travelling, at least not during working hours.'

Bernard hesitated, but only for a second - he realised the novelty had worn off and it really wasn't that much fun travelling that way on your own. 'Of course, Margaret.' And they continued their walk happily discussing brochures, and advertising, and places to go to.

Fortified by a late lunch, and the urge to take some exercise, Arnold was also out walking, a course of action he found strangely enjoyable and he wondered why he hadn't done it more in the past. Ingrid had sometimes suggested it, but he had always poo-pooed the idea.

His strolling was fairly aimless, a fact that didn't go unnoticed by Stella and Sidney, who were a few yards behind him. They couldn't work out where the alleged Australian was going, but were determined to follow him until he reached his destination.

After trailing him for over an hour they were surprised to find themselves back in Whitehouse Road. Sidney said gloomily that he supposed that was because the Aussie didn't know the area and was trying to get his bearings.

As they both had aching feet, they headed into Stella's for a reviving cup of tea. While it was brewing Sidney took a stroll round Stella's back garden. He was less interested in the flowers, than in what was going on next door. But there was no chance of seeing anything because a six-foot fence separated the two plots.

Had the fence been lower, and had he had X-ray eyes, he would have seen David who was, once again, slumped on the settee having gorged on burger and chips. A meal which he now found to be a strangely tasty and satisfying.

He knew he should get up and do something, but was overcome with lethargy. He thought about the visit from the private investigator, which in turn reminded him of Suzie. If only he could talk to her about himself then he was sure his memory would come back – and he was convinced that escaping from Arnold's body all hinged on that.

As soon as Arnold returned David outlined his plan.

'You want to do what?' Arnold was tired after his unaccustomed walk and wanted nothing more than to sit down with a cup of tea.

'I can't talk to Suzie looking like this. I need to buy some trendy clothes and have my hair cut.'

'My hair, if you don't mind,' Arnold's happy frame of mind had quickly dissipated. 'I thought we'd agreed not to make any alterations to each other's bodies.'

'But this will be an improvement, Arnold.'

'So was shaving off your moustache, but look at the fuss you made about that, sunshine. No, it's not going to happen, I like my hair the way it is.'

David sighed, why couldn't Arnold accept this was the first step to getting back into their own bodies. 'I'm going to hang the washing out, while you think about it.'

Arnold followed him into the kitchen. 'There's nothing wrong with my clothes, just pick one of my suits.'

David sighed again. 'Look on it as an investment,' and he took the laundry basket out into the garden and started haphazardly hanging up the clothes.

Arnold watched for a moment and then took over from him and did it properly. When he was satisfied, he headed back indoors, pausing on the way to stroke next door's cat – which surprised them both, as normally he fired a water pistol at it.

Realising what he'd just done, Arnold resisted the urge to be polite and shouted from the back door, 'No, Daveyboy you are not having my debit card again.'

PART FIVE – MONDAY

CHAPTER 33

Right up until they reached the men's wear shop on the High Street, Arnold moaned about spending money on trendy clothes he wouldn't be seen dead in. And David continued to explain he had to look presentable to meet up with Suzie in an attempt to regain his memory, and reiterated that Arnold should look on it as an investment.

Monday morning had started better than they could have imagined. Pretending to be his own GP, Arnold had rung the Trouble-Free Insurance Agency to say that Mr Collins was still too ill to come into work. Instead of getting Delia telling him Cyril Britten was on the warpath, he got a recorded message saying that the Agency was closed for the day while the paper work was being computerised. It wasn't happening of course, and Cyril Britten was at home spitting venom because it was a day wasted, but it was too late to get the staff back in and tell their clients it was business as usual.

In all the stress of the last few days, Arnold had completely forgotten he would be getting Monday off.

Despite that reprieve he was still whingeing on about the cost as they stood outside Montague Burton's, peering in the window. David had really wanted to shop somewhere trendier, but he thought, rightly, that Arnold would create a fuss.

The jeans and leather bomber jacket David had his heart set on could be seen hanging on the rails at the back. 'Come on the sooner we get it over with the better.' And David walked into the shop.

The assistant looked them up and down, decided they weren't eccentric millionaires dressed as tramps and asked if they had come to the right place. Looking at David he said pointedly, 'There's an Army and Navy store at the other end of the High Street, ducky.'

Arnold was outraged at the slight to his body and said his money was as good as any one's, which surprised the assistant because in his experience it was usually the older man buying gear for his younger boyfriend not the other way round. David left them to it and selected a pair of 'grandad' jeans, a trendy t-shirt and a denim bomber jacket – he didn't think he dared risk buying the leather one.

Having seen off the assistant, Arnold casually wandered over to a rail of suits and idly looked through them. Then he wandered into the changing room to see what David had chosen. Although he would have died rather than admit it, he thought his body looked pretty good in the new clothes. In fact, it looked so good, he went back and picked out a suit in his size for David to try on and said he'd have that as well.

David couldn't wait to get out of Arnold's old clothes so put the jeans, t-shirt and jacket back on and asked the assistant to put his old clothes in the carrier bag. He was surprised at how little fuss Arnold made about paying for all the new gear and wished he'd gone for the leather jacket after all. When he said he needed some new shoes as well, Arnold scarcely blinked and they headed for the shoe shop where a pair of white sneakers was added as well as a pair of smart lace-ups to go with the new suit.

David hoped that Arnold's good mood would extend to his having a haircut.

Earlier, much to Greta's horror, Ingrid had put on her pink gingham overall, ready for another morning on the Co-op tills. 'My goodness Ingrid, surely you're not going into work - not after what Arnold put you through yesterday.'

'Well, the extra money is useful and I enjoy it.' That wasn't strictly true, but Ingrid was pretty desperate to get out of her sister's house, and going to work would seem like a holiday. Greta had spent most of Sunday itemising Arnold's faults and how Ingrid was to bring him to heel.

'As soon as I was expecting Jonathan, I stopped working in the store and I never went back, I made sure of that.' Greta paused to flick an imaginary fleck of dust off the coffee table where they were having a post-breakfast cuppa. It was Ingrid's suggestion to avoid sitting on the kitchen stools again. 'And as soon as Arnold has come to his senses you must do the same.' Another imaginary fleck of dust went flying. 'And then we can go shopping together like we used to, and have coffee mornings. I'm thinking of joining the Women's Institute, and you could come to that as well.'

Ingrid wasn't sure the W.I. was really her thing. And she preferred her coffee mornings with Stella, who was a lot more fun than Greta.

'While we've got a moment on our own…' Greta was unusually hesitant, 'this friend Arnold brought home…has he shown any tendencies in that direction before?'

'What direction?'

'Well, you know…men.'

'I don't think so.' Ingrid still liked to tell herself that the young man was a work colleague.

'And you've never found Arnold wearing any of your clothes.'

'No of course not Greta.' Ingrid was appalled.

'Well, just to be on the safe side, you'd better keep your wardrobe locked.'

Sidney Spraggs was up early, and in his office, ready to send a fax to Cameron Baker-Brown on his progress so far - plus a running total of how much it was costing. Yesterday, in Stella's garden, as soon as he overheard a man's voice shouting out 'no Davey-boy you are not having my debit card,' he knew he was on the right track.

Just to be on the safe side, he said in the fax that he was close to finding David Telford and just needed final confirmation that he had the right man, which he expected to have later in the day. As he pressed the send button on his fax machine, he assumed Cameron would be very happy.

He couldn't have been more wrong Cameron Baker-Brown was furious. He'd picked Spraggs because he thought he was incompetent and that it would be days, even weeks before he tracked David down. He immediately rang Sidney and asked for photographic proof. Sidney pointed out that he could take Mr Baker-Brown to the house where David was hiding out and he could see him with his own eyes.

'I haven't got time to run all over the town on a wild-goose-chase. Take a polaroid photo of the man and fax it to me.' He slammed down the phone and immediately rang his lawyer to check that they had started proceedings to sue Alastair Grey. He anticipated the money he made from that law suit would cover the cost of the P.I.

Stella waited for Ingrid outside the Co-op. Most of what she wanted to tell her she was keeping to regale the shoppers with as well, but she thought she ought to tell Ingrid in private that DC Radcliffe wanted her to go to the police station.

Ingrid immediately turned bright pink. 'Oh, my goodness, what's Greta going to say.'

'You don't have to tell her - we'll pop along in our lunch hour.'

But Ingrid was so flustered she made a mess of opening-up her till and the manager had to come and sort it out. Meanwhile the queues to both tills were getting longer and more restive as they waited to hear the next instalment.

When everyone had settled down, Stella picked up the first item to be scanned, took a deep breath, and then described in detail how Arnold and his friend left the house presumably to go to the pub. 'And then this man knocked on my door,' she paused for dramatic effect, 'a private investigator.'

That information was quickly passed down the lines, although the ones on the end were puzzled as to why a privet hedge was knocking on Stella's door.

'He was looking for a missing man called David Telford and he was convinced that he was Arnold's new friend.'

Ingrid felt a surge of relief. 'See Arnold was just being kind and trying to help someone.'

'I don't think so,' said Stella, who didn't like her story telling being interrupted, 'because me and Sidney, that's the private investigator, went round to your house as soon as they came back and you'll never guess what Arnold said.'

Again, she paused for dramatic effect, which went on several seconds because no one could guess. 'He said the man was his cousin from Australia called Gerald Seymour over on a surprise visit.' And on that triumphant note she carried on scanning while the two queues discussed this latest development.

'But he doesn't have a cousin in Australia.'

'Exactly, Ingrid, that's what I said to Sidney.' Stella kept to herself the arrival of DC Radcliffe and being shown the door by Arnold. There are somethings the queues don't need to know.

When David said that to complete his new look he would need a decent haircut, Arnold didn't say no, but steered him towards the barber's shop he very occasionally frequented.

David took one look at the haircuts coming out on the heads of customers and refused to go in. 'You need a decent haircut to go with your new clothes, Arnold, we'll find somewhere else.'

Luckily there was a trendy salon a few doors along. An hour later they both emerged with new haircuts.

After he'd got over the shock of Wayne running his fingers through David's curls and explaining what he planned to do, Arnold enjoyed every minute of having them washed, cut, styled and blow dried as well as having conditioner and some scented gel applied. He looked across at David and saw his body now had layered hair in a style which reminded him of Tom Cruise.

Outside, Sidney Spraggs, who had followed them from the moment they left home, was waiting with his polaroid camera. But polaroid cameras are bulky and obvious so before he could take a sneaky picture the two men had walked away with their backs to him and were heading down the High Street.

Their movements were also being followed by Ingrid and Stella, who were on their way back from the police station. Fortunately for Ingrid, DC Radcliffe was out looking for clues at a suspected burglary so the sergeant on duty at the front desk noted down that Ingrid had reported, as asked, and told her, in the most kindly way, not to waste police time again. 'Now don't you worry, love, it happens all the time. It's just DC Radcliffe gets these bees in his bonnet.'

As they were heading towards the Co-op Stella nudged Ingrid hard in the ribs. 'Look, there's Arnold's so-called cousin with another man.'

Ingrid looked at the two men who were studying the menu outside 'The Cloak and Dagger' pub. There was something very familiar about the taller one. If he hadn't been sporting a trendy bomber jacket and a fashionable haircut, she could have sworn it was her husband.

The same thought also struck Stella, who gave Ingrid another hard nudge. 'As I live and breathe, that's Arnold.'

'But it can't be, he doesn't have any clothes like that and his hair's different.'

'It's him alright.' Stella pursed her lips knowingly. 'He's had a make-over that's what he's done. And we all know why.'

Ingrid felt a wave of sadness sweep over her, Arnold never dressed up for her, and she couldn't remember when he'd last had a proper haircut. When it draped too far over his collar, she trimmed it up herself with the kitchen scissors.

'His cousin still looks as scruffy, although his hair's a bit tidier.' Then Stella gasped, 'Look Arnold's been to Montague Burton, you can see the carrier bag. Well, he's certainly spending his money.'

Ingrid felt even sadder as she watched her husband and his cousin enter the pub. She couldn't remember when he'd last taken her out for lunch.

'And what's he doing home from work? He'll get the sack if he isn't careful.' Stella was on a roll. 'You need to start divorce proceedings. We'll go and find a solicitor when our shift is over. And tomorrow we'll go to the estate agents, you need to get your bungalow on the market.'

But Ingrid didn't want to sell her home and get a divorce. She thought Arnold looked very dashing in his new clothes, and the haircut had taken ten years off his age.

But she didn't get a chance to say that because Stella grabbed her arm and gasped. 'Them polaroid photos you found in the bin - Arnold must have taken them for an estate agent not a woman. He's planning to sell your bungalow without telling you.'

CHAPTER 34

As soon as David and Arnold were sitting in the pub eating pie and chips, reluctantly paid for by Arnold, the same argument that they'd been having all morning, started up again. Arnold wanted to go back to Astral Travel to have it out with Bernard Hornby and to threaten to sue him - while David thought that was a waste of time and he wanted to go to try to find Suzie.

'Why don't you go and get your car if you want to go gadding off to see your fiancée?' Arnold knew why, but he couldn't resist saying it.

'Because, it's probably damaged and I don't know which garage has it.'

'Well, you could hire one.'

David looked at him in exasperation, 'Because I can't show them my driving licence and I don't have any money.'

'You seem happy enough spending mine,' Arnold muttered.

'And I will pay you back with interest when I'm back in my body.'

Finally, it was agreed that David would drop Arnold off in Gasworks Road while he went off to the Baker-Brown's home in the hopes of seeing Suzie.

The only problem with the plan was how Arnold was going to get home, and to the amazement of them both, he said he would walk.

Sidney tried to take a photo of the men through the pub window but it came out blurred. As he was desperate for a pint of beer and a packet of crisps, he pulled his hat down as low as possible and went into the public bar and waited to be served. He'd no sooner started his drink when the two men left and headed towards the carpark. Cursing, he set off once again, jumped in his Mini and managed to catch up with their car at the road works.

A few minutes later the Escort stopped outside a building in Gasworks Road. Sidney parked a few yards away and watched the man he believed to be David Telford get out and go into the building. As soon as the door had closed behind him and the car had driven off, Sidney positioned himself across the street, ready to take a photo as soon as the man came back out. He was surprised to see the man had gone into a travel agency and wondered whether he was barking up the wrong tree, and that perhaps the man really was this Australian cousin and he was booking his flight home.

David headed to the Baker-Brown's home, but the closer he got to it the more he worried about what he was going to say to Suzie. The last time she'd seen him he was in a prison cell, so would she even give him the time of day. He nearly turned round and went back, but the horror of being stuck in Arnold's body for ever kept him going.

As he approached the gates, they opened and the Baker-Brown's Bentley pulled out without stopping. David jammed on the brakes, but before ducking down, he saw that both Suzie's parents were in it.

Heaving a sigh of relief that at least he wouldn't have to face them he drove through the gates only to meet Suzie driving the other way. They sat facing each other for a few seconds until Suzie politely beeped her horn and indicated he should back out. Then with a wave of her hand in thanks, she drove off after her parents in the direction of the next town.

David waited a few seconds and then followed her. As they approached the town's outskirts, the streets looked vaguely familiar and he wondered if he had ever lived there.

Suzie stopped outside a florist's, locked her car, and went in. Assuming she was going to buy some flowers, David parked a few yards back and waited – and waited. He couldn't remember ever buying flowers from a florist, but he was sure it shouldn't have taken Suzie forty-five minutes. There was nothing for it, if he was going to talk to her, he'd have to go into the shop.

Margaret looked up in surprise as Arnold came into her office. She had been busy cancelling all the clients' appointments, explaining that due to unforeseen circumstances Mr Hornby could no longer offer 'out of body experiences', but that Astral Travel would soon be offering coach trips instead, and as valued customers they would have reduced rates for six months – so far no one had taken up that offer.

'Oh, it's you. And who are you today - Mr Collins, Mr Telford or someone completely different?' she said tetchily.

'I'm still Arnold Collins and I'm still in the wrong body,' replied Arnold, equally tetchily.

'Yes, well, I happen to be very busy. We're in the process of setting up a new business, so unless you are interested in a coach trip...'

Arnold glared, 'No, I'm not. But I'll tell you what I'm interested in and that's suing your boss for every penny he's got.'

Margaret stood up and pressed her hands down hard on her desk ready to launch into a fierce defence of Bernard when Lettice came into the office. 'Ah, Miss Long, I've been trying to get hold of you. I'm afraid Mr Hornby is no longer offering astral holidays.'

'I'm not surprised,' Lettice said snappily, 'I think this whole thing was a con.'

'So do I,' Arnold was pleased to find a fellow supporter.

'Mr Hornby got the idea out of a book and it doesn't work.' And with a flourish, Lettice pulled 'Out of Body Experiences' out of her bag and slammed it down on Margaret's desk. 'I borrowed it from the library after you returned it on Saturday and it's a waste of time. No matter how hard you try nothing happens.'

'Here, here,' agreed Arnold, 'it's just a money-making scam.'

Margaret quickly saw the flaw in his argument. 'So, are you now saying Mr Collins that it isn't possible to release your astral spirit?'

'Ah, no, obviously it is, which is why I'm in the wrong body.' Arnold backtracked hurriedly as realised he could hardly sue Bernard Hornby for what had happened while at the same time accusing him of taking money under false pretences. So, he drew himself up as tall as possible and said, 'You will be hearing from my solicitor.'

'Bearing in mind that you have never paid a penny Mr Collins, I'm not sure what grounds you have for suing us, but I shall be interested to hear what your solicitor has to say.' And with that winning riposte Margaret also drew herself up as tall as possible and added, 'Shut the door on your way out.'

Arnold glared, but couldn't think of a suitably withering reply. With as much dignity as possible he went out into the street, closely followed by Lettice, who hung onto his arm.

'So did you really come out of your body?'

'No.' Arnold wasn't feeling up to discussing what had happened to him with Lettice, who reminded him of his least favourite aunt, and he tried to unhook her.

But Lettice wasn't easily unhooked and hung on even tighter. 'You did, didn't you? What was it like?'

'A bloody nightmare.'

Lettice was now pink with excitement. 'I want to hear all about it. Let's go and have some tea and cakes, my treat.'

Sidney was surprised to see his quarry come out of the travel agency with an old lady hanging on to his arm. As soon as they had disappeared down the road, he eased out of the alleyway he'd been hiding in and entered Astral Travel.

Margaret met him in the hallway where she'd gone to check that Arnold had definitely left the premises. 'I'm sorry, but the we are currently closed at the moment, but give me your name and contact details and I will let you know when we are starting our coach trips.'

'No, sorry ma'am, but I'm not looking to go on any outings, I just want to know the name of that man who just left.'

'Collins, Arnold Collins.
'Not David Telford?'
'No.'
'And not Gerald Seymour?'

But Margaret had had enough for one morning. It was well past her lunch break and she was hungry. 'No, and if you're not interested in our outings then perhaps you would kindly leave, I want to lock up.' And she firmly pushed him out of the door.

Suzie looked up as the shop door opened and hoped that the customer wasn't going to ask for anything complicated. She hadn't wanted to come into work as there was still no news of David - she really wanted to stay at home by the phone, even though her father had told her that the private investigator was nowhere near finding him. But the owner had to go to a funeral and asked her to take over for the afternoon.

The trendily dressed man walking towards her with a smile looked vaguely familiar, but she couldn't place him. 'Can I help you, sir?'

'I hope so,' said David, who was smitten all over again as he took in her fetching floral overall and curly blonde ponytail.

Suzie waited, but David was tongue-tied. 'Do you want some flowers for your girlfriend or wife.'

'Yes.'

'Okay…so what are her favourite flowers?'

'What are your favourites?'

Suzie smiled, 'I love lily-of-the-valley, but you should choose what she likes.'

'That's what she likes - lily-of-the-valley, I remember now.' And David realised that he did remember that - it was working, by talking to Suzie, his memory was slowly coming back.

'Would you like me to make up a small posy for you?'

'Is that what you would like?'

'But they're not for me, sir.' Suzie smiled - the poor guy seemed hopelessly inept about buying flowers. 'Or I could put them in with some tiny rosebuds and make a larger bouquet.'

David squirmed, he didn't really want to talk about flowers, he wanted to talk about him and Suzie, and the fact that they were engaged, and to find out where he lived and how old he was. 'What time do you finish?'

'Why?' there was a note of suspicion in her voice.

'I was hoping I could take you out for dinner.'

'But I don't know you.'

'Yes, you do.' David nearly blurted out that he was really her fiancé in another man's body, but managed to stop himself in time. 'We met at the hospital when I came to visit David.'

Suzie stared at him and slowly he could see the recognition dawning on her face.

'And you were in the prison cell at the police station.' She glared. 'You were pretending to be my fiancé.'

'No, I wasn't pretending to be him. It was all a misunderstanding.'

'So, they didn't keep you in then.'

'Good heavens no, as soon as you and your father left, they apologised and let me out.'

Suzie paused. The man certainly looked a lot more presentable than he had on Saturday, and if he was a friend of David's he might have some idea of where he might be. He might even be looking after him.

'Okay, Mr...?'

'Collins, Arnold Collins.'

'Right, Mr Collins, that would be lovely. I finish at six-o-clock.'

David looked at Arnold's watch, he had nearly two hours to kill. He could use that time to see if he recognised where he lived. 'Actually...I hadn't seen David for ages when I visited him. Does he live round here?'

Suzie burst into tears. 'Yes, but he's missing, he walked out of the clinic that was looking after him and I've no idea where he is.' She pulled out a hankie and dabbed her eyes, 'I was hoping you might know.'

David decided it was safer not to answer that - it would only mean another lie and he was trying to avoid telling any more. 'That's terrible...do you have his address? I'd like to pop a note through his door...for when he comes back.'

'Yes,' and Suzie tore a page out of the order book and wrote it down. 'Do you know the area?'

'Not really, Suzie.'

Suzie glanced up at him. 'How do you know my name?'

David could have kicked himself - it had just slipped out so naturally. 'I...heard your father call you that...at the police station.' He really hoped that was true.

Suzie smiled and wrote down the instructions on how to find the flat.

'Thank you. See you at six then.' He could see she was looking hesitant again. 'It would mean so much to me, more than you could ever imagine.'

CHAPTER 35

Back outside Astral Travel, with the door shut firmly in his face, Sidney couldn't decide whether to follow his quarry on foot or in his car. When he saw the pair heading towards the High Street, he thought it was safe to drive to the carpark and hurry back towards them.

Again, he wasn't the only one watching them with interest. Stella had caught sight of Arnold's cousin with an elderly lady hanging on to his arm like grim death, going into 'The Singing Kettle'. She leaned across and announced to Ingrid and the queue that Gerald, Arnold's so-called cousin, was about to enter their favourite café with a strange woman.

Ingrid sighed and several shoppers nobly abandoned their trollies and said they would eavesdrop on the pair and report back.

Sitting in front of toasted teacakes and an excited Lettice, Arnold tried to explain what had happened. It sounded ridiculous, even to himself, and he was living the nightmare.

But Lettice was once again a believer. 'So, what was it like, travelling round the world?'

'It got a bit boring.' Arnold slurped his tea. 'And I never wanted to come out in the first place.'

'But where did you go?'

Arnold tried to remember. 'Hawaii'

'Hawaii! Is that all?'

'And Benidorm…but I didn't stay there long, too many people.'

Lettice sighed. 'I would have gone to see the pyramids and the museum in Cairo and Australia and Borneo...'

'Yeah, but you can't talk to anyone or do anything or even sit down properly. No, Hornby's astral holidays weren't all they were cracked up to be, take my word for it.'

Lettice guessed she'd have to take his word for it as she was never likely to know now, so changed the subject. 'So, where's the young man who has your body?'

'He's gone to see his fiancée. He's convinced that if he can get his memory back, we'll be able to swap bodies.'

'And he definitely didn't come out at Astral Travel?'

'No, it was because of a car crash.'

'Where?'

'In in the High Street, and it caused a traffic jam, which was why I was late getting to Astral Travel and got caught up with you lot trying to come out of your bodies. He has a lot to answer for.' And he bit off a chunk of teacake and chewed it vigorously.

Lettice was too intrigued to eat her teacake. 'It must be to do with where the accident took place.' She nodded excitedly, 'And possibly, String Theory.'

Arnold knew he'd regret asking what String Theory was, and he was right. Lettice went into great detail, and Arnold munched his way through his teacake and then hers, convinced she was completely batty.

'So, when we come down to it, we don't really exist, we are all just a bunch of vibrations – yeah right.' He held up the last piece of teacake. 'This exists, I can see it and touch it and now I'm going to taste it.' And with a final flourish he popped it in his mouth, chewed vigorously and swallowed, 'And it didn't taste a bit like string.'

Lettice smiled, 'I know it's hard to understand, but I'm sure David's astral body, which is just a vibration, must have gone through some other dimensions, there are supposed to be ten you know, which stopped it coming back into his corporeal body.'

Arnold had given up trying to understand the physics of the situation, he just wanted a resolution. 'Look, stop with all this quantum mechanics stuff, all I want is my own body back.'

'It will take a special energy, but I think I know where to find that.'

'You're not suggesting we plug ourselves into the national grid, are you?' Arnold had once experienced a mild shock peeing on an electric fence on a school outing to a farm, and wasn't keen to repeat the experience.

'No, not the grid - ley lines.'

Once again Arnold knew he'd regret asking and he didn't even have a teacake to alleviate the boredom. But he asked anyway and Lettice told him about the article she'd read and the ley lines running up and down the High Street. 'Two of them cross there, and I'm sure that's where David had his accident.'

David followed Suzie's instructions and soon found his flat on the first floor of a small block. It certainly looked familiar and he had a strong feeling that he kept a spare key on the ledge over the front door.

Checking that no one was watching he felt along the door frame until he touched a piece of cold metal – his key. He pushed open the door, which wasn't easy as there was quite an accumulation of junk mail behind it, and stepped inside.

Slowly, as if he was focusing after coming out of a particularly deep sleep, the hall resolved itself into its familiar lines. He recognised the carpet and the photos on the wall – taken when he was going through his photography phase. He knew the door at the end led into his sitting room and then into the kitchen. The door to the right led to his bedroom and next door was the bathroom. On the other side was the spare bedroom which he had turned into a computer room. Of course, he thought, that's where I run my business from.

He wandered round the rooms, stroking his sofa, touching his small dining table and opening his kitchen cupboards. He checked in the fridge – yes there was the smoked salmon and an avocado – going a bit soft - and tasty salads and chilled Chablis. But although he was relieved to see them, he didn't actually want to eat any of them. What he really fancied was a beef burger. He sighed – his memory was coming back but he was still in Arnold's body and Arnold's body still wanted junk food.

He wandered into his bedroom and opened his wardrobe. He wasn't surprised to see very similar outfits to what he was wearing, hanging there. He rang a finger alone his shirts and set them swinging on their hangers. He almost wanted to kiss them he was so relieved to see that he had some decent clothes to wear.

He still has another hour to kill before meeting Suzie so headed back to his computer room and saw the light on the ansaphone was winking.

Most of his messages were from Delia Stratton calling from the Trouble-Free Insurance Agency, a name he immediately recognised as Arnold's workplace.

The first one was polite asking what time he was expecting to arrive. After that they got more agitated and, finally she said that Mr Britten was, spitting tacks and could he please let her know where he was.

He booted up his computer and checked his files and saw that he had given a quote to computerise the company's paperwork and was booked to start on Friday the fifth of May working through the weekend and all day Monday. He checked the calendar above his desk, although he knew, from the sudden chill running through his veins, that it was the eighth of May today.

But before he could ring the company and try to explain, there was a ring on the doorbell. Without thinking he opened it to find his neighbour Dennis standing hesitantly on the mat.

Dennis looked surprised when David greeted him warmly and asked how he was. 'Do we know each other?'

David quickly tried to retrieve the situation. 'Well sort of... David has told me all about you.'

'Has he, right.' Dennis wasn't entirely convinced. 'So, you're a friend of his.'

'Yes...a very close friend.'

'And you're staying in his flat? It's just that I heard someone moving around in here. I live next door by the way.'

'No, not staying, just visiting.' David was rapidly regretting answering the doorbell.

'So, how is he? We were told he'd had a fatal accident.'

'Not fatal, no, in fact he's out of hospital and well on the road to recovery.'

Dennis still didn't look convinced. 'I suppose I'd better tell the vicar then - he'd pencilled in the funeral for next week.'

'Next week!' David could feel the panic rising until he remembered that he wasn't actually dead, so couldn't be buried, no matter what the vicar had in his diary. 'Well, if you could tell the vicar that David is still very much alive, I'm sure he'll be very grateful...David that is, not the vicar, although he will probably be grateful as well.'

'So, when will he be back in his flat?'

'Soon,' said David, 'very soon...I've just come to collect some clothes for him.' And he gently shut the door.

Back in his office he saw his old computer games on a shelf. And he remembered they were what got him interested in computers and programming when he left school.

Then slowly, like a melting waterfall, a trickle of more memories poured into his head. They gathered speed and volume until finally they were gushing in, almost overwhelming him. He held his head in his hands, it was difficult to take in a lifetime of memories all in one go.

He concentrated on Suzie. He remembered them getting engaged, much to the obvious disappointment of her parents. He couldn't remember when their wedding was going to be, but perhaps the Baker-Browns had insisted they wait a while. Thinking of the Baker-Browns, and in particular Suzie's father, he felt the familiar feeling of panic.

He quickly turned his thoughts to his own parents. They had retired to Spain two years ago, only coming back to England for a few weeks in the summer.

He wondered if they had been worried about him and then remembered he'd only lost his memory - and his body - five days ago so they wouldn't have even noticed. Five days, he thought, it felt more like five months.

He checked the time on his computer, he wanted to be outside Suzie's shop before six-o-clock in case she decided to slip away to avoid their dinner date – so no time to ring Trouble-Free Insurance. But he reasoned it was probably too late to explain anyway.

Driving back to the florist he wondered whether to tell her what had happened to him or whether to wait to see if he and Arnold could now swap back.

CHAPTER 36

Sent over by Stella to 'The Singing Kettle' on a spying mission, the shoppers had got as close as possible to Arnold and Lettice, but it was difficult to hear what they were saying over the clatter of tea cups, and they only caught the odd word here and there. So, when they reported back to Ingrid and Stella, all they could say was that the conversation was about lines, strings, Cairo and Hawaii.

None of them could make head nor tail of it, but Stella said that Arnold's cousin was obviously a well-travelled man.

Suzie was locking up as David arrived. 'Oh, you're back Mr Collins.'

'Yes, here I am, on the dot. Now where would you like to go?' David had the uneasy feeling she had hoped to slip off before he arrived, but was now too polite to say anything.

'Could we just make it a quick drink, my parents rang and they are expecting me back for dinner.'

At the mention of Suzie's parents, David's stomach lurched. How had such a terrifyingly rude couple ended up with a daughter like Suzie. He had to get back in his own body. The thought of not getting married to her was too much to bear. 'Oh, I was really hoping we could spend the evening together.'

'I'm sorry,' and she gave him a sad little smile, 'But we'll have at least an hour to chat, Mr Collins.'

As they headed into the nearest pub, David remembered to his horror that he didn't have any money or cards on him. Arnold had been paying all day, and at the flat he'd found nothing apart from a couple of pound coins in an ashtray. 'I'm so sorry Suzie, but I... I've left my wallet at home.' David gulped, he'd told another lie, when would they end?

Suzie gave him a long look and then said, 'Don't worry, I'll buy our drinks.'

Feeling totally mortified David said he'd get them a table.

Suzie brought two glasses of red wine over. 'I hope you like Merlot.' She seemed less friendly now and David couldn't blame her.

He lifted his glass in a toast, 'To you and David. So, how long have you been engaged?'

'Over a year now.' She took a sip of wine. 'I thought I knew all David's friends, but he's never mentioned you. So, how do you know him?'

'Oh, we go way back, right from when we were little, very little. But we haven't been in touch for somewhile,' he quickly added. So have you named the day yet?' Knowing full well they hadn't.

'Not yet.' Suzie's eyes suddenly filled with tears. 'I'm sorry Mr Collins, but I was hoping you might know where he is, but if you haven't seen him lately, I guess you don't.'

Rather than tell yet another lie, David decided not to say whether he'd seen him or not. 'But when he comes back, you'll get married won't you?'

'I hope so, but my parents are against it and David won't stand up to them.' She delicately blew her nose. 'You know Mr Collins, I sometimes wish he was a bit more assertive.'

David knew Arnold would be assertive in that situation and hoped he would be able to take some of that with him when he got back into his own body. Then he'd tell the Baker-Browns he and Suzie were getting married - whether they liked it or not.

As if a sudden thought had struck her, Suzie put down her wine and stared at him. 'If you haven't been in contact with David for quite a while, how did you know he'd been in an accident and which hospital he was in?'

David was thankful he wasn't Pinocchio as by now his nose would be several feet long. 'A mutual friend told me. Gerald...Gerald Seymour.'

Suzie, wrinkled her brow. 'I don't think I know Gerald Seymour.'

'No, he's from Australia...over on a visit...he's going back soon.'

Lettice was more than happy to walk back to Arnold's house with him. She was dying to try out her plan to return him and David to their own bodies.

Trudging behind them Sidney Spraggs was starting to wonder if this job was really worth all the shoe leather. He still hadn't managed to get a decent photograph with the polaroid camera, and he was itching to try out his new camera with the telescopic sight and powerful flashlight, which had arrived that morning.

As soon as he saw them go into number twenty-seven, he decided to take the risk and dash back for both his car and his camera.

David touched his cheek where Suzie had kissed him before getting into her car. 'As soon as David has been found, I'll tell him I met you and I'm sure he'll be in touch.' And with that she drove off, giving him a wave.

He watched her car disappear out of sight and then wondered where to go. There didn't seem any point in going back to his flat. He had his memory back but was still in the wrong body. So, he headed back to Arnold's which now felt more like home than his flat did.

He was surprised to be greeted by an excitable old lady and a cynical Arnold. But as he too had read Stephen Hawkin's 'A Brief History of Time' he wasn't as dismissive of string theories and quantum mechanics as Arnold, and was prepared to try anything, especially now he'd spent time with Suzie.

Arnold ignored their conversation about quarks and gluons, wormholes and black holes, but his ears pricked up when they discussed Heisenberg's Uncertainty Principle. 'I don't know who this geezer Iceberg is, but if he's uncertain what makes you think your idea is going to work?'

They both tried to explain that Heisenberg was a theoretical physicist who said it was impossible to know both the speed and position of a particle with any accuracy. Arnold wished he'd kept quiet.

Sidney Spraggs missed David's arrival at the house, but Stella hadn't and soon brought him up to speed when he knocked on her door and asked if he could continue his stakeout from the comfort of her front room. It was a long wait, but the time passed comfortably. Stella made them coffee and sandwiches and they told each other their life stories.

Next door, having exhausted the subject of Einstein's Theory of Relativity, David made a meal for the three of them and they sat and chatted until one-o-clock in the morning when they thought most of the traffic would be gone.

After parking the car, the three of them walked slowly up and down the High Street until David thought he'd recognised where he'd crashed. 'I'm sure it was near here. A dog ran out in front of me and I swerved to miss it.'

'Well, next time - don't,' muttered Arnold

'I hope there won't be a next time.'

They waited until it looked as if all the traffic had cleared and then Lettice started walking up and down, the pearl pendulum, swinging. When she found the ley lines' crossing point, she beckoned them over. 'This is where the energy is strongest - David needs to stand in this exact spot.'

David stood where she pointed and immediately remember hitting his head on his car's windscreen...and then nothing. 'Yes, this must be where it happened.'

'Get closer to him, Arnold. Don't move David.' Lettice was on a roll.

Feeling more than a little self-conscious David, his heart thumping, did as he was told. Arnold stood facing him, unconvinced that it was going to work.

Using her pendulum, Lettice gave their positions another slight adjustment, much to the bemusement of an urban fox on his perambulations, and then said, 'Get on with it then.'

Both men took a deep breath. David concentrated on hitting the windscreen and Arnold said, 'What a load of rubbish.'

Their astral bodies shot out, stared at each other in astonishment and after a bit of pushing and shoving, shot into their correct bodies.

The two men continued to stare at each other, unable to believe what had actually happened.

'Well,' demanded Lettice, 'Did it work?'

'Yes, it did.' And David flung his arms round her, lifted her off the ground and hugged her. 'Thank you, thank you, thank you.'

Arnold checked that his body hadn't suffered any damage, or stretching, then he flung his arms round both of them and whirled them into a mad dance.

Their exuberant celebrations were brought to an abrupt halt when an irate driver of a white van leaned out of his window and shouted, 'What the effing 'ell are you lot doing in the middle of the road? Get out the effing way.' And with a loud blast on his horn, he roared off, leaving the three of them feeling strangely deflated,

'Now what do we do?' David felt slightly disorientated being back in his body. It felt the same, but there seemed to be a residual element of Arnold about it.

But before the others could speak. they were all blinded by a bright flash of light, followed by the sound of running feet.

Sidney Spraggs' patience had at last been rewarded. After watching the strange ritual in the middle of the road, he'd fired off his camera with its mega-powerful flashlight, and then legged it, leaving three people wondering what the hell had hit them.

Once they had got their sight back, Arnold drove Lettice back to her flat and then they returned to number twenty-seven as Arnold wasn't prepared to drive over to David's to drop him off.

'You can spend the night at mine again, Davey-boy because I'm knackered. It's been a weird sort of day.'

David agreed and headed towards the spare bedroom. 'You can go in the bathroom first, Arnold. See you in the morning.'

In his darkroom Sidney looked at the photo he'd developed. All it showed were three washed out faces with their mouths open and their eyes shut – they could have been anyone. He decided to tell Mr Baker-Brown to stuff his job.

PART SIX – TUESDAY

CHAPTER 37

At the same time that Arnold and David were reunited with their own bodies, Ingrid turned over for the seventeenth time and looked the bedside clock, it was twenty-eight minutes past one and she hadn't slept a wink. She had convinced herself that it was her nagging and constant demands for affection that had driven Arnold into the arms of another – another who she couldn't quite work out. Was it the woman from the travel agency or Arnold's supposed cousin, or perhaps someone else entirely.

Then a tiny spark of hope was ignited in her heart. She became more and more convinced that the scruffy jumper Arnold had been wearing the past few days was the one she'd knitted him all those years ago. She couldn't remember the last time he'd worn it so there had to be a reason he pulled it out of the back of his drawer. Did he remember what a labour of love it was - and was he sending her a message? Perhaps she hadn't lost him to another after all.

She had spent yesterday afternoon at work listening to Stella, who insisted that she divorce Arnold, and all the evening, listening to Greta who insisted that she made him suffer. Well, she was going to do neither, she was going to win back Arnold's affections.

In her lunch hour she would buy a trendy skirt and top and after her shift at the Co-op she would have a full make-over, including highlights. Then she would go back home and cook Arnold's favourite meal.

Having settled on a course of action she gave the pillow another punch to make it more comfortable and immediately fell asleep.

In the adjacent bedroom, Greta was awake with a pillow jammed over her ears to cut out Graham's snoring. But she was happily passing the time planning her new en-suite and pushing Graham into the box room.

Stella was also lying awake, but she was thinking about Sidney Spraggs. He had spent the evening at her house, ostensibly keeping watch on next door. He could have done that sitting in his car, she thought. And why did he tell her he was a lonely widower if he wasn't romantically interested.

But just when she was about to suggest a late-night cup of cocoa, or rather an early morning one as it was nearly one-o-clock, when Arnold, his cousin and an old lady had come flying out of next door and driven off at high speed and Sidney had rushed off after them.

Neither Arnold nor David slept well. They were both finding it difficult to adjust to their own bodies. Arnold was still convinced that David had somehow stretched his round the waist, which is why it felt different.

Finally, he got up early and spent a lot of time looking in the bathroom mirror from all angles trying to find where the damage was. He then spent an even longer time admiring his new hair style, although he would have died rather than admitting it.

David had spent most of the night thinking about Suzie and how to explain his sudden reappearance. Both he and Arnold had agreed that they would never tell a soul about what had happened to them. And Lettice had been sworn to secrecy, although they didn't think anyone would believe her anyway. He knew any explanation he gave would involve telling more lies, but felt they were justified – and they would definitely be the last.

'Now what do we do, Davey-boy?' Arnold leaned back in his chair after polishing off a full English fry-up, cooked by David, and followed by toast and marmalade.

David finished his yoghurt topped with fruit, which didn't seem as satisfying as usual. He guessed his body still retained some of Arnold's preferences for fatty foods. 'I've made a list.'

'Of course, you have, Davey-boy' said Arnold, 'of course you have.'

'We both need to go to your 'Trouble-Free Insurance Agency' first and explain about my accident and how you've been looking after me. Then I need to sort out my car or hire another one if it needs to be repaired, then I can get back to my flat.'

'So, you don't want to stay here for a few more days.'

David looked at Arnold in surprise. 'I thought you couldn't wait to get rid of me.'

Arnold shrugged, 'I thought it would be easier if I took you into the office every day for you to work your magic, then you wouldn't need to hire a car.'

'Well, that's a very kind thought, but I need to go home.' David couldn't wait to get back into his own clothes. 'And I need to check my ansaphone.'

'I could drive you over and then bring you back.'

'No, I don't want to put you to any trouble.'

'It's no trouble.'

'Also, I have to see Suzie as soon as possible, and you should go and see your wife.'

Arnold glared, 'This is your list not mine, sunshine, I'll see Ingrid when I'm good and ready.' He stood up, 'And I'm going in the bathroom first.'

David stared after Arnold's back, which was exhibiting all the signs of being in a huff. Then he went back to planning what he was going to tell Suzie.

He'd decided to say he'd lost his memory in the accident, which was true, and couldn't remember anything until he was found late Monday evening by his old friend, Arnold Collins, who took him home and looked after him, which was slightly less true.

If Suzie, or her parents, treated this story with suspicion he would remind them that the famous crime writer, Agatha Christie, had disappeared for several days in equally mysterious circumstances.

As he picked up the phone to ring Suzie, he could feel dozens of butterflies flapping about in his stomach. Her mother answered in her usual haughty way. When he said who he was there was a loud scream followed by a crash. After a short silence he could hear Suzie in the distance saying, 'Mummy! Are you alright?'

Ingrid was also up early. She wanted to call into the hair stylist to make the appointment for a make-over before starting her shift. She didn't want to ring them from Greta's because she knew her sister would tell her not to be so silly. And she also wanted to have a quick browse in the boutique before work.

Telling Greta, she had to get into work early, she managed to get out of the house before her sister could ask too many questions. As she was closing the front door, she could hear Greta shouting at Graham to come out of the bathroom at once and tell her what he'd done to upset Ingrid.

Arnold felt his first day back in the office since last Thursday had gone better than expected. Mr Britten calmed down when David explained about the accident and how wonderful Arnold had been looking after him and helping him get his memory back. 'I don't know where I would have been without him.'

Cyril Britten was highly suspicious of this explanation, but was immediately appeased by David's offer to reduce his original quote.

Maurice also had his suspicions that they weren't getting the full story, but had no evidence to back them up. When he got Arnold on his own, he asked if he'd managed to sign up Astral Travel.

'No, mate, the guy's a nutter. Total time waster. Off his head.'

'He seemed quite normal to me. He said he had big plans to get people travelling round the world.'

'What a load of…' Arnold just managed to stop himself completing the sentence. He couldn't be sure he wouldn't pop out unexpectedly, and he didn't want to take the risk. That was his favourite saying and now, because of Astral Travel, he would never be able to use it again. 'Hornby is a total menace and should be locked up. So, thanks a bunch for sending me there.'

'You were pretty keen to go last Thursday. Anyway, what are you moaning about. You're Britten's blue-eyed boy at the moment.'

Ingrid not only managed to get an appointment with Jason to have her hair cut, restyled and blow-dried in her lunch hour, but Kelli, his assistant, who looked all of fifteen in her lilac overall, was going to do her makeup.

She'd even had time to overcome her fear of entering Sasha's Boutique and had come out with a smart dress, a skirt and a fitted jacket which went with both of them.

Smuggling her bags into the staff room she wondered how she was going to tell Stella that they couldn't have lunch together. For once, she wanted to keep what she was doing a secret – and Stella did have a habit of telling the queue all about Ingrid's business and asking for their opinions.

But she was in luck, no sooner had she sat down at her till than Stella leaned across and said, 'Sorry Ingrid, I can't have lunch with you today,' she looked round triumphantly at the queue, 'I've got a date.' The queue immediately wanted to know every detail and Stella was more than happy to accommodate them. 'It's with Sidney Spraggs, the private eye who's looking for some missing guy. Do you remember he was convinced Arnold's cousin was him. Well, I was able to help him out on that score…'

Ingrid tuned out Stella's voice and the gasps from the queue, and made a mental list of what she needed to pick up for Arnold's favourite dinner of steak and chips with all the trimmings, followed by Arctic Roll.

David and Suzie sat either side of a candle-lit table in the Marlborough Manor Hotel gazing into each other's eyes. Suzie had accepted David's explanation without question. The same could not be said of her parents, who distrusted the whole memory loss thing, but couldn't prove otherwise. And they also made it quite plain they didn't want a son-in-law who had multiple personalities tucked inside his head.

But David, channelling his inner Arnold, had told them in no uncertain terms that he and Suzie would be getting married as soon as possible – in a register office if necessary.

At the words register office, Deidre capitulated. Even if she wasn't getting the son-in-law she wanted, there was no way on this earth she wasn't going to master-mind the wedding of the year.

David lifted his glass and clinked it against Suzie's, 'To us darling.'

Arnold replete with steak and chips sank back on the settee, while Ingrid made a pot of tea. Then they were going to watch 'Rocky IV' on the video Ingrid had rented from the recently opened Blockbuster Videos. Her new look had come as a bit of a shock to him, but a good shock.

His strange behaviour over the past few days was blamed on his cousin Gerald Seymour turning up unexpectedly, and who, luckily, had gone back to Australia. Ingrid may have had her suspicions, but sensibly ignored them.

When she sat down next to him, Arnold put a tentative arm round her shoulder and said, 'I'm glad you're home Ingrid,' and realised he really meant it.

EPILOGUE

Arnold and David stuck to their stories and their kith and kin accepted their explanations with only a few reservations. The police were less accepting, but in the end all David lost was his 'no claims' bonus.

Arnold and Ingrid spent two weeks in Benidorm at the end of July to celebrate their twentieth wedding anniversary. Better late than never as Arnold wasn't slow to point out. And Ingrid was very impressed that he could find his way around the resort so easily having only been there once before. Now that they had the travelling bug, he wondered about going back to Hawaii! He was slightly disappointed that they couldn't attend David and Suzie's wedding, but he and David both agreed they would be pushing their luck.

David and Suzie had a spectacular wedding and Deidre was able to impress all her friends at the golf club. Suzie was surprised that David didn't invite Arnold to be his best man, but accepted he had moved away. But first, David had to agree to see Alastair Grey and apologise for running away from his private clinic Safe Haven, even though he had to pretend he had no memory of the event. Alastair, who had been reading up on multiple personalities told him he needed to live in harmony with the other people inside him, which David was happy to promise he'd do.

Margaret and Bernard had a quiet register office wedding and Margaret and her mother moved into Bernard's house. Their coach holiday business blossomed, and Lettice, who after hearing about the problems caused to Arnold by astral travelling, forgave Bernard and became one of their regular customers.

Greta finally managed to get her en-suite, but lost her husband, Graham, who refused to move into the box room and, like his mother before him, ran off with a traveller in cutlery – a Ms Marie McDonald.

Stella and Sidney became an item and he moved into her bungalow. He was so impressed with her tracking skills that he also took her on as his part-time assistant so she always had a good story to regale the Co-op queue with.

And, finally, Cameron Baker-Brown dropped his lawsuit against the Safe Haven clinic when Sidney said he wouldn't be charging him for finding David – not that Cameron had intended paying him anyway.

THE END

Acknowledgements

I'm lucky enough to have a husband, John, and two daughters, Nicola and Linda, who are not only encouraging but prepared to read what I've written, and a good friend Lesley Hudswell who proof read it for me. An onerous task because it was full of typos

Printed in Great Britain
by Amazon